For Philip and Elias

Owl Eyes

A Fairy Tale

Molly Lazer

F&I

ISBN: 978-1-68046-616-4

Fire & Ice Young Adult Books
An Imprint of Melange Books, LLC
White Bear Lake, MN 55110
www.fireandiceya.com

Published in the United States of America.

Cover Design by Caroline Andrus

CHAPTER 1

$\mathcal{I}$ sat at the window with the sun on my face, slicing tomatoes I picked from the vine that climbed the back of the kitchen house. On the other side of the room, Greta hummed an old tune. The words tickled at the fringes of my memory, not quite making their way to my lips. I hadn't heard them since she used to sing me to sleep almost seven years ago. When I was six, old enough to hold my knife, hearth-lit songs and dreams had been replaced with work.

Tomato juice sluiced across the cutting board as I bore down with my blade. The carvings that covered its handle had practically tattooed themselves on my palm. I imagined it had been the same way for my real mother—the knife had once been hers.

"Nora, Robert stopped by while you were outside," Greta said, arm-deep in a bowl of dough. "He said there's a new woman and her son coming sometime this week. They're going to work here with us."

"Why?" I said, glancing up from the mess of tomatoes on my board. The kitchen house already felt small with Greta, Peter, and me living there.

Greta shrugged. "Sir Alcander must have thought we needed the help."

Bright pain burst through my hand. I drew a breath and looked down at where my knife had bitten into my finger.

"Are you okay?" Greta asked.

"I'm fine." I hid my finger under the table until she turned back to her dough. I didn't want her to take away my knife.

"Anyway, we'll need to clear out some space in the loft."

"Mm-hmm." I held up my hand and stared at the red teardrop of blood glinting in the sunlight. It was beautiful, I decided. Like a jewel. I wrapped a rag around my finger before Greta could see it.

A chirrup of delight sounded outside. Siobhan and Annabelle had come out to play. Even though they rarely acknowledged me, I swore that the girls, the daughters of Sir Alcander and Lady Portia, played in view of the kitchen house just to remind me that they had the time and leisure to play when I did not.

"Greta!" Siobhan ran up to my window and leaned inside. "Do you have any chocolate?" Her voice was sweet, a voice that tried to please.

Greta knew better. "No dessert before tea."

Siobhan's innocent mask fell off. "I said give us some chocolate. I'll tell mother if you don't."

There was a fleeting moment when I thought Greta might say no. Tell them to say please. Make them ask nicely like she would make me do if I ever talked to her like that. Instead she shook her head and went to the shelf to get the chocolate. She never would have given in to me, but my mother wasn't the lady of the house.

"Ella-Della!" Annabelle peeked her head through the window as she reached for the chocolate.

"Not Ella-Della," I said. "Nora." Della was the name of the simple milkmaid in one of Annabelle's favorite stories. Her stupidity always got her in trouble with the lord of her household. Once I had the misfortune of walking by with a bucket of water while Portia was outside, telling the story to the girls.

"Look, there goes Della now," Portia said. At the time, I didn't even know what the name meant, but the way she laughed let me know it wasn't a compliment. Siobhan and Annabelle echoed her laughter and her words, and the name stuck.

"Ella-Della, we heard a secret," Annabelle said through a mouthful of chocolate.

Siobhan shushed her. "I said I was going to tell her!"

She picked up a piece of tomato from my cutting board and threw it at my face. Warm, acidy juice trickled down my cheek. I wiped it off with my rag. Annabelle murmured in disgust at the blood that streaked the cloth.

"You're going to want to hear it," Siobhan said as I moved the cutting board out of her reach. "It's about you." She looked at Greta, who pretended not to pay attention, then back at me. "Meet us by the tree."

"Race you!" Annabelle shouted and ran into the field. Siobhan followed. I imagined them tripping in their silk slippers and staining their dresses with dirt.

As much as I didn't want to admit it, I was curious about what they had to say. But I also knew Greta would not let me leave until my work was done. I picked another tomato out of my basket, cut a slit into the side, and squeezed it so the slit cracked into a mouth.

"I have a secret! It's about you, Ella-Della. Now give me chocolate!" Pulp lolled out of the tomato-mouth.

I wished Peter were here. His stories full of chivalrous heroes, brave maidens, talking animals, and the occasional fairy always made time go faster. But Peter was up on top of the main house, patching the roof again. I wished I were up there with him, outside and above everything, but Greta had insisted I stay with her.

"What if you fell off the roof?" she said as we ate breakfast.

"Then you'd heal me and make me all better," I replied.

"Lucky." Peter grinned as he drank the last of his tea. "She'd leave me for dead."

"You know that's true," Greta said, and we all laughed. She and Peter had been married for so long that she liked to say their jokes about killing each other were sometimes serious.

I looked out the window at where Siobhan and Annabelle had settled themselves under the hazel tree in the middle of the field.

"Greta?" I said. "Can I go outside?"

Greta tsked and shook her head. "You know those girls don't have anything worthwhile to say."

I bit the inside of my cheek. I wanted Greta to be right, but there had been a wicked delight in Siobhan's eyes that made me think that she really did have a secret to share. There was no way I was going to let her keep it to lord over me later.

Greta waved her hand. "Put the soup on, then go."

I diced the rest of the tomatoes and carried the cutting board to the pot that hung over the fire in the hearth. The tomatoes went in on top of the carrots, parsnips, and rosemary that I threw in earlier that morning. I poured a pitcher of water on top of the vegetables and wiped my knife on my apron. The tomato pulp left an orange swath across the fabric.

"Now?"

Greta nodded. Her long braid fell over her shoulder as she worked. She pushed it back behind her. "Go. But you're a glutton for punishment. And I'm not going to stop your soup from boiling over."

I untied my apron and hung it over my chair by the window. I usually took my knife outside with me so I could use the handle to smash open the skins of the hazelnuts. Greta watched me with a raised eyebrow and the hint of a smile on her face. I left the knife behind.

I could feel Greta watching from the window as I crossed the field behind the kitchen house. Smoke meandered from the chimney, a reminder of the soup that would boil soon. The kitchen house was a squat brown-and-grey stone block compared to the massive size of the main house next to it. I could walk to the main house in minutes, but it felt like it was miles away. I'd never been inside. Greta always murmured something about my being too young when I asked if I could help bring in dinner.

Siobhan and Annabelle sat on the grass under the hazel tree. I bristled at their presence. I claimed the tree for myself long ago. It was close to the rest of the forest but set off by itself, pulsing with a secret, solitary life. I used to climb over its branches, rubbing my feet over the smooth bark and leaning my ear against the trunk to listen for a heartbeat.

It was my tree, alone and proud. I didn't want them playing near it.

Siobhan sat with her legs tucked under her skirt, pulling up blades of grass, knotting them, and throwing them at Annabelle. She threw a clod of roots and dirt at me. It landed harmlessly an arm's-length away. I was sure that if I hadn't already gathered most of the hazelnuts from the ground that morning, Siobhan would be throwing them instead.

"What took you so long?"

"I had work to do." I put my hands on my hips, trying to look imposing. Siobhan stood up and brushed off her skirt. Even though I was more than a year older, she was taller and always managed to look down on me.

"Of course," she said, miming forgetfulness. "Ella-Della is our servant."

"Della, Della, Ella-Della," Annabelle sang. "Fetched some milk and met a fella." She was ten, a year younger than Siobhan. Her face screwed up in an expression of intense concentration as she tried to remember the next part of the song.

"What is it?" I asked. "You said you had something to tell me."

"You need to earn it, Ella-Della." Siobhan pointed to the top of the tree where the tail end of one of Annabelle's bird-shaped toys stuck out between the leaves.

"Why don't you get it yourself?" I said.

Siobhan snorted. "Climbing trees is not ladylike, Ella-Della."

Annabelle, having given up on the song, fit a chain of clovers on top of her golden curls. As she and Siobhan waited, ladylike, on the ground, I grabbed the lowest branch and swung up into the tree. There was a curved branch halfway up that I liked to sit on. I stopped there, balancing with one hand against the trunk. The toy was stuck between the branches far above my head.

"Just because it's a bird doesn't mean it can fly," I called down.

Cocooned among the dark, jagged leaves, I couldn't see Siobhan. But the leaves didn't stop her voice from reaching me.

"Just because you look like a horse doesn't mean you can run."

I continued to climb. Greta was right. They didn't have anything useful to tell me. They just wanted someone to get Annabelle's bird.

The cloud-dappled sky came into view near the crown of the tree. The toy's red body stood out from the green around it. I stood on my tiptoes on a thin branch and stretched to reach it. My fingers brushed against the painted wood, and it plummeted out of the tree, hitting branches and smashing to the grass below. I climbed down as slowly as I could.

Annabelle held the bird's wooden body in one hand and the wing that had broken off in the other. Her cheeks were reddened with anger. She started to speak, but Siobhan brushed her off.

"Father will buy you a new one," she said. "Tell him that Ella-Della broke it. He'll take it out of her wages."

I shuffled my feet, which smarted from landing on the ground. What did they even know about my wages? I'd never seen any of the money due to me—I always assumed Peter and Greta kept it safe for when I was older. What did I need it for, anyway? When he went to the Market, Peter used his own wages to buy me small toys or the charcoals and chalk I used whenever he or Greta had time to give me lessons. Did Sir Alcander take from my wages any time I did something he didn't like? I'd only ever seen the man from a distance, but he seemed imposing enough that I could imagine him doing it.

"Ella-Della," Siobhan said, "don't you want to know the secret?"

"No." I turned back to the kitchen house.

"I heard Mother and Father talking in the parlor. They thought I was in bed, but I was getting those black biscuits from the servants' rooms."

Annabelle dropped her toy back on the ground. "You said I could come with you! I wanted biscuits, too!"

"Those were for the house servants," I said. Greta and I made the thin bilberry biscuits a week ago. It was my idea to smash up the berries to give the dough its dark color.

Siobhan went on as though she hadn't heard me. "Mother and Father were talking and Mother said, 'Someday she's going to find out, and when she does, she's going to want to know why, Alcander.'" She did a pitch-perfect impression of her mother, cocking her head just like I'd seen Lady Portia do.

Curiosity won out. "Why what?"

Siobhan opened her mouth to answer, but Annabelle got there first.

"Why you live in the kitchen house when your father is in the main house." She gasped and clapped a hand over her mouth. Siobhan looked around. Her haughty expression was gone, replaced by guilt. She was not good at burying her thoughts. They were telling the truth.

Siobhan's moment of humility didn't last long. "I always thought your father lived in the oven," she said. "That would explain why your arms are all messed up."

I crossed my arms behind me, trying to hide the pink burns scarred onto my skin.

"You're lying," I said. Even if they actually heard Lady Portia say those words, what she said wasn't possible. Greta and Peter were my parents. My real mother died in childbirth, and my father followed her to the World Apart soon afterwards. That's what Greta and Peter always said. But the hazel tree brightened behind Siobhan's head, and my feet felt lighter than before, like they weren't quite touching the ground. It might have been hope.

"Am not," Siobhan snapped. "I'm being nice. I just thought you'd want to know that your father threw you away in the kitchen house so he wouldn't have to see your ugly face every day. See if I ever do anything for you again."

She turned on her heels and hauled Annabelle back to the main house. I stood there for a moment, letting the colors of my small world return to normal. I couldn't go back to the kitchen house, not yet, not if what they said was true. Why would Greta and Peter tell me that my father had passed? Was his presence the reason I wasn't allowed in the main house? He could be there, waiting for me to come find him. Did he know who I was? Did he even want me?

"Nora!" Greta's voice pierced through the fog of questions swirling around me. "The soup is burning!"

I ran back to the kitchen house and hefted the pot off the fire. I hadn't put in enough water, and what I did add had boiled away. I poured in two pitchers this time and put the pot back on the hearth, hoping no one would notice the vegetables' smoky taste. I barely heard Greta's reprimands as I ran through the list of men who worked in the main house. There were three male servants: Matthew, Sir Alcander's valet, was married to Sarah, the head maid. They came to work at the Runes when I was eight, so it couldn't be Matthew. Victor, the footman, was only seventeen. The only one left was Robert, the butler. He began working at the Runes before Greta and Peter, and he was certainly old enough to have a daughter my age. He had only ever been kind to me when he came to deliver messages or get food from the kitchen house.

Someone knocked at the door. Greta opened it, and there he was. Breath caught in my throat.

"Robert." Greta nodded, and he came inside.

"The new kitchen maid will arrive from the Vale tomorrow."

"From the Vale?" Greta sounded surprised, but I didn't understand why. "Is she Kindred?"

"She and Alcander are like-minded when it comes to"—he glanced over at me—"the goings-on at the Vale."

I held Robert's gaze for as long as I could, scrutinizing his features. He carried himself with a dignified air, stately even. He took pride in his work, which was probably why he'd been employed at the Runes longer than any of the other servants. His hair was wiry and grey. I ran a hand through the scraggily, dark red tangle on my head. I'd never met anyone else with my thick, ratty hair. Greta's braid, while heavy, was smooth and dark. Annabelle's and Siobhan's curls were always brushed to perfection. Robert's hair reminded me of trees I had seen in the woods that had been struck by lightning, an image I often associated with myself when I looked in the mirror. I could imagine his hair being the same color as mine once upon a time. His eyes were grey instead of gold like mine, but I could have gotten my eyes from my mother.

Had Robert ever been married? He wasn't now. Maybe he had a wife who died in childbirth, and he couldn't bear to have the child near him because she—I—reminded him too much of her. It was all very romantic. I wanted to rush over to him, but I held back. What if I were wrong? I would just embarrass myself.

Robert and Greta's conversation ended with the determination that Peter would meet the new servants in the woods west of the Runes proper the next day. Robert brushed past me on his way out.

"Nora." He nodded at me.

I wanted to follow him back to the main house, but as soon as the door closed behind him, I turned to Greta.

"My parents," I said. "My real parents—do you know who they were?"

She startled at the abruptness of the question. "Why are you asking this now? Did the girls say something?"

"I just want to know."

Greta beckoned for me to sit down with her.

"You know the answer. The couple who worked in the kitchen house before us gave you to Peter and me."

"But those people weren't my parents," I said.

"They didn't say who your parents were," Greta continued. "Only that they'd passed, and you needed someone to take care of you. We always wanted a child, and—" She stopped talking when it became obvious I wasn't listening. This was a story I knew by heart, but it wasn't mine anymore.

Greta narrowed her eyes. "What did the girls say to you?"

I stood up. "Nothing."

I went back to my seat by the window, put my apron on, and began to mash up a pile of sprigberries that Greta had put on the table while I was outside. If she and Peter knew anything about my real parents, they would have no reason to hide it from me. They gave me my mother's knife, after all. Sir Alcander and Lady Portia obviously knew, but I couldn't ask them. Lady Portia's visits to the kitchen house were rare and always came with demands. Less salt in the soup or an extra dessert tart for Siobhan and Annabelle. She gusted in and out, never staying for longer than her words and never looking in my direction. Sir Alcander never even set foot near the kitchen house. The only times I'd laid eyes on him had been through a window when I brought something to Peter while he was patching the exterior of the main house. I knew Sir Alcander more by his maps. Peter had one in the kitchen house, and he used it to teach me the geography of Colandaria. Sir Alcander's intricate compass roses were more familiar to me than his face.

No, I would not get answers from either of them. But I would go to the main house. I had to talk to Robert.

~

"Good morning, early riser. Any chance you made breakfast while we were sleeping?" Peter said as he climbed the ladder down from the loft and joined me in the kitchen, where I'd been trying to quiet the pounding of my heart since before sunup. He put his arm around me and kissed my forehead. The bristles of his short beard tickled my chin. All fathers should feel like this, I thought.

I had to keep myself from trailing behind him when he brought breakfast to the main house. I would have to wait until everyone was doing their work before I could go inside. I'd seen Greta and Peter go in the back door of the main house as often as I'd seen Robert, Sarah, or one of the other servants come out of it on their way across the field. The servants' quarters were supposed to be right near the entrance. There had to be something there that would tell me about Robert.

I picked at my breakfast. The nervous flutter in my stomach made me too nauseated to eat. I'd occasionally thought about my real parents resting in the World Apart. Their ashes would have been given to the wind somewhere meaningful. Someone would have held me nearby to ensure that their spirits would watch over me. Growing up, though, I had the parents I needed. Greta and Peter gave me a fire burning in the hearth, a garden to pick food from, and stories to fill warm nights in the loft.

Now, with just a few words from Siobhan and Annabelle, I needed more.

No one would be in the main house servants' quarters after breakfast. I waited until Peter went outside to repair the fence around the chicken coop and Greta began making her daily bread at the counter that faced away from the window.

"I'm going to see if any more tomatoes are ripe," I said as Greta took out caraway seeds and flour and put them next to the eggs that I gathered from the coop before breakfast.

She nodded, and I headed out, glancing back to make sure that she had started on the dough. While she was busy measuring ingredients, I ran across the field to the main house and went in the back entrance. Once inside, I cracked open the first door I came to. The room I entered was about the size of the floor of the kitchen house, large enough to fit six beds. Some belongings—probably Victor's, since Peter always complained what a mess Victor was when he came back from bringing in supper—were strewn about the floor, while others sat on shelves or against the wall. The largest bed would belong to Matthew and Sarah. That left only a few beds that could be Robert's. A green satin vest with gold edging hung on a stand across the room. That had to be his. He would wear it to serve at Sir Alcander's and Lady Portia's banquets. Robert's shelves were bare except for a few books and a tin of my bilberry biscuits.

I warmed at the thought that my father had a stash of my cooking. There was something else on the shelf, something flat enough that I couldn't see what it was. I stood on my tiptoes and retrieved a palm-sized agate cameo. The carving was of a young woman not more than twenty years old. She was lovely, with long, wavy hair tied back with a large bow.

Was this my mother? In profile, it was difficult to make out anything specific about her features. I wished her image were in color so I could see if she had my gold eyes. I had to talk to Robert before I lost my nerve. I went back to the hallway with the cameo clutched in my fist. I didn't know where to go, but I did know that I would be in trouble if I were caught roaming the halls. I picked a direction, glancing around each corner before proceeding as I looked for a shock of steely grey hair.

Portraits lined the hallway. All of the subjects wore the same shade of dark green that marked them as the noble family of the Runes. I stopped in front of a painting that depicted Sir Alcander and Lady Portia posing with younger versions of Siobhan and Annabelle. The artist captured the girls' smug expressions well. The paint in Siobhan's eyes shined with mischief. Lady Portia's every hair was defined. The painter had arranged his light source to highlight her sharp, elegant cheekbones. Sir Alcander's eyes were duller than those of Lady Portia or their daughters. Even Annabelle's eyes twinkled with specks of white that were missing in her father's.

"Nora?"

I wheeled around to face Sarah, the head maid.

"What are you doing here?"

I looked at the floor. The grey and green grain of the marble flowed like the lines on one of Sir Alcander's maps. I ran the tip of my shoe along one of the paths.

"I'm looking for Robert," I said. "I need to talk to him. It's important."

"He's taking dictation for Sir Alcander." Sarah looked past me down the hall. "He'll be done soon. Come with me."

She put a hand on my back and ushered me in the direction from which I'd come.

"You're not supposed to be in here," she said.

"I know." I tucked the cameo into my pocket. "But it's important. Don't tell Greta, please."

Sarah glanced behind us. The pressure of her hand on my back became more urgent.

"It's not Greta I'm worried about." She opened the door to the servants' quarters and pushed me inside. "Stay here. I'll get Robert."

She left the door open a crack and hurried down the hall. I sat on Robert's bed. A long piece of straw poked out of the mattress. I pulled it out from the fabric and broke a piece off the end. By the time Robert arrived, shutting the door behind him, there was a small pile of straw on my lap. I leapt off the bed, spilling it on the floor.

"Sorry." I bent down to sweep the straw into my hand. Robert knelt to help me.

"Nora, what are you doing here? You're not supposed to be—"

"I need to talk to you," I said. "It's about my—" The word stuck on my tongue. "Um, Siobhan and Annabelle said that…" I took the cameo out of my pocket. "Who is this?"

Robert snatched it out of my hand. "What are you doing with this?"

My cheeks burned. "I found it on the shelf. Is it your wife?"

The angry lines on Robert's face softened. "No, it's my sister. She died a long time ago. Why do you ask?"

I sat on the bed. I felt heavy enough that I might sink into the straw and never come out.

"Siobhan and Annabelle said they heard Lady Portia and Sir Alcander talking, and they said that my"—I choked out the word —"father was in the main house. I thought that you might be—"

Robert moved away, dropping the straw into a bucket next to the bed. I sank farther into the mattress. Being poked with spindles of straw was preferable to the silence in the room.

"Your father?" Robert said. "Nora, the man who was your father is long gone."

"But you have to be," I protested. "Your hair, it's just like mine."

"What, this old mess?" Robert ran a hand through his hair and sat down next to me.

My voice dropped to a whisper. "It has to be you."

"I'm sorry, Nora. I don't have any children. Peter's been a good father to you, hasn't he?"

"Yes." I could feel each razor of straw jabbing into my skin. "I just thought—"

Wait. What did he say?

"You know who my father was!" It came out as a statement, not a question. Robert jumped up from the bed.

"No, Nora, you misunderstood. I—"

"Yes, you do!" I leapt up after him. "You said he was gone, but you know who he was. Tell me!"

Robert's eyes darted back and forth as if he were looking for a way to escape the conversation before fixing on a point behind me. Panic tinged his voice.

"She was just bringing a message from the kitchen house."

I turned to see Lady Portia standing on the other side of the door. I hadn't heard it open. Waves of anger passed through her cold ocean eyes. I had only ever seen Lady Portia angry, but this was different. This was rage, and it was aimed squarely at me.

Robert put a protective arm around my shoulders.

"I'm sending her back right now."

"Eleanor." Lady Portia's voice was ice cracking. "You are not permitted in here."

"I'm sorry," I croaked. "I'll go back." This was different from Sarah's confusion at finding me in the hall or Robert's initial anger at discovering his cameo in my hands. Different, and infinitely more dangerous.

Before I could move, Lady Portia was in the room, grabbing my arm and wrenching me from Robert's grasp. I could feel her breath on my cheeks as she pulled me close.

"You are supposed to stay in the kitchen house," she hissed. She jerked me out of the room and down the hall.

"Ma'am—" Robert started after us.

"Stay where you are," Portia said without turning to look at him. "This is none of your business."

I looked back, panicked, as I flailed in my attempt to keep up with Lady Portia's long stride. I heard the sound of the back door being thrown open. I could only hope Robert was going to get Greta or Peter.

Lady Portia's fingers burned on my arm as she pulled me behind her, making a series of turns through the hallways. Anytime I opened my mouth to protest, to apologize, to cry, she jerked me forwards, and my words were swallowed in a yelp of pain. She finally stopped in front of a plain, wooden door. It felt out of place next to the other doors in the hallway, which were lacquered and covered in carvings. Its austerity didn't belong, just like I didn't.

My wrist glowed red when Lady Portia let me go, and I rubbed my arm to quell the pain. My mouth ran ahead of me, spitting out every apology I could think of. She ignored me as she sorted through the keys on a ring she took from her dress pocket and fit a large iron key into the lock. The door creaked open. I couldn't make out anything inside—there were no windows to let in the light. The darkness in the room felt different than when the kitchen house darkened after sunset. This darkness was hungry. I turned to run.

Portia caught my wrist and shoved me into the room. I fell on my hands and knees. Small pieces of something—dust? ash?—rose up around me, making their way into my throat. I started to cough.

"Never ask about your father again." She slammed the door, plunging me into the dark. The door fit so snugly in its frame that there wasn't even a sliver of light shining at the bottom.

It was a moment before my shock allowed me to react. The room smelled scorched with death, like it hadn't been opened in ages. I coughed again, trying to get out the pieces of the room that had infiltrated my throat, my nostrils, my eyes. I shuffled forwards until I reached the door and felt for the knob. It was cold to the touch. I pulled as hard as I could, but it would not turn.

"Robert!" I screamed. "Sarah! Peter! Greta!" I kept screaming their names until my throat was raw. The fine powder that covered the floor stuck to me wherever my body touched the damp ground. There were voices down the hall, but they were too far away for me to hear what they were saying.

"Father?" I whispered.

My arm ached where I could feel a bruise blooming around my wrist. I wanted Peter and Greta. I wanted my father and my mother, but I didn't know their names. Only the darkness held me as I cried.

CHAPTER 2

I didn't know if my cries echoed from the walls for moments or hours. The darkness sucked up time. When my tears dried up, I stayed as quiet as I could, pressing my ear to the door. Soon, I could tell the difference between the footsteps in the hallway: heavy ones, light ones, and feet that clicked against the marble floor. I didn't know what I was waiting for. A familiar gait, perhaps, friendly feet that would come and take me out of the dark. None of the steps even slowed in front of the door. It was as though it, and I, were invisible.

Panic prickled my skin. I pounded at the door, screaming, and still no one came. I was hungry and so, so thirsty. I lay down on the floor, which was, impossibly, both damp and bone-dry at the same time.

I didn't know if I was asleep or awake when I began tearing at the walls, scraping my fingers against the stone even when warm blood coated my hands. There had to be another door, a key, something that would get me out. I had covered three walls when my finger caught on a slot between the stones. The mortar took a chunk of my nail with it, and I whimpered with new pain as I felt around the tiny crevice. One of the stones was loose.

I rocked the stone back and forth until it came out and jumped out of the way when it thudded to the ground at my feet. I reached into the wall, hoping for a key, an axe, cup of water. My hands closed around something wooden roughly the size of a loaf of bread.

I ran my blood-slicked fingers over the box. Its surface was warm, much warmer than the stone behind which it had been entombed. The box was covered in carvings, but I couldn't find a latch to open it. Grey stars danced in front of my eyes, and blood rushed to my head. The box slipped from my hands. The dull thump of its impact echoed in my ears as I joined it on the ground.

～

*L*ight spilled into the room. I opened my eyes into small slits and peeked through my fingers. I could just make out a female figure, waist tightly corseted and gown flaring out at the hips.

"Mother?"

"Don't be daft, Eleanor," Lady Portia said. "Get up."

If I had the strength to move, I would have run from the room as fast as my feet would carry me. Instead, I curled into a ball on the ground. Even though I squeezed my eyes shut, I could still see the orange glow from the torches in the hall.

"I said get up." Lady Portia grabbed my arm in the exact spot where she bruised me before. I cried out as she hauled me to my feet.

"Have you learned your lesson?" Her breath was sweet, like lavender. I wanted to retch on her shoes. I could feel the darkness reaching for me with sticky-slick fingers.

"Yes, ma'am," I whispered as loud as my dry throat would allow.

"I can't hear you." She tightened her grip on my arm, and it was all I could do not to whimper as my eyes finally adjusted to the light.

"Yes, ma'am," I repeated, louder. My head pounded. She released my arm.

Gold eyes stared at me from a mirror that hung on the opposite wall, daring me to make a move. The girl in the mirror had swallowed the darkness of the room; my shadow-self stared out from the glass. Her skin was dead black. I looked down at my arms. They were covered in ash from the floor of the room with no windows. I screamed.

Lady Portia's hand cracked across my cheek. "Stop that," she hissed.

I scraped my arms with hands that were just as black. I smelled ash every time I breathed in.

Siobhan and Annabelle's laughter echoed through the hall. I had to get out of there. Lady Portia grabbed the back of my shirt as I braced to run.

"Girls!" she barked as Siobhan and Annabelle rounded the corner. "No running in the hall."

The girls skidded to a stop in front of us.

"Ella-Della!" Annabelle said. "What happened?" She looked up, appealing to Lady Portia. "Mother, she didn't really break my bird. It was an accident!"

"Don't call her that name, Annabelle," Portia said. "You sound like an imbecile."

"An imbecile who got her own toy stuck in a tree." Siobhan swatted Annabelle's sleeve and cocked her head at me. "You look like an owl with those yellow eyes. You're so dirty they're all I can see. Are you hungry, Owl Eyes? I'll see if I can find you a mouse for supper."

She laughed and began to hoot. Annabelle joined in, and Portia sighed with disgust.

"Take her back to the kitchen house," Portia said. "And get these two ready for dinner."

I hadn't noticed Sarah and another servant standing there. Sarah ushered Siobhan and Annabelle back down the hall.

"Bye, Owl Eyes," Siobhan called over her shoulder.

"You," Portia said to the other servant. "See that she stays where she belongs."

The woman crouched down next to me. "You must be Eleanor," she said. I didn't know who she was, so I just nodded. "My name is Liana. I'm working with you and Greta and Peter now. Shall we go back to the kitchen house?"

I wanted to correct her, to tell her that I wanted to be called Nora, not Eleanor. Only Portia called me Eleanor, and it always sounded like a punishment. The room swam as Liana took my hand and we left the main house.

"Where's Greta?" I asked. Tingling heat spread through my body. I could barely put one foot in front of the other to cross the field.

"Come on," said the woman whose name I'd already forgotten. She scooped one arm around my back and the other under my knees and lifted me up.

"No!" I struggled in her arms. She was taking me back to the room with no windows. The darkness that was already pushing its way into the edges of my vision would return.

I heard a door open. The ashy scent in my nostrils mixed with the familiar scents of baking bread and the burning hearth, alive in all the ways that the room with no windows was dead.

"Shhh, you're home now." Greta's voice was accompanied by a cool cloth on my forehead. I stopped struggling.

"You're making bread without me."

"Tomorrow." Greta held a cup to my lips. "You can help tomorrow."

I tried to sip the cold liquid, but most of it dribbled down my chin and onto my shirt. Greta and the other servant's conversation floated somewhere above my head as they washed me off and tried again to ladle water into my mouth. Greta gave me a few tasteless crackers that I took without opening my eyes and chewed until they dissolved down my throat.

Then, a new voice: "Who's that?"

"This is Nora."

"What's wrong with her?"

"Shhh. She has a fever."

"Why's she all black like that?"

"Never mind that. We're taking care of her."

"Oh." The voice got quieter as it moved away. "I'm going to sleep. Tell Nora I hope she feels better."

The voices lifted farther and farther away until I felt like I was straining to hear them through ashy stone walls. Even though I fought it, the darkness took me.

$\sim$

I climbed through an inky blackness that was not just the absence of light—it was the absence of everything, the absence of me. Only the branches under my feet told me I still had legs. The familiar bark of my hazel tree was under the pads of fingers I could not see. Leaves brushed against my face, their surfaces smooth, their edges razor-sharp. I couldn't escape them as I climbed up and up and—

"Nora!"

I shot up from the ground. Sunlight filtered through the kitchen house windows. I was sitting on the floor next to the hearth. The pillow next to me was grey and damp with perspiration. I clenched my eyes shut, refusing to look down and see my arms. I knew that when I did they would be ash black.

"Nora?" The voice said again. I opened one eye. A woman stood in the doorway holding a basket of herbs. She touched her chest. "It's Liana. It's okay if you don't remember."

I swallowed, and saliva scratched my throat. I looked down. My arms were clean and tan. Never before had I been so grateful to see the puckered, pink-white scars that burned across my skin.

"I'm all wet." I plucked at the shift that stuck to my legs.

"Your fever must have broken," Liana said. "I'll get Greta."

She turned to go back outside, and I smelled ash.

"Don't leave." The words came out as a quiet breath.

Liana stuck her head out the window instead. "Greta!" she called. "Your patient is awake."

Greta hurried in, and with five long steps she was beside me. I buried my face in her shoulder and breathed in the earthy scent of her hair.

"It was so dark," I cried. "Why didn't anyone come get me?"

"We tried," Greta said. "Portia wouldn't let us in the main house, not even to bring in meals. So we stopped cooking." She smiled to herself. "They didn't much like that."

I let go of her and scratched at my arms. The white lines my nails left darkened to a rosy pink.

"How long was I—?"

"A little more than a day," Greta said. "We tried to get in there, Nora, we really did. I won't let her hurt you again."

I shook my head. I knew this wasn't her fault.

"Let's get you a bath," she said.

Liana brought in water for the washbasin, and I separated myself from my sweaty shift. I stepped into the basin and sank below the water, relaxing as the nothing sounds filled my ears. Greta reached under the water and tapped me on the head. When I surfaced, she handed me a steaming cup of tea. I smelled it before taking a sip. Greta looked at me and raised an eyebrow. She was testing me. This was good. This was normal. This was home.

"Dandelions…fellberry leaves, mint, and—" I took another sniff. "Milkweed."

Greta grinned. "Very good."

"It's for a fever," I explained to Liana, who stood on the other side of the kitchen, dusting lavender sugar crystals over a tray of pastries. "Greta is a healer. She's teaching me what plants are good for helping sick people. It's like magic."

Liana flinched. "I should hope not. I was told there were no Kindred here at the Runes."

I looked to Greta for help. I'd only ever met the Kindred, Colandaria's practitioners of magic, as characters in Peter's stories.

"There aren't," Greta said. "These are herbal remedies I learned from my mother."

"Peter says Greta can stop a cold in two days flat," I added, trying to be helpful.

Liana muttered something about potions and went outside.

"Did I say something wrong?" I asked. A few pieces of ash floated on the surface of the water in the tub. I picked up the sponge that was tied to the side of the washbasin and scrubbed my arms.

"No." Greta put Liana's pastries in the oven. "There are just some people who think magic is bad or that practicing it is wrong."

"Do you?" I kept scrubbing.

"No. But I grew up in the Summit, where we were closer to the sorcerers in the Farlands. They would come with the traveling shows. My favorite was when they would turn someone's hair strange colors. My mother went around with blue hair for a fortnight before the spell faded."

"If I could do magic, I'd make it so that dough rises faster. We could make twelve loaves a day."

"That's a nice idea." Greta flicked water at me. Her brow furrowed as she looked at my arms. I had scrubbed them hard enough that the sponge's rough surface abraded the skin. I winced, drawing a quick breath as blood twinkled on my forearm. Greta took the sponge away.

"I think you're done." She held up a towel for me to step into.

I dried off and put on a nightgown even though it wasn't time for bed. My serving clothes hung on a line outside. I could still smell the ash on them when I stuck my head out the window.

"Where's Peter?" I asked.

"He took Jack to the Market," Greta said. "Liana's son," she added, noting the question on my face. "They went to get supplies for the banquet."

"Oh," I said. I tried to wind my hair up over my head in the towel like I'd seen Greta do, but the towel kept flopping onto my face. Peter had never taken me to the Market before. It was in the middle of Colandaria, almost a full day's journey from the Runes. He'd never even taken me to the local market, which was closer to the Runes proper. My whole life was tied up in the kitchen house.

I pushed the towel out of my eyes and looked into the glass on the wall. Gold eyes—"owl eyes," according to Siobhan—stared back at me. They had to have come from somewhere, and that somewhere was the main house. The girl in the mirror was no longer just Nora, daughter of Peter and Greta, who lived in the kitchen house. She was a puzzle that needed solving, a shade of a person, missing a history. I had to fill in the missing pieces.

∼

By the time the sun disappeared under the tree line, my heart was trying to beat its way out of my chest.

Greta lit the candles in the kitchen, and when Liana came back from bringing dinner to the main house, the three of us sat around the table for our own supper. The sound of my fork shaking against the clay plate rang in my ears, blotting out Greta and Liana's conversation. I pictured candles going out one by one, sending ribbons of smoke trailing towards the ceiling. The light on Greta's face grew dimmer until she was lit only by the embers from the hearth. A powdery gasp sounded from the chimney, and I spun around in my seat. Ash spilled from the hearth onto the floor, over the slate, almost touching the legs of my chair. I pulled my legs up and buried my face in my knees. I couldn't breathe.

"Nora?" Greta put her hand on my shoulder.

I gasped, filling my chest with shallow, painful breaths. There was no ash on the floor. The fire blazed in the hearth.

"Nora, why don't you lie down? You don't look well."

The ladder that led up to the loft seemed taller than before. I imagined falling from its rungs like Annabelle's bird toy, cartwheeling down until I broke. Darkness gaped above the ladder. Even though my bed was in the center of the loft, no light reached it from the main floor.

"No." I grasped at my nightgown. "I can't. It's too dark up there."

Greta handed me a candle from the table. "Take this. No, wait." She went to her herb shelf and sorted through bottles of essence before finding the one she wanted and pouring a few drops into the oil.

I smelled it. "Motherwort. For calm."

"And to help you sleep," Greta said. "Because this mother is a worrywart about you. Take the candle up with you."

Greta held the candle as I climbed the ladder and passed it back to me when I reached the top. I carried it in two hands, holding on to the metal base and focusing on the flame that burned inside. As long as the fire kept burning, I'd be okay. I could keep the dark away.

I settled down on my mattress, turning on my side so I could watch the flame dance.

~

"*Hi*." I shot up from the bed, screaming, and scrambling backwards before falling off the mattress onto the planked wood floor. A boy crouched next to me with his elbows balanced on his knees and his chin resting against his palms. He wore an old, light blue shirt that was much too large for his small frame. A piece of hay stuck up from the mop of brown hair on his head.

"Jack!" Liana called from the kitchen. "Don't wake Nora."

"Too late," the boy called back.

"Who are you?" I pressed my hand to my chest to keep my heart in place. "Why were you watching me sleep?"

"I wasn't watching you sleep," the boy said. "Peter and me just got back from the Market, and I got up here and found you on my mattress."

"Your—" I sputtered. I took a deep breath and tried to inhale the motherwort from the candle. "This is my bed."

"Well, no one said it was yours, did they? I claimed this bed when I got here, and no one made a peep." He crossed his arms and looked at the floor. "They were probably too worried if you were okay to care about where I was sleeping. You looked pretty rotten."

"I was sick," I said, staking my spot on the mattress again.

"No, I mean you actually looked like you'd rotted. Your skin was all black. Are you sure you're not a spirit who's talking to me now?"

I grabbed his arm and pressed my palm to his.

"No spirit," I said. "I'm here."

He grinned. I shoved him on the floor.

"I'm Jack," he said as he picked himself up.

"Nora."

"Are you Greta and Peter's daughter?"

"No." I regretted the words as soon as they came out of my mouth. They were true, but I chewed them like a lie. "I mean yes. Sort of."

"How are you only 'sort of' their daughter?"

"I mean, yes, I'm their daughter. They're just not my real parents. My real parents are dead. Or gone. Or something. My mother is dead." I was rambling. I pulled the candle closer to the mattress, hearing Greta's voice in my ear warning me that the flame could catch the straw on fire. I didn't care. I lowered my face and breathed in.

"Does your ma's spirit ever talk to you?" Jack asked.

"What?" I stared at him. "That's stupid. How old are you that you still think that can happen?"

"I'm thirteen." Defensiveness crept into his voice. "And I only asked because I can talk to my pa anytime I want to. Or at least I could when we lived in the Vale. His spirit lives in the river there."

Sir Alcander had hired a crazy person to work in the kitchen house.

"No, he doesn't."

"He does so! I'll show you sometime, and you'll see."

I flopped back down on the mattress and rolled over so I was facing away from him, pulling the candle to the other side with me. I could feel Jack watching me.

"Your ma is nice," I said, still not facing him.

"Thanks. I think so too." There, finally, was something we agreed on. "I'm going to bed now. You can keep your spot. I didn't want it anyway."

I peeked over my shoulder. Jack lay down on a new mattress I hadn't noticed next to the wall.

"Thanks," I said. In the dim light of the candle, his eyes looked almost gold. I smiled.

"It's all right," he said. "I can sleep almost anywhere as long as I've got enough space. I don't like feeling closed up in small places."

The dark room pulsed behind me. "Me neither."

Now we had two things in common.

CHAPTER 3

*T*he soft glow of morning brightened the loft. Greta, Liana, and Jack were still asleep. Peter was missing, probably gone off to start his work before dawn. I crept down the ladder and lit the fire, stepping over boxes and crates that weren't there the day before. After a trip to the well for a bucket of water, I put the kettle on the hearth and went out to the chicken coop. The chickens made their usual row, clucking and kicking up feathers and straw when I entered. The coop smelled terrible. Someone would have to clean it out. I sucked in the rancid air. At least it smelled alive.

Outside, I shielded my eyes from the sun and the sight of the main house. I wished I could believe that I would never go in there again, but there were answers inside those walls. Answers locked up in rooms, in cabinets, in people who knew but just needed the right key to unlock them. If only I could breathe when I felt the stone walls looming over me.

By the time I got back in, Greta had woken up and started making bread. Our morning ritual had taken on a familiar ease. Without looking, I knew exactly when she would be ready for the herbs I chopped and how brown the loaf needed to be before taking it out of the oven. So many memories of bread and work and Greta were burned onto my arms, just as they were on hers. Greta, my mother, but not.

Liana peeled vegetables while we worked.

"I take it you met Jack last night. I'm sorry he woke you up."

"It's okay," I said. "He does talk a lot."

"I think he's making up for lost time," Liana said. "We went almost a year with hardly a peep from him after his father passed." With a muffled grunt, Jack climbed down the ladder into the kitchen. Liana laughed and shook her head. "Hey, sleepy. Here in the Runes, we get up with the sun."

Jack stumbled to the hearth and poured a cup of tea.

"His father couldn't start the day without his tea either." Sadness glimmered in Liana's eyes. It was like her loss was a mask that had clouded over her true self. Did everyone who lost someone look that way? Did I? I'd never seen a funeral pyre, and the only times I'd heard the verses for the dead were in Peter's stories. I never knew to miss my parents before. They were figments, stories that I never really felt the need to hear. But now I was closer to something I couldn't begin to grasp. I rubbed my thumb over the handle of my knife. My mother's hands had touched that same wood. I pictured her fingers, warm over mine, showing me how to chop, mince, and dice. When I looked up, she vanished, a ghostly remnant of my imagination. If I could find my father, maybe I could find her too.

Liana leaned over to look at the carvings on the handle as I chopped the rosemary and sage on my cutting board. She frowned, disapproval written all over her face.

"Where did you get that? That's not a kitchen blade."

"It's mine. I keep it here." I showed her the leather sheath that Peter made for me to wear on a belt around my waist.

"You're allowed to carry a knife around?"

"She's quite good with it," Greta said, nodding in my direction. I minced the herbs on the board and looked to Liana for approval. Her expression softened.

"Not bad. I could teach you a thing or two if you want."

I shrugged. "Sure."

Loud thumping sounded above us, and I jumped in my seat.

Greta looked up. "That would be Peter. He's got some new project he won't tell me about. I swear that man is going to fall off the roof someday." She looked over at Jack. "He'll probably go out and check his traps later, if you want to go with him."

Jack perked up. "What's he trapping?"

"Quail and pheasant, mostly. Sometimes rabbits or a turkey."

A frown of jealousy wormed its way into my chest. If I wasn't needed in the kitchen, I was the one who would check traps with Peter. He showed me how to reset them once they sprang, and I made sure he would free any wood sparrows, which we called dumbirds, that wandered into the traps.

The thumping overhead changed to the harsh rubbing of a saw.

"What is he doing up there?" I got out of my seat to look.

Greta shook her head and motioned for me to sit back down. "Never mind him. We've got work to do."

We spent the rest of the morning opening packages and sorting through the food that Peter bought for Lady Portia's banquet. Unfamiliar meats were packaged in crates of ice that I moved to the icebox, stuffing everything in until my hands turned blue. Jack delighted in naming some of the fruits and spices I didn't recognize.

"That's a stalk of flickersweet. And this"—he pointed to the large, bumpy, purple fruit in his hand—"is a snow lemon." Gingerly placing the snow lemon on the table, he reached over and grabbed a pale blue fruit from the box. "These are my favorite! They're from the Vale." He started to put it in his mouth. "It's—"

"Not for you," Greta interrupted, taking the fruit and shooing him away. "Go help Peter."

Jack bounded up to the loft, where the sawing had changed to a loud, staccato hammering. When he was gone, Greta, Liana, and I looked over Lady Portia's banquet menu, and Greta delegated tasks to each of us. She put the snow lemons in front of me.

"Open them and smash up the insides."

I took my knife out of its sheath, steadied the fruit, and bore down with the blade. It wouldn't pierce the tough skin. Liana tried to hide her laughter as I attempted to slice through the lemon, smacked it repeatedly with the handle of the knife, and stabbed it with the tip of the blade. The purple shell was not even dented, and my fingers, still tender from clawing at the walls of the room with no windows, throbbed. Finally, with a shout, I threw the lemon on the floor. It cracked in two perfect halves, and cold, white powder shot up from the flesh to cover my skirt and apron.

"Snow lemons," I said. "I get it."

Lady Portia came into the kitchen house without knocking.

"Well?" She looked around for a response.

I couldn't catch enough air to breathe.

"Where is Peter?" Portia paced around the kitchen, ruffling through piles of food and opening the icebox to look inside. "Did he get everything?"

Peter peeked over the edge of the loft. "Yes, ma'am. Everything you asked for." His face blurred as my vision swam. I grabbed the edge of the table. My wrists burned with phantom pain.

Lady Portia gusted by, looking everywhere but at me.

"Are you sure? Even the diamond conchs? Queen Catalina loves them, and so help me, if they aren't perfect—"

"We have everything you asked for, ma'am," Liana said. She put a hand on Portia's shoulder and steered her back to the door. "Don't worry. Your banquet will be just splendid."

I'd never seen anyone talk to Lady Portia like that, as though she were simply a nuisance to be managed. My muscles unclenched. Liana closed the door and went back to her work without another word. I wanted to applaud.

By the time Peter sent Jack down from the loft, I had opened all of the snow lemons and was sitting in front of a large, cold pile of frothy pulp. Greta had me shaving bits off the peels with a small razor.

"He wants you," Jack said as he sat down next to me.

I dropped the razor and hurried to the ladder. In the loft, Peter was hammering nails into the roof around a window that hadn't been there when I woke up that morning. The glass was positioned right above my bed. Perspiration shined on his brow.

"Do you like it?"

There had been no discussion about my time in the dark room, about my fears of the darkness coming for me at night. He had just known. I could find an escape in the stars that would shine above me, in the light poking through the sheet of hungry blackness. I threw my arms around him.

"Thank you."

Peter, my father. But not.

"Are we still going to check traps?" Jack stood at the top of the ladder.

"If your ma says it's okay." Peter rapped his knuckles against the window to make sure it stayed in place. I stood on my tiptoes and did the same, but when my hand hit the glass, it was for luck.

"You'll make sure he's safe?" Liana said when we came back down into the kitchen.

"I'll do my best." Peter put his tools back in their box behind the ladder. "I make no guarantees the ogres in the woods will do the same."

Jack's eyes widened. "Are there really ogres?"

Liana stepped between them. "Of course not. Don't go putting silly ideas in his head, Peter. He's too old for that."

Peter winked at Jack. "We'll be back before you start dinner," he said. "They're having pheasant in the main house tonight, provided you and I find some in the traps."

"What about all the meat you bought?" I asked. I wanted to keep Peter in the kitchen with me.

"That's for the banquet," Peter said. He ruffled my hair, strapped his bow and quiver of arrows over his back, and gestured for Jack to follow him. A pang of disappointment dampened my smile. I sat back down and picked up my razor. The lemons weren't going to zest themselves.

Peter and Jack came back with three pheasants later in the day. Jack was telling Peter a long story about a time when he had almost fallen in the well at the Vale proper. Greta smiled a thin, secret smile.

"I think he's going to tire poor Peter out," she whispered in my ear.

We stopped our banquet preparations to make dinner. Liana laid the roasted pheasant on plates and placed baked apples that she had carved into floral shapes next to them. Greta fished a loaf of bread out of the oven, setting half aside for the next morning's breakfast, and slicing the other half into thick pieces. Peter readied the cart with a pitcher of wine for Sir Alcander and Lady Portia and a pitcher of water for Siobhan and Annabelle. As soon as Liana put the plates on the cart, he pushed it towards the door.

"Are you coming?" he asked, looking in my direction. My tongue tied with surprise, and my head began to pound. How could he ask me to go back to the main house?

"Yep!" The voice came from behind me as Jack followed Peter out of the kitchen. Why was he allowed to go when I never had been? It wasn't my age that relegated me to the kitchen, I was sure of it. Lady Portia's venom was proof.

I sank so deep into my thoughts that I didn't hear Greta telling me to sit down for supper. Everyone else was already at the table. I trudged over to join them, feeling the weight of everything I was missing drag me back into the dark.

CHAPTER 4

*R*outine was a fact of life in the kitchen house. Bread was made in the morning, tea poured in the afternoon, and silver plates brought out for dinner in the evening. I found comfort in this; there was something nice about knowing what to expect. But the day before the banquet, the routine stopped. In the morning, Peter took Jack out to the forest with his bow and arrows. Greta was relying on them to come back with deer slung over their shoulders. She needed the bones for the stock for the burdock and spring pea soup favored by King Philip. She was not amused when I suggested that Jack was so small that he would have to ride the deer back to the kitchen house instead of carrying it.

Liana puzzled over what to do with the strange vegetables from the Ken that Portia called diamond conchs. She poked and prodded them with the tip of her knife until one jumped off the table and we realized that they were actually mollusks in a transparent shell.

"Throw them in the pot and boil them," Greta said as Liana chased one around the floor. "We'll serve them with butter and snow lemon cream."

I sat at the window, chopping whatever Greta put in front of me and watching Siobhan and Annabelle, who were once again playing under the hazel tree. Annabelle tiptoed behind a wood sparrow that hopped across the grass, oblivious to her presence. Siobhan sat on one of the lower branches of the tree, singing. I was too far away to hear what the song was, but her voice was lovely. It was a nice contrast to the hurried shouting around me as another one of the strange ocean creatures got away from Liana's pot and Greta dissolved in laughter. Siobhan stopped singing when Annabelle climbed up next to her.

By the time Liana's pot stopped hissing, the conchs' shells had become translucent and begun to sparkle. She lifted one out with a pair of tongs, cracked its shell open, and butterflied it faster than I thought possible. I had just gotten up to ask her to show me how she worked so fast with her knife when a heavy thump came from outside.

Annabelle screamed on the ground below the tree. Her face was bright red, and her left arm hung at an awkward angle. Greta ran up behind me. I could tell from the look in her eyes that the soup she had been so worried about was the furthest thing from her mind.

"Mash up valerian root and mead-wort. And get her a piece of white willow bark to bite down on," she said and ran outside.

I'd seen Greta in full healer mode before, when I was seven, and Peter had been bitten by a silverhead snake in the garden. It was as though she ripped away the mask that made her a kitchen servant and revealed a truer self underneath. I wished I could do the same, but my hands started shaking the moment I heard Annabelle fall.

I hurried to the herb garden and pulled up one of the tall mead-wort stems, then ran back into the kitchen and grabbed the bottle of valerian root oil from the shelf. Outside, Greta tried to coax a hysterical Annabelle up off the ground as Siobhan stood idly behind them. I poured the oil into the mortar on the table, plucked the leaves and flowers off the mead-wort, and threw it all in together. Greta gave up niceties and dodged kicks as she lifted Annabelle off the ground.

I took the white willow bark out of its jar, put one piece in my pocket, and chopped the other. I'd had enough scrapes and falls to know that even though she hadn't asked for it, Greta would want to give Annabelle white willow tea. I threw the chopped bark in the kettle already on the hearth. At the last moment, I added honey to the mead-wort and valerian oil mixture.

Liana blocked the doorway, that disapproving look back on her face.

"I've helped Greta plenty of times," I said. "I know what to do." I bore down with the pestle, macerating the ingredients in the mortar.

"Making potions?" she said.

She thought I was practicing magic. There wasn't time to argue. Greta was calling me. I threw the pestle aside.

"It's healing, not magic." I grabbed a bottle of castor oil, put it in my pocket with the bark, and dashed past Liana with the mortar in hand. Greta was already at the back entrance to the main house, struggling to open the door with Annabelle taking up both of her arms.

"Nora, get the door," she called.

Halfway across the field, I stopped. She wanted me to go to inside. Cold pricked at my skin. I couldn't go back in, not now. My shadow self, all black soot, yellow eyes, and dark that eats people alive was waiting on the other side of that door.

"I can't go in there."

"You're coming," Greta said. "I can't do this without you."

I shook my head, clutching the mortar to my chest. She had to understand. The dark room was still there. Once it was open, it would have infected the entire house. I'd lose her to the darkness too.

"Nora." Greta was insistent, nodding at the door. "I need your help."

Siobhan poked Annabelle's foot. Annabelle moaned in pain.

If I couldn't take off a mask like Greta could, I'd have to put one on. A mask of bravery and strength, even if underneath it was cinder black. I pushed open the door, and Greta carried Annabelle inside. I followed close behind in case Greta's courage was contagious.

Siobhan bumped into me as we walked, trying to knock me over. I kept my eyes on the floor, holding tightly to the mortar as I followed the hem of Greta's skirt into what had to be the dining room. In the center, there was a long, bare table that had yet to be prepared for the next day's banquet. Greta lay Annabelle on top of it as Lady Portia rushed in.

"What happened?" She ran to Annabelle's side. Gone was the woman who threw me into the room with no windows. This was a mother afraid for her hatchling who had fallen out of the nest. She stroked Annabelle's cheek, whispering words of comfort.

"It's her shoulder," Greta said.

"I can see that," Portia snapped, but her tone was frantic, not angry. Annabelle's shoulder jutted forwards much farther than it should have under the puffed sleeve of her dress.

Siobhan snorted, looking at Annabelle through narrowed eyes. It might have been a laugh. It occurred to me that Annabelle's swift exit from the tree might not have been an accident.

"What happened?" Portia looked to Siobhan.

"She fell," Siobhan said without expression. She glanced at me as Portia turned back to coo at Annabelle. Did she want me to back her up, or was she worried I would contradict her story? I frowned at her. Darkness crept in at the edges of the room as she glared back at me. She could easily say that I was the one who hurt her sister, and Portia would believe her.

"She was climbing the tree outside," I said. "It was an accident."

I squirmed as Lady Portia looked at me for the first time since she entered the room. For a moment, the lights shifted, and flames burned behind her eyes.

"What are you doing here?" She started towards me.

Annabelle grabbed her with her good arm, tethering Portia to her side.

"Mother!" she cried. "It hurts!"

"Nora, the mortar." Greta eyed Lady Portia until she moved aside. "Annabelle, you need to eat some of this. It doesn't taste good, but it will help your shoulder." She took a spoon out of her pocket and scooped up the sticky mixture. Annabelle wrinkled her nose at the green-brown color but opened her mouth and swallowed.

"It's sweet," she said. Greta looked back at me.

"I added honey," I said. "It will help her heal faster, right?"

Greta gave me a curt nod and turned back to Annabelle. "I'm going to put your arm back in place now," she said. I handed her the piece of white willow bark from my pocket, and she put it in Annabelle's mouth. "Bite down on this. Nora, hold her down."

She ripped Annabelle's sleeve open and shifted her over so that her left shoulder hung off the edge of the table. Portia yelped in surprise. Annabelle whimpered in pain. Her eyelids began to sag; the valerian was already tiring her out. I put my hands on her good shoulder.

"Talk to her," Greta whispered as she lifted Annabelle's forearm.

"Hi, Annabelle." I tried my best to sound calm. Her eyes were red from crying. Greta slowly rotated her arm outwards. "Are you excited for the banquet?"

"Mm-hmm." Annabelle gritted down on the bark.

"We're cooking some weird sea creatures from the Ken. Liana is chasing them around the kitchen now. I hope they taste good, because it's a lot of work to wrangle them into the pot."

While I babbled, Greta lifted Annabelle's arm, and Annabelle clenched her teeth harder against the bark. She squeezed her eyes shut as Greta rotated her arm back in until a pop echoed through the room. Tears slipped from the corners of her eyes.

"You did a good job," Greta said, brushing Annabelle's hair from her forehead. I let out the breath I didn't realize I was holding as she looked at me. "You too."

I fished the castor oil out of my pocket. "I put willow tea on the fire. And I brought this, too. I thought that since Peter uses it for his knees when they hurt—"

"Very good, Nora," Greta said. She looked towards the door. "Does anyone have a rag?"

I turned around to see Sarah and Matthew watching us.

"Of course." Sarah passed us a cloth she had tucked into her apron. Greta soaked it in castor oil and wound it around Annabelle's shoulder. She used her apron to fashion a sling for Annabelle's arm.

"She'll be fine," she said to Lady Portia. "Have her lie down for the rest of the day."

Lady Portia nodded. "She won't have to wear that sling tomorrow at the banquet, will she?"

Greta wiped off the table. "She needs to rest the arm for the next few days."

Portia's eyes widened. "Days? That can't be. The Queen will think I don't take care of my children."

"Queen Catalina is a mother. She'll understand." Greta picked the mortar off the table. "I'll be back with the willow tea in an hour."

"Thank you," Portia said as though it pained her to do it.

"I couldn't have done it without Nora." Greta passed me the mortar. "The honey and castor oil were her ideas. Good ones too."

I couldn't help smiling, even when Portia's eyes told me I shouldn't take pride in any of this.

"Come on, Nora. We have a lot of work to do." Greta beckoned for me to follow her. "We'll see you tomorrow for the banquet." She looked at Portia with a gaze that would harden stone. "Both of us."

With that, she turned on her heels and left the room. I hurried after her, not wanting to see the expression on Portia's face.

CHAPTER 5

ith just three words, Greta had condemned me to serve at the banquet in the main house. I felt like the deer Peter and Jack stalked in the forest. Vulnerable. Exposed. I couldn't sleep even with the stars shining down into the loft from the new window in the roof.

In the morning, I followed her around. The words, "Do I have to?" hovered on my lips as Greta paced around the kitchen, shouting directions and making sure everything was getting done according to her timetable.

"Peter, I said sage and rosemary on the venison, not felberry hips. Nora, cut the greens evenly, would you? Jack, take your hands off the sprigberries and put them in the pie."

"I can't put them in the pie if my hands aren't on them." Jack popped a berry into his mouth. I cringed. He didn't know Greta well enough to realize that this was not a time to be mouthy. As far back as I could remember, Portia and Sir Alcander only had minor lords from the Runes over for dinner and occasionally hosted nobles from nearby provinces. They'd never thrown a banquet of this size, with the King and Queen and nobility from all over Colandaria expected.

Greta stopped pacing. "Get out of my kitchen."

Jack shrugged and ran outside. I moved over to the seat he vacated and picked up where he left off with the pie. Greta was so tightly wound that one wrong word could make her burst. "I don't want to serve at the banquet" was a whole sentence's worth of wrong.

It wasn't just that I was afraid of Lady Portia. I imagined the long list of mistakes I could make that would land me right back in the room with no windows. I could over-season the soup. I could put one too few berries in the pie. I could breathe on Portia's slice of bread. She'd know, I was sure of it.

"Nora!" Greta grabbed the fork that I was using to crimp the edges of the pie crust. The doughy border was a mess of slash marks. "You too. Get out. Come back when you can hold a utensil straight."

Tears sprang to my eyes. What happened to the Greta who had been such a comfort just a few days ago? I needed a mother who would keep me out of danger, not one who was going to thrust me right into it. I gripped the edge of the table to quiet my shaking hands.

"Greta, I don't want to go to the banquet."

Greta stopped her work and turned to me. "We need you there. Portia does too, even if she doesn't know it. You just wait until you see the King and Queen eating those bilberry biscuits of yours, and it will all be worth it." She dotted my nose with a berry-covered finger, an old gesture from when I was young. It was meant to be reassurance. I wiped off the berries with my sleeve. Streaked on the fabric, they looked like blood.

"Now get out of my kitchen," Greta said.

I ran outside, where the sky was open. Why couldn't she understand? If there was one thing that had been made abundantly clear, it was that I was not supposed to be in the main house. There was no way that helping Annabelle was enough to earn my way in, and Greta was too preoccupied to see it.

"Hey!"

I looked up to see Jack sitting on the roof, dangling his feet over the edge.

"Greta kicked you out too? What did you do?"

I didn't want to explain myself to him. "Nothing. She's just stressed out." So was I. I hugged my arms around my chest. Greta would call for us to come back in any time now; there was too much work to get done. I just wasn't sure I could do everything she asked of me with the main house hovering in the distance like a promise I desperately wanted to break.

Jack gestured to the ladder that leaned against the side of the kitchen house.

"Come on up! You can see clear into the forest from here."

A pair of black horses trotted out of the woods, down the southeastern path towards the main house, pulling a large carriage behind them. Any time Lady Portia and Sir Alcander had guests over, I would watch the carriages arrive, crossing in front of my window on their way to the front of the main house. Without knowing who they were, I made up stories about the lords and ladies who came to visit.

This would be good. This would be routine.

I climbed the ladder and held my arms out to steady myself as I walked across the roof to Jack. The dark blue coat of arms on the door of the carriage that drove past meant that the guests were from the Summit, the province northwest of the Runes where Peter and Greta grew up. Liana hurried towards the main house with a cart loaded with pastries and a pot of tea. A second carriage appeared on the path bearing a red coat of arms, no doubt from the Fall.

"They had to travel for more than a day to get here," Jack said. "Can you imagine being stuck in a carriage for that long?"

The Fall was the northernmost province, buried among the mountains in the western corner of Colandaria. Even though I'd never left the Runes proper, Peter had seen to it that I could point to the major areas of the country on Sir Alcander's maps. The nobles from the Fall had to pass through the Summit to get to the Runes.

"They probably stayed over at the Summit," I said. "Maybe they're friends."

"I wouldn't want to be stuck in a carriage for that long," Jack said. "You probably have to sit real close to whoever is next to you. I bet you'd bang knees all the time."

He scooted closer and knocked his knee into mine. I shifted away.

"Maybe that's why the ladies wear so many layers," I said. "To keep their knees from getting bruised."

Jack laughed. He had a good laugh, easy and natural, like water running over a rocky stream. "If I were a lord, you wouldn't see me with a servant driving my carriage," he said. "I'd ride the horse myself."

I laughed this time. "No way you would. That's only in stories—the handsome lord rides through the forest and meets a beautiful maiden. In real life, the lord would have a servant guiding his horse, and he wouldn't even see the maiden because the curtains of the carriage would be shut. Do you even ride?"

Jack frowned. "No. Sir Milton started to teach me—he's the Lord of the Vale. But then we left to come here. Do you?"

"Mm-hmm. Peter taught me how."

"Maybe he can teach me sometime." He stared longingly at the horses as they trotted away.

"Maybe," I said. Jack's hair ruffled in the breeze. He looked shrunken in his clothes. "Why doesn't your shirt fit?"

"Ma made it so I could grow into it." His cheeks colored as he pulled on the sleeve. "It's not so bad, is it?"

"No, it's not that bad. Look." I pointed at the next carriage that appeared on the path, another painted Summit blue. "I bet that one has been chasing the first two the whole time. The lord from the Summit must have forgotten his handkerchief. This is his lady bringing it to him." I waved an invisible scrap of fabric in the air. "My lord! Your hankie!"

Jack grinned. "Yeah, or maybe the lord can't wait to eat Ma's cabbage rolls, so he left the Summit early. He must like bad food." The first carriage, the one with the black horses, came back around the side of the main house on its way to the stable. "I don't think I'd want to be invited to a banquet."

I couldn't imagine not wanting to go to a dinner like this. When I was cooking, I always fantasized about getting all fancied up in a sparkling green dress, putting emeralds in my hair, and eating gourmet courses until my stomach burst. Siobhan and Annabelle got to do that all the time. I doubted they ever dreamed about eating a simple meal in the kitchen house.

Jack continued, "It's the table. Banquet tables are too long, and the person who sits at the head is so much more important than everyone else. It's not fair. And you can only talk to the people on either side of you. What if you don't like them?"

"I've never been to any of the banquets here," I said. "I'm—" I hesitated for a moment. "I'm not supposed to be in the main house." I stared at the coarse green fabric of my skirt, pinching it between my fingers. "Did Sir Milton have a lot of banquets at the Vale?"

"He had a few. Nothing like this, though. Nothing with the King." Jack ran his hands over the shingles on the rooftop. "I miss him a lot. My pa too."

I leaned my chin against my knees. I didn't even know to miss my father until now. I couldn't imagine having him and then losing him. That must hurt even worse.

"Do you like it here?" I asked.

"It's fine. But Sir Milton was nicer than Lady Portia or Sir Alcander. I've never even seen him, and she's…" He trailed off, searching for the right words.

"I know," I said. "She is."

He smiled. "There weren't many other kids around in the Vale, but Sir Milton's daughter Bess was my friend. The girls here—"

"I don't even think they're each other's friends."

Jack nodded. Flecks of green shined in his hazel eyes. "I guess we're stuck being lonely together, then."

"I guess we are," I said. Jack opened his mouth to say something, but I shushed him and pointed to where Siobhan followed Annabelle around the side of the kitchen house. They were both dressed for the banquet in green silk dresses with bows around their waists. A thick emerald ribbon kept Siobhan's hair off her face.

"I'll ask Greta," Annabelle was saying. "You'll see."

Siobhan grabbed the sling that held Annabelle's arm in place. "Mother says you have to take it off!"

"No!" Annabelle wrestled away and ran into the kitchen house.

Jack's foot scraped against the shingles, and Siobhan looked up at us. She put her hands on her hips.

"What are you looking at, Owl Eyes?"

"Nothing," I said.

Annabelle came back out of the kitchen. "She says I have to leave it on."

"Who are you going to listen to," Siobhan said, "Mother or some servant?"

"Some servant?" I stood up, balanced on the pitched roof. Jack stood up behind me. Greta was more than just some servant, and if she said something was the case, that meant it was. She meant what she said about Annabelle wearing the sling, and she also meant what she said about me serving at the banquet. She might not have been able to protect me from the room with no windows, but if she believed I could serve at the banquet, then maybe I could. Her belief would scare my shadow-self away.

"Go scavenge for some mice, Owl Eyes." Siobhan pulled Annabelle away by her injured arm.

"I'll put mice in your soup," I muttered.

Jack chuckled. I climbed back down the ladder and went inside to help Greta.

~

When it was almost time for the meal, everyone went up to the loft to change. Liana shooed me behind a dressing screen that she brought from the Vale, where I changed into a new dress made of smooth, green material. It was a sharp contrast from my usual skirt. I wondered when Greta had time to make it. Peeking around the side of the screen, I could see Jack tugging at the brown britches with white stockings that Liana gave him to wear, and I couldn't hide my laughter behind the hand that covered my mouth. He smirked as Greta tried to brush down my hair and fastened a white cap to my head. I tied my apron, which had been washed and starched so that it was crisp and white, around my waist.

Greta assigned each of us a cart with the first courses. Jack's was filled with breads and jams. He raised an eyebrow at me and plucked a fingerful of plum jam out of one of the bowls and popped it in his mouth. I slapped his hand away when he went in for a second taste.

Peter opened the kitchen house door, smooth on hinges he oiled that morning. The pathway to the main house was lined with torches. I went last, wheeling my cart as slowly as I could so as not to upset the drinks that were arranged on top. The cart did not agree with me. Liquid rumbled and pitchers threatened to tip over with my every step. It felt like a sign telling me to turn away. I had only made it halfway down the path by the time everyone else stopped at the door. Jack doubled back to help me.

"Now I get why no one let you into the main house before," he said, steadying the pitchers while I pushed the cart. "You're terrible at this."

His ribbing was different from Siobhan's—there was humor in his eyes when he spoke. But it didn't quiet my nerves or make the shadows that danced at the corners of my eyes go away. Together, we made it to the door that Liana propped open. I held my breath as I crossed the threshold.

We wheeled the carts through the halls until we reached the dining room. Greta put the carts in order at the back of the room as we filled goblets, straightened place settings, and put bread and jam on the table. A rich, forest-green cloth was laid out for the meal, and the house servants had set out fine copper plates and bowls. Each cream-colored napkin was embroidered in green with Sir Alcander's family crest: a quill, ivy leaves, and a unicorn.

Greta nodded to Robert, who went to announce that the table was ready, then lined us up along the wall.

"Stand up straight," she said to Jack. "Nora, fix your apron."

I looked down at where my apron hung askew and straightened it just as Lady Portia and Sir Alcander led their guests in. There must have been thirty or forty nobles trailing behind them, each wearing the colors of his or her province. I couldn't take my eyes off the woman who walked next to Lady Portia. Her violet-and-gold dress matched the amethysts that dotted her hair and hung around her neck. Her small gold crown reflected the light of the candles on the table. Queen Catalina. King Philip was next to her in a matching amaranthine tunic. The Prince and Princess, twins, followed behind them. They were flanked by royal guards who spread out around the room. Jack poked me in the side, and I exhaled.

I had been so worried that Lady Portia would be watching my every move, waiting for me to make a mistake so she could throw me back in the room with no windows, but she walked by us as though we were just part of the furniture. The rest of the lords and ladies were so engaged in their conversation that we remained invisible as the procession passed. It was a thrilling feeling—I could watch without being watched. I drank in as much of the sight as I could, trying to commit everything to memory. Then I felt it, a tingle up the back of my neck. Someone was looking at me. I searched the crowd until I found him: a balding lord with a large nose in a pale-blue-and-silver tunic standing at the back of the group. He stared at me with narrow, curious eyes.

Jack brightened. "Sir Milton!"

The lord's expression changed to a smile, and he offered Jack a small wave. Before that, I was sure that I was the one he had been watching. I didn't like the feeling.

King Philip sat at one end of the table, Sir Alcander at the other. Queen Catalina and Lady Portia sat next to their husbands with their children opposite them. Annabelle's sling was missing. She winced as she picked up her fork.

King Philip raised his glass. "A toast to Sir Alcander and Lady Portia for inviting us into their home again after so long. May this be the resumption of many banquets to come."

"To King Philip and Queen Catalina," Sir Alcander responded, "and to all of you for eating with us tonight. And, finally, to my wife, Lady Portia, for organizing this banquet for you all to enjoy."

Lady Portia beamed. I bristled. She may have done the inviting, but Greta was the one who organized the meal. King Philip nodded, and everyone drank.

Liana pushed out the cart with a large tureen of the soup we had finished that morning. Peter followed with a ladle and spooned the soup into bowls. Jack gave each guest a piece of salty bread.

"The wine, Nora." Greta pointed to my cart and gestured to each pitcher. "Blackberry, elderberry, and cherry. The King first."

Though she had not acknowledged us as she entered, Lady Portia watched with hawk-like attention as I wheeled the cart to the table. The candles on the wall flickered for a moment, plunging the room into darkness. The nobles sitting at the table kept up their laughter and conversation as though nothing happened. It was my fear that put the lights out. I couldn't let it win, not in front of Lady Portia. I tightened my grip on the cart. My knuckles were white by the time I stopped next to the King.

"More wine, Your Highness?"

King Philip turned to me. His dark beard was cut short to his face. Up close, he looked almost youthful.

"What is your name?" he asked. The floor quivered under my feet.

44

"Eleanor, sir."

"Yes, Eleanor," he said. "I would like some wine."

The pitchers stared up at me. Yellow candlelight flickered on top of the liquid.

"Blackberry, cherry, or—" I couldn't remember the last one.

"Cherry. And cherry for the Queen too. It's her favorite."

He moved his goblet so I could fill it. I looked over at Portia, who was still staring me down. She thought it was a mistake that I was here. If I were ever going to rid myself of the room with no windows, I had to prove her wrong. I tipped the pitcher, and the wine poured into King Philip's cup. I breathed a sigh of relief as Portia turned back to the woman seated next to her.

I filled the Queen's goblet and made my way down the row. The lord in blue, Jack's Sir Milton, sat on the other side of the table, watching me. I didn't know what else to do, so I smiled at him. He nodded at me and turned to talk to his neighbor.

At the other end of the table, Portia was talking up the food as though she had cooked it herself. "Oh, Abigail, just wait until you try the diamond conchs. I know you're used to having them in the Ken, but we've done a traditional Runes preparation, and they're just delightful."

She knew very well that we'd never cooked diamond conchs before. She was lucky that all of the creatures even made it into the pot. And the traditional Runes preparation she boasted about had ingredients in it from the Ken and the Summit. I wondered if Lady Abigail would say anything when she figured that out. It was too bad I would miss Portia's embarrassment.

Portia thrust her wineglass at me. "Elderberry."

I filled it to the brim without spilling a drop.

Sir Alcander was next. I stopped to take him in now that I was seeing him up close for the first time. His hair, dark brown with a few streaks of grey, was tied back with a thin green ribbon. His short beard covered what Greta would call a noble chin, which tilted up as I approached. It seemed like he made an effort not to look at me. It was a sharp contrast to Lady Portia's casual disdain. I wanted to see if his eyes were as dull in person as they were in the hallway portrait, but he turned away to look at Siobhan and Annabelle.

"More wine, sir?"

He stiffened. "No. Not now."

Siobhan tittered next to him. "Hoot-hoot," she said. She poked Annabelle's arm, making her cringe. My cheeks burned. My small feeling of triumph at having proven myself to Lady Portia was gone. I continued around the table, filling glass after glass without looking at the guests. Something about the way Sir Alcander had so pointedly ignored me made me think that this would be the last banquet at which I'd be serving.

I made my way back to Greta, who took the wine cart and gave me a tray with Liana's cabbage rolls. They looked suspiciously like something I might find while cleaning out the stables. The King and Queen each took one and thanked me. I offered my tray to Prince Edward. He glanced at the cabbage roll, then at his sister. They both burst out laughing. I stepped back, mortified.

"Edward, Callista," Queen Catalina snapped. "Take what is offered to you."

Prince Edward held out his plate.

"Thank you, Eleanor," King Philip prompted.

"Thank you, Eleanor," the Prince repeated in a tone that indicated he would not be eating the roll when I walked away. Even so, part of me warmed at hearing him say my name.

We served course after course. There was far more food than I remembered making over the last few days. Peter kept going back to the kitchen house to get yet another dish or bowl. Liana left to bring food to the servants' quarters, where all of the carriage drivers had been seated at a long table that Peter and Robert set up in the morning. When she returned and there was only dessert left to serve, Greta pulled Jack and me aside.

"You did a good job," she said. "We'll finish here. You go to bed."

Jack started, "But I want to talk to—"

"To bed," Greta repeated. "You've had more than your share of excitement for the day."

Jack headed out of the dining room with his shoulders slumped in defeat. I followed behind him. As soon as we were out of view of the royal guards who had stationed themselves at the entrance, Jack grabbed my hand and pulled me in the opposite direction.

"Where are we going?" I pulled my hand back.

46

"Where do you think?" he said. "This is the time to explore!"

"Are you out of your mind?" I looked around. The hall was empty, but I could feel the crush of danger, tendrils of shadow slicking their way towards me. "Someone will catch us."

Jack motioned back to the dining room. "Everyone is either eating or serving. If we do get caught, what's the worst they can do? Send us back to the kitchen house?"

He didn't know, not about the room, not about the darkness, not about the shadow-girl who hung on my back. I wanted to tell him, but I feared that if I opened my mouth to speak, I would only let out a puff of ash.

Jack grinned and turned down the hall. "Come on!"

From somewhere deep inside, a small voice urged me to follow him. There was something hidden in this house, something Lady Portia didn't want me to find. Something that might lead to my parents. And Jack was right—there wouldn't be another moment like this, when everyone else was occupied. It had to be now. I had to outrun the shadows.

With everyone in the dining room or the servants' quarters, the halls belonged to us. We slid on polished floors and craned our necks to see the marble swirls on the ceiling and the molding carved with ivy leaves that topped the walls. The farther into the house we went, the more I felt the air clear around me.

"Lady Eleanor, I do think we need to tell the maid to polish the ceiling," Jack said, putting on airs. "The mica doesn't sparkle quite enough."

I straightened up, doing my best impression of Lady Portia. "Get the kitchen servants to do it. They don't have nearly enough work. Especially that ugly one with the yellow eyes. She's just atrocious. Put her up on the ladder. No one will care if she gets hurt."

Jack stared at me.

"What?" His expression made me uncomfortable, like I'd said too much.

"Why did you say that?"

"Well, Portia certainly thinks I'm atrocious. Did you see the way that she watched me in there?" I glanced around, sure that someone hid just around the corner, waiting to report back to Lady Portia.

"Not that. Why did you say you're ugly?"

"Come on." I pulled him down the hall. I could hear the walls hooting at me.

We peered into room after room. I yanked Jack away from the pianoforte in the music room as soon as he crashed his fingers down on the keys. A dissonant chord echoed from the ceiling, and I froze, gripping his hands and listening for the footsteps that would mean we were caught. When no one came, my relief was so great that I burst out laughing.

I followed Jack into another room farther down the hall. Framed maps and shelves lined the walls. A large, furry rug stretched out over the floor in the vague shape of the animal it once was. Parchment was strewn over every surface, and quills perched in inkwells on a canted desk. A half-finished map was laid out with weights holding down the corners. The map showed the Fall, each mountain detailed in red crosshatching and the river and the giant waterfall that gave the province its name drawn out in blue.

"Look at this!" Jack pointed to a suit of armor in the corner of the room. We knelt down to look at the plaque below it.

"Sir Alcander of the Runes, Knighted by King Philip for Exceptional Service to Colandaria in Her Time of Need," I read.

"What did he do?" Jack asked.

"He made maps and he fought. All the knights did." Sir Alcander was often away, traveling through Colandaria, even as far as the border of with the Farlands where the war was fought, to make his maps more precise.

Jack leaned against the desk. "Sir Alcander didn't say anything to me tonight. Sir Milton did, though. He said my pa misses me." He took a quill from the desk and ruffled the feather. "It was good to see him. I just wish we had more time to talk." He looked over at the cabinet on the other side of the room. "What's in there?"

My stomach fluttered as he opened the door and began taking out books and pieces of parchment. Even though the room was a mess when we arrived, we'd have to put everything back in its place before we left. I peeked out into the hallway, half expecting to see Sarah or Robert coming in our direction. They would just escort us back to the kitchen house, but if Lady Portia caught us on the way—

"Ha!" Jack shouted as he opened one of the large books he'd put on

48

the desk. I shushed him. "It's Alcander's logbook. Do you want to know how much everyone gets paid?"

Now he had my attention. Robert said that my father was no longer at the Runes, but if the logbook were old enough, maybe his name would be there. I leaned over Jack's shoulder.

"How far back does it go?"

Jack flipped backwards through the pages. "A long time—back before the Border Wars. Look." He pointed to the page where someone, Sir Alcander or the Lord of the Runes before him, began numbering the years at zero as King Philip had ordered when the Border Wars were won. I was born a few years after that. Of all the servants' names that were listed, I only recognized Robert's. He worked alongside servants named Carlton, Yllianne, Arelys, and Marc Charles. Could either of the men be my father? And the women—perhaps one of them was my mother. Where was she on these pages? In the fifth year after the war, the names changed, with only Robert remaining as a fixture in the house. Greta, Peter, Matthew, Sarah, and eventually Victor appeared as the entries went on.

I pointed to the spot where the names changed. "There were almost all new servants starting twelve years ago. What happened?"

"Maybe you scared off the old ones when you were born," Jack said. I thumbed my nose at him. He flipped forward in the book.

"No wonder Ma can't make me a shirt that fits." He gestured to where Liana's name appeared in the log's most recent entry. Her wages were listed as twenty lil per month, as were Greta's and Peter's. "That's not nearly enough. She made thirty lil a month in the Vale."

Jack's name had the number ten next to it. My name was at the bottom of the list. The space for my wages was blank.

"That's weird," Jack said. "Don't you get paid?"

I turned back to earlier entries in the log. Going back twelve years, each month, my name was written at the bottom of the list with no number next to it. My assumption that Greta and Peter held my wages for me was dead wrong.

"That's not fair," Jack said, echoing my thoughts. "How come we get paid and you don't?"

I didn't have a chance to respond. Footsteps came down the hall. I dashed to the door.

"They're coming this way." Jack yanked me back into the room. I looked around for somewhere to hide. There was only one place to go.

"In here!" I slammed the logbook shut and shoved Jack into the cabinet ahead of me, ignoring his protestations that it was too small and shutting the door just as the footsteps entered the study. As soon as the cabinet door closed, I had to quiet the urge to scream. Jack was pressed against my back. I could feel his panicked breath on my neck.

This is not the dark room. And you're not alone. There was small comfort in this. On the outside, the cabinet was smooth and polished, but the inside of the door was just as rough and unfinished as the door to the room with no windows. My wrist began to throb where Portia had grabbed it. The only saving grace was the small chink in the wood that let in the tiniest glow from outside. I pressed my eye to it, trying to drink in as much light as I could. I could see Sir Alcander enter the room with Sir Milton behind him.

"...a wonderful banquet, Alcander," Sir Milton was saying.

"Thank you, Milton. Philip is pleased that you attended."

"Sir Milton!" Jack whispered a bit too loudly. I squeezed his hand, hard. He squirmed behind me, making the cabinet feel even smaller. The temperature rose around us.

Sir Alcander rifled through the papers on his desk. "You should have a banquet of your own sometime. I'm sure everyone would like to come out to the Vale."

"Perhaps when Bess has finished her studies," Sir Milton said.

"Studies, yes." Sir Alcander fell silent. Sweat beaded on my forehead. The cabinet walls were too close. It felt like we were hiding in an oven.

"You can dispense with the formalities, Alcander." Milton dropped his cordial expression. "You wouldn't have invited me tonight if Philip weren't coming. Don't want to make a bad show, am I right?"

Sir Alcander bristled, and I couldn't help but smirk. Maybe this was his comeuppance for ignoring us during the meal. For a moment, the walls pulled away.

"That servant," Sir Milton continued. "The girl with the dark red hair. She looks an awful lot like—"

I gasped in stale air. I was right—Sir Milton had been watching me. I lurched forward, knocking my forehead against the cabinet door. It opened a crack, and I held my breath.

"Your map," Sir Alcander interrupted, thrusting a rolled-up parchment from his desk at Sir Milton's chest. "Pay and be done."

Sir Milton fished coins out of his pocket and handed them to Alcander. "She looks like Izella," he finished.

I was looking for my father, but here was my mother's name, spoken by someone who had obviously known her.

"Izella," I breathed. Jack clapped his hand over my mouth.

Sir Alcander gripped the edge of his desk. "Her child is dead." His voice tried to be flat and emotionless, but there was an undercurrent of rage in it that unmoored me.

"Eleanor?" Milton asked. "I remember that's what she wanted to name her."

Something was wrong. Very wrong. I had to get out of the cabinet, to get somewhere where this conversation wasn't happening.

"Take your map and go."

Milton sighed and shook his head. "Izella's daughter deserves better. Your daughter deserves better."

I was back in the darkness again. The pinpoint of light coming into the cabinet from the knot in the wood was not enough to keep it at bay. Sir Alcander looked as though he might rush across the room and stab Sir Milton with a quill. Milton walked out without looking back.

"Let go," Jack hissed in my ear. I was still clutching his hand. I didn't want to let go. I couldn't. I had to hold on to him. If I didn't, I was sure that this would all be revealed as a dream. Jack yanked his hand, clammy with sweat, out of my grasp.

Sir Alcander picked up the logbook we left on his desk and walked towards the cabinet. Jack buried his face in my hair. "No, no, no," he breathed. I dared Alcander to open the door, to find me there, to know I heard every word.

He reached for the handle.

"Father!" It was Siobhan, calling from the hall. Alcander put the logbook back on the desk, took a breath, and fixed a smile on his face.

Siobhan peeked into the room. "Edward and Callista have to leave."

"Let's go see them off, then." Alcander took her by the hand and led her back into the hall. It was the sort of thing a father would do.

As soon as Alcander left, Jack pushed his way past me and threw open the cabinet door.

"Too small," he panted. His face was ashy white.

I stayed in the cabinet. Just moments before, I couldn't wait to get out. Now I was nailed in place. He was here. Sir Alcander: my father, but not. Not at all. My father, lord of the manor, and me, his servant. No wonder Lady Portia didn't want me in the main house. I should always have been there, sitting next to Siobhan and Annabelle by my father's side, instead of being ignored as I offered him a drink.

"I thought you said your father was dead," Jack said. "Why would Alcander say *you're* dead?" His face softened as he looked at me. "Are you okay?"

"Shut up." I got up and walked out of the room.

"Nora—" Jack called. I kept walking. "Hide!" He pushed me behind a column just in time to avoid being seen by the procession coming down the hall. The royal family was leaving. Lords and ladies lined the hall by the front door to bid the King and Queen good night. Sir Alcander bowed before King Philip, who nodded back at him. Siobhan and Annabelle curtseyed. Portia whispered to Annabelle, and she curtseyed even lower, grimacing in pain as she held her skirt up. Prince Edward smiled at them as he and Princess Callista followed the King and Queen outside.

Realization roiled in my stomach. Siobhan and Annabelle were my sisters, and they didn't even know it. Or maybe they did, and their daily routine of reminding me I was their servant was a way to keep me in my place. I had a real family, and all I wanted to do was to put as much distance between myself and them as possible.

"Thank you for coming," Portia said to the crowd once the royal family left. "One of the servants will escort those of you who are staying to your rooms." She and Alcander remained at the door to bid farewell to the nobles from the Vale and the Summit as they went to their coaches. Sir Milton walked out without acknowledging either of them. Sarah, Matthew, and Robert circulated among the guests from the Fall and the Ken and the minor lords and ladies who lived around the Market, taking them to the rooms on the second floor.

My vision clouded over as I followed Jack to the back door. The torches that lit the path were already extinguished. I didn't want to go to the kitchen house. From across the field, I didn't recognize it as home. The main house wasn't home either, even though it should have been.

I had almost crossed the field when I realized that Jack was no longer with me. I looked back to see him standing by the main house with Sir Milton. Moonlight reflected off their faces, giving Sir Milton's balding head and prominent nose a blue glow. Jack's face was lit with a wide smile as he gesticulated wildly while talking to the knight.

I wasn't jealous of him, not exactly. Sir Milton wasn't his father. But it still wasn't fair. As Lord of the Vale, Sir Milton treated Jack far better than Alcander ever treated me, and I was his daughter. Why wasn't I curtseying to the royal family with Siobhan and Annabelle? The hole in my life was supposed to be filled when I found my father. Instead, it felt so deep that I couldn't claw my way out.

Jack hugged Milton goodbye and jogged back over to me.

"Sir Milton asked about you," he said. The knight went back around the front of the house to get his coach. "He wanted to know if you were okay. I told him I was watching out for you."

"Mm-hmm."

Jack looked at the ground, shuffling his feet. "You know, if you want to talk about it, I'd be happy to—"

"Jack! Nora!" Liana's voice cut across the field.

Jack's lips quirked up into a smile. "We're in trouble."

"I don't care." I tore the white cap off my head and thrust it into his hands. "Go back to the kitchen house. I'll be there in a bit."

He glanced at the window where his mother stood, then back at me. "They're going to ask where you are."

I started towards the main house.

"Tell them I went to talk to my father."

CHAPTER 6

I didn't know where to find him. I wasn't sure I wanted to. There were too many things to say. Twelve years of things.

The house servants were busy escorting guests to their rooms, but they still managed to take the time to order me back to the kitchen house when they passed me in the hall. As if I needed a reminder.

Robert hurried by with a candle snuffer. "Nora." He ran a hand through the grey hair I once hoped matched mine. "You shouldn't be here. Go back to the kitchen house and tell Greta that Sir Alcander wants his tea in his study."

I curtseyed, keeping my gaze on the floor so that he couldn't see the tears swimming in my eyes. I would have been happy if he were my father, even if I had gone twelve years without knowing it. Even now, I felt closer to him than I did to Sir Alcander. Robert and I were the same. The knight, the master of the house, was so far above us. The part that hurt the most was that this was his design. I wasn't born a servant. Alcander made me one. I needed to understand why.

"Yes, sir."

Robert continued down the hall, and I headed in the direction from which he'd come, straight to Alcander's study. With each step, more of my numbness turned to pins and needles of hot anger. I had to release it before I was riddled with holes.

The door to the study was closed. I pushed it open without knocking.

My father sat at his desk, hunched over a map with a quill in his hand. In the shadows cast by the few candles that remained lit, he looked not like a man but like a mountain, one that I could never get over.

He didn't look up from his work.

"Yes?"

Now that I was there, I didn't know what to say. The only thing that would come out was, "Sir."

His eyes met mine for the barest moment, and shame flooded through me. I should be calling him Father, Papa, Daddy. But if I did, I would tether myself to him in a way that I could never break, in a way that I longed for just as much as I feared.

Alcander looked back at his parchment. Pained lines carved themselves into his face. He knew why I was there. He knew everything.

"It is not proper for a kitchen servant to address her lord alone in the main house."

He named me what he made me. A servant, nothing more. But it wasn't the truth, not my truth. It couldn't be.

"Daughters"—I stepped farther into the room—"can address their fathers any time they want."

I stared at him until he looked up. His eyes were cold, iron grey.

"You don't know anything about being a daughter. What do you want, Eleanor?"

I felt nothing at hearing him say my name for the first time. There was no emotion in his words, no warmth, not even the calm father voice he put on for Siobhan when she came to this same room before. We were strangers. I wished I could feel nothing, too, but everything was bubbling up inside me.

"You're my father."

"No." He turned back to his work.

I rushed to his desk.

"You are! Robert knows it. Sir Milton said it. Lady Portia locked me in the room with no windows for even asking about it."

"She did what?" He looked up, alarmed.

I took a step back, surprised at the panic on his face. He didn't know.

I'd been so close to him, just a few doors down from this one for more than a day, and he didn't even know. Now maybe he would do something about it.

"She did! It was awful and dark and—"

"You shouldn't have been in that room," he said. "You're not supposed to be—" He glanced around, looking for an escape. I couldn't tell if he was upset that Portia hurt me or anxious that I'd been somewhere I wasn't supposed to be.

I gripped the edge of his desk. "I was! You should have helped me!"

Alcander stood, knocking his inkwell to the floor. Black liquid splashed onto my skirt.

"I owe you nothing," he barked.

"You owe me a father," I cried. "You owe me a home."

"You have a home. And a father. I could have left you out for the wolves."

I bit the inside of my cheeks to keep from crying. Blood burst onto my tongue. The pain told me I was really here, really hearing him. My father.

"Sir Milton said I deserve better."

Alcander crossed his arms in front of his chest. "That meddler needs to keep his mouth shut."

I leaned in. This was my only chance.

"Who is Izella?"

Alcander grabbed my arm and pulled me close. I was as near to him as I would ever be.

"She's dead," he hissed. "Don't you dare foul this house with her name."

"She's my mother," I cried, wrestling my arm away. His fingerprints stood out scarlet on my skin. His mark was on me, whether he wanted it or not. It always had been.

"She's dead." He turned to the window. "You killed her."

The darkness returned. I knew my mother died in childbirth, but this accusation condemned me. I would never be a daughter to Alcander. I was a murderer. The new identity settled over me like evening fog.

We stood in silence until I asked the only question I could. "Do you wish I were dead?"

Alcander didn't respond.

For just a moment, he had been my father. Now I knew he was not. I didn't have his eyes, his hair, his home. This moment was all I would ever get from him. He waved his hand in a useless gesture.

"Go back to the kitchen house. Don't bother me anymore."

Hot, angry tears ran down my cheeks.

"I hate you," I said. I spat in the puddle of ink at my feet. Sir Alcander did not even turn around to watch me run out of the room.

I ran through corridors of the house that would never be mine. Outside, I followed the northwestern path away from the Runes. I couldn't stay here, not with the main house pulsing like a living thing, mocking me from above.

I wiped the tears from my eyes and looked up. Branches cut the white and grey moon into pieces. I wasn't sure I could traverse the fragmented path alone. Cool wind shivered my shoulders. I knew that if I turned back to the Runes proper, I might never be able to leave. But I'd never left the estate before. I had nowhere else to go.

"Nora?"

I turned back. Jack stood on the path behind me.

"Where are you going?"

Dark trees surrounded me. I was lost.

"I don't know," I said.

"So let's go home." He extended his hand and pressed his fingers to mine just as I had when I tried to show him I was a person, real, whole. Not a spirit, not dead at all. I didn't know what else to do. Heaving sobs erupted from my chest. I cried on his shoulder as we stood together under the tree-broken moon.

CHAPTER 7

We were older, then.

Five summers passed, their patterns sewn with stitches I could not break. Five summers with bread baked in the morning, gardens tended in the afternoon, and dinners prepared in the evening. At twelve, I had only made it as far as the entrance to the woods. The Runes proper was home, whether it welcomed me or not. But the comfort of the kitchen house was preferable to the uncertainty of a country I only knew from maps. At seventeen, I had gone a bit farther, to the local market with Peter and Jack. But at the end of the day, my path always led back to the kitchen house. It was the only place I had.

"Watch your head!" I shouted as I sawed through the rope that held our net trap in the air. The net landed on the ground next to Jack, who knelt down to check our catch.

"Finchlings," he said. I groaned.

Our nets used to catch pheasants and turkeys, but this summer their numbers had dwindled. Peter said it was due to the weather. The ground was dry from lack of rain, and dust stuck to our bodies like a second skin. I imagined that if I could slough it off, I might reveal someone new underneath, someone whose daily routine involved music lessons and teatime instead of kitchen work that only added another layer of sweat to her dusty veneer.

Jack's shoulders sagged as he stared at the small green birds fluttering in the net. It was a look I was used to seeing. Even though he was a good shot and a smart trapper, Jack preferred tending the garden to hunting. He occasionally came out with Peter and me, but he never seemed to master the art of unobtrusiveness in the forest. Sometimes I thought he scared rabbits and deer away on purpose. Closer to the kitchen house, the garden flourished under his care. Even without the rain, the only plants that grew were the ones he tended.

Peter came out from behind the trees with three skinny rabbits slung over his shoulder. His sigh echoed Jack's.

"Let them go."

I loosened the knot that held the net closed and was almost knocked backwards by the flurry of little green birds that flew up and away. Jack and I reset the trap, and, together, we left the woods.

~

The night of the banquet, Peter had been waiting for us when Jack and I came back to the kitchen house. Unable to keep it inside, I told him what I discovered about my father. His words did little to mask an anger I already understood well.

"That man is nothing," he said as he folded me into his arms. "I'm your father."

"I know," I said. But it wasn't the same. Nothing was anymore—it couldn't be, not when I knew I should be in the main house, sitting next to my sisters as Sir Alcander's firstborn. I loved Greta and Peter, but more and more often, I found myself hanging back and watching as the others laughed and worked, feeling apart from the parents who actually wanted me. An invisible wall had risen up between us, and even when I laughed at one of Peter's jokes or basked in the glow of Greta's praise, it didn't feel quite right. Not when my real father walked around choosing to see everything but me. Not when my real mother was nothing more than a knife and a name.

I didn't talk about it with Peter or Greta. I couldn't put the jumble of emotions I felt into words that made sense.

Maybe Peter couldn't either. Maybe that's why he almost lost his position soon after the banquet for barely missing Alcander with an arrow when the lord's coach drove by him in the woods. The arrow went in one window and out the other, a hair's breadth from Alcander's nose. It was only Greta's insistence that the coach must have come between Peter's bow and a deer on the other side that saved his job. Peter maintained he never missed a shot.

~

*N*ow, Peter's knees popped when he knelt down, but his aim was still as good as ever. The rabbits he carried over his shoulder were shot clean through the eye. Their heads bobbed with his steps as we went back to the kitchen house. Jack walked next to me, knocking his hip into mine as I made a game of trying to step on his toes. When he was thirteen, I had been taller, but now, at eighteen, Jack stood a whole head above me. His strides were longer than mine, and I had to rush to keep up. I was already off-balance when he knocked into me too hard and sent me flying to the ground.

"Oops." He grinned and offered a hand to help me up. Peter waited for us, shaking his head. I laughed Jack's offer away, got up, and jumped on his back. He carried me the rest of the way back to the kitchen house.

As soon as we came inside, Greta sent Jack out to the garden and handed me a tray with tea and biscuits to bring into the main house.

I groaned. "That's Liana's job!"

"She's resting in the loft."

I blew a piece of hair off my forehead and took the tray. Since the night of the banquet, I'd been in the main house plenty of times—Portia saw to it that I was added to the rotation of servants bringing in meals. Now that I knew who my father was, she took every opportunity to remind me of my place. I was at the bottom, lower than Greta or Peter, whom she awarded a certain measure of respect. I was the abomination, her husband's bastard child who hung on like a growth she couldn't remove.

I wondered why Alcander hadn't just put me out. He could have, a hundred times over. I imagined it was because of Izella, my mother, whoever she was. I preferred to think that he loved her enough that he still felt some responsibility towards me. It was better than thinking that he kept me at the Runes as punishment for a crime I never intended to commit.

Portia, on the other hand, threatened to get rid of me anytime I did something she didn't like. If her meat was overseasoned, it was, "Do your job or leave." If it was undercooked, it was, "You're not *my* child. I don't have any great need to keep you around." But there I was, still around.

Even if I had somewhere to go, I couldn't leave yet. Somewhere in the Runes proper were traces of my mother. She was not in Alcander's logbook, not on the paintings on the wall or in the whispers of the house servants. Even Robert was tight-lipped when I asked about her.

"There are some things it's better not to know," he said, hurrying me away. "This is one of them."

But by keeping me around, Alcander hadn't completely erased Izella from the Runes. Each night as I fell asleep, I would imagine what she looked like. Sir Milton had said something about how I looked like her. Did she have my gold eyes, my dark red hair? Or did I resemble her in some other way? Was she a kitchen servant or head of her own household, a traveling sorceress or a lowly stable girl? My mother was so many different women; I didn't know which was real. She had to be there, shut up in some secret corner of the house. I just had to find her.

Today, though, the midsummer air was oppressive, and I was not in the mood.

"Do you want to go?" I asked Jack, who knelt in the middle of the garden, pulling up the weeds growing between the cabbages.

"To the main house? I went the last two days. Yesterday, Siobhan threw a fork at me. It's your turn. Do it for Ma."

I glanced up at the window in the kitchen house roof. Since the heavy snow this winter, Liana could usually be found in the loft, resting as she recovered from a horrible cough she'd contracted after spending too long outside, searching for pine needles to line the jackets she made each of us. Jack and I took on more of her work to compensate. He did it without complaint, even going so far as to try to mimic Liana's intricate knife cuts so that no one in the main house would know it wasn't his mother's handiwork. Under Liana's tutelage, I had become more adept at using my knife than Jack had, so after he got frustrated, he usually ended up passing the plates to me.

"Please?" I said. "I'll clean the stable for a week if you go."

"I'd rather take the stable."

"Ugh." The tea and scones were for Siobhan and Annabelle's quarters. There were no hints of Izella there, only pointed looks and biting words.

Inside, the dulcet tones of the pianoforte sounded through the halls. Siobhan took up the instrument a few years ago and had become quite accomplished. She was often invited to neighboring estates to play. Portia encouraged Annabelle to take up an art as well, but nothing she tried really stuck. Her hands were not deft enough for music, and her failed attempts at drawing ended crumpled and strewn across the floor. More recently, Portia hired her a dance instructor. When I peeked into the music room, she was dancing barefoot in time to Siobhan's minuet. She leapt off the ground, twirling and landing gently on her toes.

"Owl Eyes." Siobhan stopped playing. Annabelle came down on her heels mid-spin.

"What's for dinner?" Siobhan asked, reaching over to the tray I put down next to the pianoforte. "These dry scones won't keep us for long."

I made the scones myself. They were as moist as they could be. I didn't like to see them wasted on the likes of Siobhan. Annabelle's eyes lit up as she sniffed the scone in her hand. Lemon was her favorite.

"Rabbit," I said to Siobhan.

She poured herself a cup of tea. "Doesn't that woman in the kitchen house know I hate rabbit? It's so gamey."

Ire rose in my chest. "That woman has a name, you know."

"Mind your manners, Owl Eyes." Siobhan glanced at my balled-up fist. "What would Mother and Father do if they heard you? Maybe they'd make you the servants' servant." Annabelle sat on the pianoforte bench with her scone, avoiding my eyes as Siobhan continued. "You could do the jobs even they don't want to do. Shine the chamber pots. Clean the chimneys. Then the dirt would hide your face. They might like it better that way. I know I would if I had to see that much ugliness every day."

The image of the rabbits slung over Peter's shoulder popped into my head, their brown eyes replaced by Siobhan's green ones. How I wished I could push Siobhan between Peter's bow and its target.

"These scones are delicious," Annabelle murmured, glancing up at me. Her cheeks were pink. "Did you make them?"

"Poor Owl Eyes," Siobhan cooed. "Her father left without her, and her mother is scattered to the wind."

Sometime during the last five years, Siobhan had settled on the notion that my father was no longer at the Runes. I didn't see the point in correcting her. In a way, it was closer to the truth than she realized.

Annabelle stood up as Portia came in, holding a rolled-up parchment. My fists were clenched so hard that my nails bit into my palms. I felt the small, warm ooze of blood on my hands. I needed to get out of there, but I had to wait until I was dismissed. Portia's entrance almost felt like a rescue. Siobhan usually pulled her claws in when her mother was around. I forced a neutral expression onto my face and clenched my fists even harder.

"Where are your shoes?" Portia asked Annabelle, who drew her feet up under her skirt. "You look like a commoner."

"It's easier to dance without them."

"You won't be dancing without them at the ball, so don't get used to it now." Portia held up the scroll, which was bound with a wide purple ribbon.

"Oh, Mother!" Siobhan almost tripped over herself as she grabbed the scroll out of Portia's hand. "This is it!" She untied the ribbon, unrolled the parchment, and read out loud: "King Philip and Queen Catalina are pleased to invite Sir Alcander of the Runes, his wife, and daughters to a ball at the Castle on the eve of the Harvest Moon in honor of their children, Prince Edward and Princess Callista." She turned to Annabelle. "The girls were talking about this last week at Lord Carson's estate. They're inviting all the nobles in Colandaria, and Edward and Callista are supposed to—" She stopped and looked at me, then at Portia.

"Seeing as you are not one of Sir Alcander's daughters, this does not concern you," Portia said. "You are dismissed. Take this with you." She handed me a folded paper and waved me away. The blood from my palm spotted the paper. Portia's eyes narrowed. "Get out."

When I got back to the kitchen house, Jack was still outside, kneeling at the edge of the garden with an exasperated look on his face as he pulled a sickly-looking carrot out of the ground. He leapt aside as I nearly plowed into him.

"Nora." He grabbed my shoulders and pulled me back before I reached the door. "Are you okay?"

"I'm fine."

"What happened?"

"The usual." I shook the tears from my eyes. "I'm ugly, and my father doesn't want me. They even threw my mother in this time." I winced as Jack wiped the spots of blood off my hands with a rag from pocket.

He put his arm around me. "At least you didn't get a fork to the face."

"A fork to the face might have been better than whatever that was."

"You take the stables tomorrow. I'll take your turn in the main house." He smiled his mother's reassuring smile, and I sagged with relief against his side. I was slotted to bring in dinner the next night. Dinners, with the family seated around the table and Alcander making a point not to look at me, were the worst. I helped Jack gather the garden's small harvest before we went back inside.

After we made dinner and Greta and Peter took the food to the main house, we gathered around our table to eat. Jack helped Liana to her seat. Her coughs echoed between the walls, and she put a hand to her heart.

"Liana, can I get you some tea?" Greta asked, moving to the hearth to get the kettle even though she knew what Liana's answer would be.

"No, no." Liana waved her hand. "I don't want any of your potions."

Greta sighed. Her remedies were no more magic potions than my knife was an enchanted sword, but Liana insisted on calling them by that name. The word "potions" made me think of sorcerers huddled over a cauldron, reciting archaic verses as their mixtures bubbled and spurted. While that was surely happening somewhere in Colandaria, it wasn't here at the Runes proper. As knight of the province, Sir Alcander had a say in who was allowed to sell at the local market. I didn't know if he was the one who decreed it or if it was just Runes tradition, but there were no spell or charm vendors anywhere in the market aisles. The Vale, one province to the west, was known as a haven for those who practiced magic. Working at the Runes must have been a more attractive option for Liana, who eyed anything that had even a hint of wonder about it with suspicion.

Even though Jack hadn't inherited his mother's disdain for magic, the only spells that we cast were in our imaginations. When we were younger, he and I staged elaborate pantomimes of the Border Wars in what little free time we had.

I would play the army of Dark Mages fighting against Jack's Colandarian forces. As I cut down soldiers with my phantom swords and cast every dark spell I could make up, I imagined I could see my father in line with Jack, who put on a flower crown to play King Philip. One dark curse, and Alcander was vanquished. If the battle reached its conclusion, playtime usually ended with one of us perched on top of the other, the one on the ground crying for mercy, and my having to go into the woods to gather herbs to treat our cuts and scrapes away from Liana's disapproving eyes. More often, we were interrupted by Greta, who reminded us that we were too old for games like this and didn't Jack know better than to irritate his mother? We were too old—there was no doubt about it. But all my earlier fantasies had been by myself. Now, I had someone to escape with.

We grew out of those amusements as we got older and our workloads got larger. But for a brief period of time, I almost felt normal. Now, every day, we took on extra work in Liana's place, and every day, Greta offered the tea that Liana refused.

Greta exchanged a glance with Peter as she returned to her seat. I sat next to her, and she opened the paper that Portia gave me. I had been too upset to read it myself.

"It's the market list," she said. "Central Market this time." I leaned over her shoulder to look. There were enough items that were foreign to the Runes that Peter would have to make the day-long trip to the middle of Colandaria to find them all. Portia wanted fern tubers, snow lemons, diamond conchs, and other fruits and vegetables we couldn't grow here or find at the local market. There were also the usual household items Robert and the other servants needed to keep the main house in order. Greta and Peter would assess our stocks of flour, sugar, and yeast, and add what we needed to the list before the morning.

"Why don't you go with Jack this time?" Peter said. It was a moment before I realized he was talking to me.

"You want me to go?" I echoed. I must have heard him wrong. Trips to the central Market were Peter and Jack's job. The Market was large enough to be considered a province itself—it only lacked a knight to represent it—and I didn't travel to other provinces.

"I have to finish fixing the stable doors." He pushed the list over to me. "You're old enough. It's about time you took some responsibility around here." He laughed and took a bite of the green pea mash I'd made for dinner.

I tried to restrain myself from leaping out of my seat. There was no way Portia and Alcander had authorized my going on the trip, but I didn't care, not when I had the promise of seeing someplace other than the Runes.

"Come on, Peter," Jack said, taking exaggerated offense to Peter's words. "Don't you trust me to go by myself?"

Peter smiled. "Absolutely not. We wouldn't want you to get lost on the trail alone."

"Better to lose both of us than just one?" Jack said.

"You got it." Peter wiped his mouth with his napkin. "Have I ever told you about my first trip to the Market?"

Greta groaned. "No one wants to hear your stories, old man."

"Who are you calling old?" Peter rubbed his chin.

"That would be you, greybeard."

"Protests notwithstanding, I will now regale you with a tale. Nora should hear this on the eve of her first trip to the Market." Peter made a grandiose gesture and waited for everyone's attention. Liana pushed her plate aside and picked up the knife she was using to whittle a hazel branch into the shape of a small tree with an elaborate branch system. She'd hardly touched her dinner.

I pulled my chair closer to Peter. Though he hadn't told this story for years, I'd heard it many times as a child. I could almost recite it along with him. Jack put his plate in the washbasin and settled next to me.

"I first went to the Market when I was fifteen years old," Peter began. "My parents and I were serving under a minor lord up in the Summit, and his son Henry and I were great friends. Henry loved nothing more than to hear his mother play the mandolin. As I was getting the wagon ready to head off to the Market, he ran out of the house with a small bag of coins. Fifty lil, to be precise. He asked me if I would buy him his own mandolin so his mother could teach him to play.

"'Get me the finest one you can,' he said. 'You keep whatever lil are left.'

"The trip to the Market from the Summit is two-and-a-half days long. First you have to travel southeast through the mountains, then true east through the forest. The local market could never compare to the one I was going to." He looked at me. "You'll see, Nora. It was a lonely two-and-a-half days, traveling by myself. But when I arrived, there was so much to see. It's easy to forget yourself in the aisles. I only got lost eleven or twelve times."

I chuckled. The number of times he got lost went up every time Peter told the story.

"I was about to leave for the day when I remembered Henry's fifty lil. Someone pointed me to the music stand, where the vendor was entertaining a group of children. He had all sorts of instruments: lyres, crwths, flageolets, drums, even a harpsichord. I asked to see his finest mandolin. It was beautiful, with intricate carvings along the edges. It cost forty-eight lil. That would leave me with only two for myself. But when the vendor plucked at the strings, I knew it was the one, and I bought Henry his heart's desire.

"With only two lil to my name, I wandered down the aisles, waiting for something to catch my eye."

"Here we go," Greta said. Peter shushed her.

"I turned around, and there she was in front of the florist's stand: a girl in a dark blue skirt, which meant that she lived somewhere in the Summit, like me. She couldn't have been more than fifteen."

"Fourteen," Greta said.

"Who's telling this story?" Peter cleared his throat and went on. "She couldn't have been more than fourteen, and she had the most beautiful long, dark hair I'd ever seen. Her face was just as lovely. I was almost too scared to utter a word in her presence. Finally, I said, 'Excuse me, miss, are you getting those flowers for your lady?'

"She said, 'Yes, sir, I am,' and the sun shone from her eyes. I used the two lil I had left to buy three yellow roses. I handed them to her and said, 'Someone as beautiful as you deserves her own flowers.' She took the roses, thanked me, and left. She didn't even tell me her name.

"Every time I go to the Market, I think about that beautiful girl and the roses I gave her." Peter looked at Greta. "And then I think about how lucky I am to have married her."

Liana smiled. "That was sweet."

"That was nauseating." Jack patted Peter on the back. "I've had about as much romance as I can take for one evening. I'm going to get the dishes from the main house."

I sent him a silent thank-you. That had been my job tonight.

"I agree with Jack," Greta said. "That was nauseating. But you're a nauseatingly sweet old man." She kissed him on the cheek and cleared the rest of our dishes. Liana's knife slipped out of her hand and clattered to the floor as she began to cough again. I ran to her, picking up the knife and taking the tiny tree she clutched in her hand.

"Let me help you up to bed." I let her lean on me as she stood. She was small and thin in my arms. Heat radiated from her skin.

"I'm fine," she said when we reached the ladder. "I can go up myself." I stood at the ladder until she reached the loft. Greta and Peter were washing dishes. I hesitated before joining them.

"Well," Greta said, looking up at me, "come on." There were tired circles under her eyes that I hadn't noticed at dinner. We worked side by side until Jack came back into the kitchen house, arms loaded with dishes.

"Go to bed," I said. "Jack and I will finish here."

Greta and Peter wiped their hands dry and followed Liana up to the loft.

"Goddess keep you," they said. We replied in kind.

Jack blew out the candle on the table and joined me at the washbasin. Our Market trip turned into whispers of possibility as a nightingale trilled outside.

CHAPTER 8

Greta and Peter were already buzzing about the kitchen when I woke up. Jack and Liana were still asleep across the loft, Jack's lips turned up in a half-smile. I crawled over and smoothed away the tuft of hair that fell across his forehead.

"So peaceful," I whispered.

I took the nearest pillow and smacked him with it.

He woke with a start. "What—?"

"Morning! It's Market day!"

He laughed at my excitement. This wasn't a new experience for him. He had gone to Colandaria's central Market with Peter many times before. But as I peeked over the dressing screen while I shimmied into my skirt, I could see his nerves betray him. He'd stopped, half-dressed, and was staring at the map Peter had given him, tracing his fingers over the Market path. I wound my eyes around the slight curl of his hair where, at its longest, it brushed the bottom of his neck.

"Hey." He looked up at me. "A little privacy? I'm changing here."

I couldn't tell if he was joking. Heat rose to my cheeks, and I ducked behind the screen. When I was dressed, I grabbed one of Jack's caps, shoved the brim down above my eyes, and climbed into the kitchen where Peter was adding last-minute items to Portia's list. I sat down at the table as Jack made a beeline for the teapot on the hearth.

Peter slid a pouch, heavy with coins, across the table to me. "Your lil," he said. "Keep them somewhere safe and look out for pickpockets."

"He won't give them to me because I lost twenty lil last time." Jack slid into the seat next to mine with his mug in hand.

"Lost? They were taken right out of your pocket." Peter sighed. "You have the map?"

Jack handed it to him. The road to the Market was plotted in a bold, dark brown. We would share the route with travelers from the Vale, who followed the same path but started out from farther west. The northern and southern provinces had their own roads to the Market.

"Keep your knife with you," Greta said, handing me Portia's list and motioning for us to hurry and eat.

"Greta, don't scare her."

She turned to Peter. "You never know what they'll encounter on the road. Better safe than sorry."

"What are you talking about?" I asked. Now I could understand Jack's nervousness. Peter was skilled with his bow and arrows and his hunting knife. I would trust him to protect me in a dangerous situation. But Peter wasn't coming on this trip. I felt for my knife in its sheath at my side and ran my fingers over the familiar carvings on the handle. I'd never used the blade for anything other than kitchen work—I couldn't imagine using it to defend myself. My imagination ran ahead of me, picturing what might wait for us on the path. Thieves. Murderers. Creatures of story. There was safety in being cooped up at the Runes, and as excited as I was to go, I was reluctant to leave that safety behind.

"Just be vigilant and stay on the path," Peter said. "Jack, you take my bow and arrows. I want everything back in exactly the same number of pieces. I left something extra for you in the pouch in the quiver."

"Yes, sir." Jack downed the last of his tea, and we headed outside. Honeycomb, Greta's palomino, was already harnessed to the wagon.

I looked at the edge of the forest with old trepidation. Once again, I was going to venture into the woods, not sure how to get to my destination. But before, I was alone. Now I had a map, a traveling partner, and the promise of home. It was enough to turn most of that fear into something good.

Liana met us at the door.

"Are you still here?" she asked and coughed. The sound thundered up from her chest, shaking her slight frame.

Jack went over to her. "Ma, are you sure you don't want me to stay with you?"

Liana replied in a low voice. He whispered back, his brows creasing with a mix of concern and anger. Next to me, Greta cleared her throat. I busied myself with checking the straps on Honeycomb's harness to make sure everything was fastened properly.

"Wait!"

Annabelle ran out from the main house, skidding to a stop in front of me. Dirt rose up from the ground to cover her shoes.

She panted, trying to catch her breath. "You can't leave without the rest of the list." She handed me a slip of paper. Siobhan came up behind her, her disappointed shoulders showing none of Annabelle's urgency.

"They're sending *you* to the Market?" She looked from me to Annabelle. "I thought it was bad when Peter and that boy went. Now they're sending this imbecile? There's no way this won't get cocked up." There it was, "imbecile," one of Portia's favorite words. Along with Portia's dark hair and graceful features, Siobhan inherited her mother's vocabulary. The way she addressed me next, though, was all her own.

"You need to follow our instructions to the letter, Owl Eyes. Well? Open it." She gestured to the paper Annabelle gave me. I bristled at the command and looked over to Greta for support, but she'd gone back into the kitchen. Jack and Liana were still deep in conversation, and from their hushed tones and Jack's beleaguered expression, I knew better than to pull him out of it. I unfolded the parchment. The handwriting was alternately purposeful and weighty, the writing of someone who was trying too hard. "Read it out loud," Siobhan said, "so we know you understand."

I had a strong urge to ball the paper up and throw it back at her.

"I'm not illiterate," I said.

Siobhan crossed her arms and tapped her foot on the ground.

"Fine." I read down the list. "Twelve lengths heavy green satin, two lengths gold brocade, two lengths silver. One length each gold, silver, and cream lace. Three pair green cords. Emerald, gold, and pearl necklaces and hairpins from Harold of the Summit. Why aren't you picking these out yourselves?"

"There's no time. Siobhan has to learn to dance before we go to the ball," Annabelle said with the barest hint of a smirk on her face. Siobhan glared at her.

"But the Harvest Moon isn't for two months," I said. "If you want to buy from Harold, can't he come here so you can pick out your own jewelry?"

Annabelle put a hand up to the side of her mouth and leaned in to me. "It might take her that long to learn how to dance," she whispered, not so quietly that Siobhan couldn't hear. I bit my lip so I wouldn't laugh.

"Shut up." Siobhan shoved Annabelle aside. "I drew what I want here so even you can't screw it up." She pointed to the bottom of the paper where she'd drawn a picture of a beaded necklace with a large, pear-cut stone in the center. "Harold has something put aside for Mother already. All Annabelle wants is some stupid pearl necklace. Get it right, or I'm sure Mother will have something to say. You know she and Father would sooner throw you to the wolves than see us looking like"— she looked me up and down—"well, like you."

I crumpled the list and shoved it in my pocket. "Coal necklace, got it."

Siobhan cocked her head at me. "It's too bad you're not invited to the ball, Owl Eyes. It would be delightful to watch Prince Edward see how beastly you are. Maybe he'd take pity and let you serve on his kitchen staff. It would be a step up from where you are now, anyway. I bet your mother would be proud. Oh, wait, she's dead."

By the time Annabelle stepped between us, I was braced for a fight. She put a hand on Siobhan's chest and pushed her backwards.

"Don't touch me." Siobhan shook her off and went back to the main house.

"I want a necklace with pearl doublets," Annabelle said to me. "She only says it's stupid because she thinks they're ugly." She looked hurt.

"I'll get it," I said. "I'm sure it will be nice."

Annabelle brightened and handed me a small purse that jingled with coins. "This should be enough for everything," she said. "Mother counted it out." She ran to catch up with Siobhan.

Greta and Peter came back outside to see us off as Liana and Jack's conversation came to an abrupt end.

"No!" she said, loud enough for everyone to hear. "And that's final. Go to the Market. I'll see you when you get back."

Jack shook his head, the slow shake he did when he was acquiescing even though he didn't want to. I wasn't sure why he was suddenly reluctant to leave. He kissed Liana on the cheek and climbed onto the wagon seat. Liana came over and pressed something into my hand.

"Take care of him," she whispered in my ear.

"Of course." I uncurled my fingers. I was holding the tree she had whittled from the hazel branch. At the center of the trunk, a tiny owl looked out from a knothole. I knew she meant well, but the gift stung.

"Thank you," I said and hugged her anyway before climbing onto the wagon. Greta and Peter waved goodbye, and Jack called, "gee-up" to Honeycomb.

We headed into the mouth of the forest and left the Runes proper behind. I fished the map out of the pocket of Jack's vest and tried to follow along with our route.

The trees became less familiar as we got farther from the Runes. The dark brown of the route on the map mirrored the colors of our surroundings; there was little greenery to be found. The drought had not just affected the Runes proper. The trees that lined the path were the color of soil, as though the ground had risen up and eaten away the leaves to make everything the color of earth. I imagined the skeletal branches reaching for us, ready to pluck us out of the wagon. Honeycomb would go on without us, and we would be left behind, hanging from the trees as pickings for the forest denizens.

My heart thumped along with the crunch of the wagon wheels against the ground. A flash of brown darted between the trees on the side of the wagon. I yelped and grabbed Jack's shoulder.

"It's just a deer." He shrugged me off.

I frowned. "What's wrong?"

"Nothing."

"Not nothing. You haven't said a word since we left."

"I don't want to talk about it." He kept his gaze fastened to the road. "I just wish we could have gone to the Market on a different day, that's all."

"Because of your ma?" I asked. "What were you arguing about?"

"Nora, I said I don't want to talk about it!" He turned on me, eyes blazing. "Leave it alone."

"Sorry." I sank into my seat. My face burned as Jack seethed next to me. I was used to that kind of response from Robert if I asked him about my mother, or from Portia if I did something—anything—she didn't like. Even from Liana, if the subject of magic came up in the kitchen house. But not from Jack.

A lone spot of green hovered above us, an elder tree that still seemed to have all its leaves. As we got closer, I could see that the green was actually a flock of finchlings hopping from twig to twig, pecking for berries that weren't there. The birds took off into the cloudless sky, leaving the tree as bare as its neighbors. There would be no relief from the drought today. The only dark cloud hovered next to me in the wagon.

Even if we didn't have Peter's map, our route, the widest road in the forest, was clear. As we went on, the path split off, with offshoots leading to small villages. I waved at people who were out chopping wood, tending gardens, or sitting in front of their homes. I knew there were villages that weren't part of Colandaria's five main provinces, but I was surprised at the number of houses we could see from the path.

At the same time that the houses began to appear less frequently, the path changed from dirt to cobblestone. Honeycomb's hooves clacked against the ground.

"Are we there?" I looked at the map. The trip was supposed to take all day, and it was barely lunchtime. On our left, the woods opened up to a rolling, green lawn. A brook babbled a short distance away. Beyond the water and surrounded by a tall stone wall, a castle rose up from the ground. Its grey stone exterior sparkled in the sunlight. Purple flags flew from the parapets.

"Wait." I traced the path on the map with my finger. There was nothing marked there, but it had to be: "It's the Castle. The royal Castle."

I grabbed the reins away from Jack. Of course the Castle wouldn't be marked on our map. The Border Wars were recent enough that the King must still fear an invasion from the Farlands. Leaving the Castle off the map was a form of protection.

"What are you doing?" Jack reached over to take the reins back. I held them to the side, out of his reach.

"I want to see the Castle," I said.

"We can see it from here." Jack nearly fell across my lap in his effort to get the reins. "We need to keep going."

"No," I said, jerking the straps so he couldn't grab them. Honeycomb turned to the right, taking the wagon off the path. I stopped her. Seeing the Castle from the road wasn't enough. The main house was already abuzz with excitement over the Harvest Moon Ball, and it was still months away. I could only imagine how much worse it would get as the day of the ball approached. If I made it to the Castle before Siobhan and Annabelle, it would be something I could hold over them, even if they never knew. I couldn't explain this to Jack—I knew how petty it sounded.

"It's just the Castle." Jack crossed his arms in front of his chest. "We're not going to make it to the Market before dark if we stop for too long. And I don't want to have to rescue you when you get arrested for trespassing."

I hopped off the wagon and looped the reins around the closest tree. "You might have seen the Castle a hundred times, but I haven't. I'm not going to waste my only chance. You can stay here if you want."

I only got a short distance from the wagon before hearing Jack's footsteps behind me.

"Fine," he said. "But I'm only coming so you don't end up in the dungeons alone." He smiled, even as he kept his head down to avoid looking at me.

I hugged him. "My hero."

The Castle grounds were enormous. The field that separated the woods from the wall was easily five times the distance between the main house and the kitchen house in the Runes. I wanted to run across the lawn and put as little distance between myself and the Castle wall as I could, but I matched Jack's even stride through the grass.

"Why is it still so green here?" I wondered, holding my arms out for balance as I stepped from rock to rock to cross a small stream. The stones were slippery, and Jack grabbed my hand to steady himself.

"Magic?" he suggested.

I shrugged, stepping onto the grass on the other side of the stream and pulling Jack the rest of the way across. He was probably right. The Castle sorcerers would see to it that the grounds looked perfect even when the rest of the country suffered from drought. We could use some of that magic at the Runes. When they didn't think we could hear them, Greta and Peter spoke in hushed tones about the dwindling supply in our well. Soon, we would have to barter for water from neighboring estates.

The Castle wall towered over us. I trailed my hand along its rough surface, catching my fingers in the slots that were left open at varying heights ("So we could get speared from the inside with a halberd or a sword if we were trying to invade, or if we're caught trespassing," Jack reasoned), being careful not to shred my skin on the thorns of the climbing roses that covered the stones.

We walked along the wall to where a number of forest paths combined into a wide road flanked by a line of white oaks. Just setting foot on that road made me feel special, like I was doing exactly what a daughter of Sir Alcander of the Runes should.

At the end of the path, a pair of large doors was set into the wall, carved with the royal insignia: a rose was emblazoned on each door, and a tall sword was split in the center. On either side of the doors, lookouts kept watch in towers.

"Nora—" Jack pointed to the tower on the left where the guard was holding a crossbow and eyeing us suspiciously. The thunder of hooves sounded behind us.

"Make way!" the guard on the right shouted. We jumped off the oak-lined road as horses galloped past. Four guards on horseback carrying halberds and dressed in mail surrounded the riders in the center. The doors opened from inside, and the horses disappeared onto the grounds of the Castle proper. The guard with the crossbow called out to us as the doors shut, gesturing with the weapon. "Shoo!"

Before the doors closed, I got a quick view of the Castle grounds. They were enormous, much larger than the estate at the Runes proper. There was as much distance between the wall and the Castle as there was between the forest and the wall. Smaller buildings dotted the grounds, and I had the faintest glimpse of servants going about their work outdoors.

Suddenly, I realized the foolishness of this endeavor. What was I hoping for? To walk into the Castle and announce my presence to His Majesty? To blend in among the Castle servants in my Runes green skirt? I wanted to see the building before my sisters did, and I probably hadn't even done that. With their status, they'd almost certainly been invited to the Castle before. As for me, there was still a giant stone wall and a pair of armed guards in my way. I'd need a title, a name, an invitation to actually go inside.

I yanked at my servant's skirt—the coarse material was hot and scratchy against my skin—and walked back in the direction from which we came. Jack pivoted to follow.

"I'm sorry," I said. "This was stupid." Stupid to think I could have gotten here first, stupid to think that we could get onto the grounds of the Castle proper, stupid to have stopped. Imbecilic, Portia's voice said in my head.

"It would have been a good story," Jack said. "A tale to rival Peter's, even if you'd been shot with a crossbow. Especially if you'd been shot with a crossbow."

He stopped walking, attention piqued.

"What?" I said. I wanted to get back to our wagon before another guard shooed us away. Jack pressed his eye to one of the halberd holes in the wall and motioned for me to come look. I pushed a rose aside to look through a lower opening. I could just make out a path and the edge of a building.

"What?"

"Shh," Jack whispered. "Listen."

Snippets of conversation mingled with the sounds of horses. The building must have been one of the royal stables.

"—can't believe you're so cavalier about this." The first voice, a man's.

"Why is everything a matter of life and death with you?" A second voice, female.

"Who is it?" I whispered. Jack shook his head and moved along the wall, peeking through the halberd holes. I followed until I had a better look at the speakers. The man paced, appearing and disappearing as flashes of brown trousers and a white shirt in my thin window. The woman stayed squarely in view, watching the man with amused detachment as she flipped her blond hair over her shoulder.

The man's voice floated in and out with his movements. "...isn't going to change what Father said…don't pick a husband, he's going to pick for you…and I have to…"

"You?" The woman laughed. "You look like you're ready to jump out the window whenever a lady comes to court!"

"It's Princess Callista," Jack whispered. His voice was hoarse.

"And Prince Edward," I whispered back.

"Let's go before we get a halberd to the eye," Jack said, tugging on my sleeve.

"Absolutely not." I strained to hear more of the conversation inside.

"I'd prefer defenestration to some of those girls," Edward said. He stopped pacing and stood with his back to the wall. "Did you know that Lady Grace actually asked to try on Mother's crown?"

"Nora," Jack said. His eyes were beginning to water. The smell of the roses around us was overwhelming.

"Just a bit longer." I ran along the wall, following the Prince and Princess. Now that they were a bit farther away, I could see them better. Their brown riding clothes were snug on their figures. Princess Callista walked with her hands on Edward's shoulders, hanging on his back and laughing. A pair of guards followed them.

"Poor Edward," Callista cooed. I ran to the next opening in the wall in time to hear, "—if you can't find someone then, you might as well let Father pick for you."

Edward wheeled around, shaking her off. "I don't want a marriage of convenience! I want to be happy." I had my first look at his face, which had changed quite a bit from how I remembered him years ago. He had grown to be tall and striking, with dark hair and handsome features. The opening in the wall wasn't large enough for me to see him well, but from what I could make out, I could easily imagine noble girls fighting over him.

"So be happy," Callista said. "And while you're at it—"

Jack sneezed. One of the guards looked back at the wall.

"Uh-oh," Jack said.

I jerked back as the point of a halberd jutted through the hole. "Run!"

Inside, the guard let out a yell, and the doors in the wall swung open. I grabbed Jack's hand and sprinted towards the forest path as two guards followed us.

Jack's long legs took him ahead of me as my side burned with effort. I gasped for air. There was no time for the careful balancing act that took us across the stream before. We splashed through the water. Jack was already on the other side when my foot caught on a rock and I pitched forwards, falling face-first into the stream. I sputtered, blinking water out of my eyes as Jack grabbed my arm and helped me up. The guards' mail jingled behind us.

"Where's the wagon?" I wheezed. It felt like I'd swallowed a lumpy rag. I couldn't find the tree where we'd tied Honeycomb.

"No time." The guards had already crossed the stream. Jack pulled me into the forest, holding fast to my hand. I pushed to keep up with him as we wove through the trees.

"Here," he said, yanking me into the hollow of a large, dead oak. We pressed ourselves against the black rot. Something wet and viscous dripped onto my back, and I pressed my face into Jack's shirt to muffle my scream. He tightened his arms around my waist and pressed his chin against the top of my head as we tried to make ourselves as inconspicuous as possible as the guards thundered by.

When we heard them stop a short distance from our tree and turn back towards the Castle, my muscles finally unclenched. Jack peeked around the tree and breathed a sigh. He leaned over, hands on his thighs, shaking his head. I thought he was crying, but when he lifted his head to look at me, I realized he was laughing instead. I laughed too. The front of his shirt and pants were wet where I had pressed against him. I wanted to apologize, but I couldn't get the words out.

"Chased by Castle guards," he said. "That's a story I don't think I'll bring home to Ma."

"Definitely not."

We walked back to the path. I knew I had tied Honeycomb's reins to an ash tree. The ash was still there, but Honeycomb and the wagon were gone.

My relief vanished. "Now what?"

"We've got a long walk home," Jack said, looking just as dismayed as I felt. "And probably a stern talking-to by Greta and Peter." He started down the path back towards the Runes. I trudged after him. "Or a flogging by Portia," he went on, "though she'd probably make someone else do it so she wouldn't get blood on her dress."

I cringed. "That's awful." No one at the Runes had ever been hurt like that, but no one had ever lost a wagon and a pony, either. "Anyway, Portia wouldn't beat us—she'd just throw us in the dark room."

Jack nodded. He knew all about the room with no windows from hushed conversations as we sat under the skylight after everyone else had gone to sleep.

"Wait," I said. Something moved down the path. "Honeycomb!" There, far enough away that we almost couldn't see her, Honeycomb pulled our wagon into the trees. I took off after her and caught up to where she stood, munching on a patch of crabgrass.

"What are you doing?" I said, patting her neck. She tossed her pale mane and whinnied. "You'd leave us behind for crabgrass?"

I climbed onto the wagon seat and led her back onto the path. Jack jumped up onto the wagon as we passed him. This time, when we rode past the Castle, we sped Honeycomb to a trot.

~

Closer to the Market, other wagons joined us on the path. I waved at a couple dressed in dark blue from the Summit.

"I don't think I could live like that," Jack said. Our excursion to the Castle seemed to have brought him out of his gloom.

"Like what?"

"Like the Prince and Princess. I couldn't stand always being surrounded by guards or having everything arranged for me." Jack took Peter's quiver from the back of the wagon and checked the arrowheads.

"Everything *is* arranged for us," I said. "We get up, we work, we go to sleep. We're not so different from Edward and Callista."

"Oh?" Jack raised an eyebrow. "You think you and your prince are so alike?"

Heat rose to my cheeks. "He's not my prince."

"I can't imagine Ma ever saying that I had one night to pick a bride or she'd choose for me."

I pictured Liana lining girls up and eliminating them one by one. She would be picky, that was for sure.

"It's romantic," I said as I watched the rise and fall of Honeycomb's haunches. "Imagine seeing a girl at a ball and knowing you want to marry her."

"It's something out of a story," Jack said, "and your prince seems to feel the same way." He flipped open the clasp at the front of the quiver and peeked into the pocket. "Oh." This time, he was the one who blushed.

"What?" I leaned over to look. Jack jerked the quiver away.

"Nothing."

"Fine. You don't believe in love at first sight?"

Jack faltered for a moment. "Nora, I hardly ever see anyone other than you, Greta, and my ma. And Siobhan and Annabelle aren't exactly the kinds of girls I can see myself marrying."

I shuddered at the thought. Siobhan and Annabelle would marry the highest-ranking lords they could find, or the Prince, if one of them could win him. I could picture Siobhan standing beside him, a self-important smile on her face and the Queen's gold crown casting a glow on her dark hair. Or Annabelle, twirling under the Prince's arm at the ball, light on her feet as her dress swirled around her and countrymen watched with approval. And me? I would be in the kitchen house, wrist-deep in dough with sweat dripping down my face. Not as beautiful, not as graceful, not as deserving.

Next to me, Jack was laughing.

"I'm picturing being married to one of your sisters." He chortled. "It's like a nightmare come true."

I pictured it myself, and my mood immediately lifted. "They'd run you ragged! Jack!" I pitched up my voice in a too-shrill imitation of Siobhan. "Get my looking glass! I have a hair out of place! Jack! Get me the seamstress! I've torn my dress with all my whining!"

Jack dissolved in laughter, and a cluster of sparrows rose up from a nearby tree.

We were close to the Market now. Vendors had roped signs to tree trunks, advertising Farland gems, fresh fish, and children's toys. There was something new in the air. New smells, new sounds, a new mood. The scents of bread and meat wafted between the trees, and if I listened hard enough, I could hear the buzz of a large crowd of voices. The cacophony had a joyful tone to it, as though whatever was about to appear held its arms out to us in welcome.

"Singing frogs, only at the Market until the Harvest Moon," Jack read as we passed a large sign painted in a pattern of yellow and orange diamonds with a fat green frog in the middle. "That's new."

My breath caught as the road opened into the Market clearing. Contained within the ring of a large, low fence, the stands made a forest of their own. Vendors stood back-to-back in neighboring aisles, each shouting to be heard over the others as customers bustled about. Another sign for the singing frogs rose over a gold tent on the other side of the field. The Market continued on farther from there; I couldn't see the stands in the back. The whole scene glowed with the light of the setting sun.

"We'll have to wait until tomorrow to go in," Jack said, gesturing to where some of the vendors had already begun to pack up their wares. "They're closing up for the night."

Hundreds of wagons were pulled into circles around fire pits at the edge of the field. People busied about, putting away packages, lighting fires, and cooking dinner. As we rode past, a father yelled at his sons to hurry as they struggled under the weight of their bundles. Closer to the forest, a man whose face and hands were wrapped in cloth mounted a white horse and rode back into the woods. A number of people had their horses with them at their wagons, but others had put them in a penned-in area across the road.

"We'll find a space at one of the wagon circles," Jack said, taking the reins from me and guiding Honeycomb around the campsite. "We rest for the night and go in tomorrow."

I looked around. "But we don't know anyone."

"You get a sense of who not to talk to here. I've never camped next to anyone who I wouldn't want to share a meal with." He guided Honeycomb to an open spot between two wagons covered in light blue cloth from the Vale. People were already gathered around the closest fire. I hadn't seen such an array of clothing since Portia's last banquet. In our circle alone, there was Ken gold, Fall red, and light blue from the Vale to go with our Runes green.

I climbed off the wagon and stretched. Jack unloaded our packs and looked for the food Greta gave us for dinner. My stomach rumbled. Lunch had been forgotten in our adventure at the Castle. Next to me, Honeycomb whined and kicked the ground. She was hungry too. I eyed the two buckets of oats in the wagon and asked a man in Ken gold who was sitting at the fire how much it cost to put a horse in the pen.

"Jack!" I called. "We can put Honeycomb in the pen for both nights for only two lil. Do we have enough?" I didn't know how much we should expect to spend inside. I tossed him the money pouch so he could count the coins. He didn't even open it.

"I don't think Portia would pay for it. Every other time I've been here, Peter's had to make a list of how much money we spent and where. Somehow I don't think Portia would be okay with seeing 'horse lodging' on the list."

I ran my fingers through Honeycomb's mane. "But she's such a good pony." I pouted. "And I'm sure she'd rather play with the other horses than stand by the wagon the whole time. It's only one lil a night. Can't we spare two?" I puffed out my lip and flashed Jack my most pitiful expression. He frowned and turned back to the wagon.

"Well," he said, reaching into the pocket of the quiver of arrows and producing two small silver coins, "Peter did give me these."

"What for?"

Jack's cheeks reddened in the firelight. "Nothing. Here." He thrust the coins into my hand and unhooked Honeycomb's harness, ignoring my curious gaze. I led her across the road to the pen and passed the money to the groom, who took a small book out of his pocket and wrote down my name and Honeycomb's description.

"Palomino, white blaze, half sock on the front left foot. Come back when you want her."

As soon as he opened the gate to the pen, Honeycomb bounded inside and began munching on the clover.

Satisfied, I went back to our camp. Jack had already laid out our dinner of apples, bread, and some dried meat and was sitting at the fire with the other travelers. I sat next to him and took an apple.

"Honeycomb okay?" Jack asked.

"Why did Peter give you two lil?" I asked in return.

He avoided my eyes. "To buy a flower for a pretty girl," he mumbled.

I laughed. "And you spent it on Honeycomb? She's pretty, but I doubt she'll return the affection."

Jack ignored me, but it looked like his face was just as red as when

I'd left for the pen. We reached for the bread at the same time, and I felt heat rise to my own face. The fire crackled. For a moment, the flames looked like a field of yellow flowers.

Jack struck up conversation with the people from the Vale who sat next to us. As he asked after Sir Milton's family at the Vale proper, I tilted my gaze up to the stars. By the time the conversation around the fire had waned, I was long past tired. Some of our circle-mates fastened strings of bells around their wagons before lying down for the night. The set of bells Greta had given us lay at the bottom of my pack—they were to warn us in case anyone tried to rob us while we slept. I left them there for now. We'd use them the next night, when we had something worth taking.

Jack spread out a blanket beside our wagon. I lay down next to him, using my pack as a pillow.

"Did we really get chased by Castle guards today?" I asked.

"I'm pretty sure we did," he said. "…'m tired."

"Goddess keep you," I said. He murmured something that might have been the same. I closed my eyes and dreamed of fire and roses.

CHAPTER 9

*W*hen I woke, the stars were winking out. I leaned back on my elbows and watched as the dusky pink sky changed to orange and the bright edge of the sun peeked over the trees. A light breeze blew through the Market camp. A few people walked around, whispering as they put away their blankets. The family from the Vale we ate with the night before had already packed up their wagon and taken their horse from the pen.

Jack woke and offered a groggy wave as they drove away. After, he mumbled something about water and gestured towards a well in the middle of the camp. As the one who was more awake, it appeared that it was my job to get it. A haphazardly placed sign in front of the well reminded patrons of the drought and asked that everyone take only a half bucket's worth of water.

Jack was leaning against the side of the wagon, reading over Portia's list when I got back. He handed me a piece of bread and an apple from last night's dinner. The bread was hard, but I ate it anyway. I poured the water into a pot over our fire for tea, and we sat with the other travelers in our circle, waiting for it to boil. Jack tossed tea leaves, wrapped in a piece of cheesecloth, between his hands. The morning air was cool, and when the water was hot enough, the tea felt good going down my throat.

A crowd was gathered at the Market gate.

"Why isn't anyone going in yet?" I asked.

"You'll see," Jack said. We stored our cups in the wagon and squeezed between the other customers until we were at the front of the crowd. Inside the Market, vendors readied their stands and laid out their wares. One of the vendors closest to the entrance was roasting a boar. My mouth watered.

"Wait for it." Jack pointed to where a man climbed the tall gateposts with a horn tied to his belt. His clothing was covered in patches of so many colors that it was impossible to tell where he was from. Since the Market wasn't technically considered a province, the people who lived in the vicinity wore whatever colors they wanted, which often meant that they were clad in motley patterns. Traveling vendors from the Market area sometimes stopped by the Runes. I was jealous of their bright, colorful clothing. It was so much more vibrant than the Runes green I always wore.

The man balanced on one foot on the top of the post and jumped, twisting in the air and landing on his other foot. With both arms held out to steady himself, he walked to the center of the crossbeam between the posts, teetering in an exaggerated fashion. Even though it was obviously an act, I gasped along with the rest of the crowd as he leaned so far to one side that I couldn't figure out how he managed to stay on the beam. Everyone clapped as he straightened up, laughing and waving at the crowd.

"That's the Zephyr," Jack explained. "He opens and closes the Market. He's a lot better than the last one. She broke her leg falling off the beam and had to do the rest of her shows from the ground."

The Zephyr put his horn to his lips and played a sweet, high-pitched melody. When he finished, he somersaulted off the top of the gate and landed cleanly on his feet, bowing before he disappeared into the Market aisles.

"And now we go," Jack said as we were hustled along with the rest of the crowd into the flow of Market traffic. Once inside, we hung back and looked at our list, deciding where to go first. Jack pointed out the aisles that sold food, which were the closest to the entrance. My stomach rumbled as we turned down the first aisle and stopped at a stand that sold mushrooms that could only be found in the Fall. I followed the example of the customer in front of me and asked for a sample to make sure the produce was fresh. The mushroom snapped in my mouth, filling it with earthy flavor. I grinned at Jack. If we could taste everything we bought, we wouldn't need the rest of the food Greta packed for our lunch.

We walked through an aisle lined on both sides with vendors selling nothing but bread: long, thin loaves; short, stumpy loaves; loaves that smelled of mint and honey and cinnamon. At the end of the aisle, a vendor sold corn that looked like it was made from gemstones, with each kernel a different color. He had heated some of the corn and was putting the rainbow of popped kernels into small bags to sell. In the next aisle were cured fish brought from the oceans by the Ken and fresh fish from the streams in the Fall. The scales on the fish from the northern Runes glittered pink and silver in the sun. Vendors laid their catches on large blocks of ice. I couldn't fathom where all the ice came from; I didn't know anywhere in Colandaria that was so cold. But ice was always on our Market lists. Our meat would go bad without it.

The weight of our purchases dragged on my arms. Jack scribbled down each item we bought and how much we paid on a cramped page in a ledger he kept in his pocket. I was in charge of Portia's list, stealing the small piece of chalk that Jack tucked behind his ear so I could cross off the items as we found them. I was too intimidated to do any bartering. The vendors here were firmer in their prices than the ones at the Runes market, who would often lower their price by a third after I chatted with them. Jack was better at negotiating here, getting us lower prices on some fruit and Portia's diamond conchs. The vendor, a large, mustachioed man wearing Ken gold, used a scoop to put the clear sea creatures into a small barrel, which Jack got him to throw in for free.

Jack grunted as he heaved the barrel onto his shoulder and water sloshed around inside. We left the Market and dropped off our purchases at our wagon. When we tried to go back in, we found the Zephyr on top of the gate.

"Lunchtime!" he shouted and played another melody on his horn. Vendors threw sheets over their wares as sales ground to a halt. Many customers headed out of the Market to eat at their campsites. Others, mainly nobles, stayed inside to eat. In the southwest corner of the Market, there was a large structure with three walls. The front was left open so that everyone could see inside. Ivy climbed over the wooden trellises, and fruits and vegetables hung from the slatted ceiling. Inside, patrons sat and ate. Earlier in the morning, Jack led me away from the structure, explaining that it was reserved for nobility. We didn't have the extra money to eat there. Neither did most of the people around our fire pit; we were all plainly clad. I was sure that if Portia or Alcander ever graced the Market with their presence, they would eat inside.

Outside, most people left their purchases in their wagons, covering them with only a blanket. There was a trusting atmosphere at the campsite during the day. At night, bells would be tied tightly around the carts.

Finally, the Zephyr appeared to signal the Market's reopening. We went back inside and made our way past the food. The next aisle was filled with chairs, tables, and beds. Jack ran his hands over the leg of a table that was whittled in an intricate pattern of slash marks and crosses.

"Ma would love this." There was a note of sadness in his voice.

I reached into my pocket and felt for the little tree Liana gave me. Its branches poked my fingers. I thought for a moment of giving it to Jack, but he was already off walking into the next aisle.

A few rows over, we found the textile stalls. After picking one that specialized in satin, I read what we needed off Siobhan's list, and the vendor measured the long sheaths of green fabric. He folded them in brown paper, which he tied up with a piece of twine. I put the package in the bag slung across my shoulders. It was heavier than I expected. We found the brocades, lace, and cords at neighboring stands.

With each purchase, I became more rankled. If Portia, Siobhan, and Annabelle wanted dresses for the ball, they should be the ones doing the shopping. I tried pretending that I was buying fabric for my own dress, but I couldn't picture myself preening in front of a mirror, clad in rich, dark Runes green. My plain skirt would never have the silver and gold accents that would cover the girls' dresses. My untamable hair could not be calmed into a delicate bun like Annabelle's, and my too-slight frame would never fill out a dress like Siobhan's. My arms and hands, covered in scars from the oven, would never be as pristine as Portia's. Even if Alcander suddenly decided I was worth bringing into his family, I could never pull off nobility.

"You look miserable." Jack pulled my hand away from where it rested on a piece of smooth, indigo fabric and hauled me towards the large, gold tent in the center of the Market sprawl. "We're taking a break."

"What are you—" I started before seeing the sign for the singing frogs. A break would be good.

Inside the tent, a woman in a yellow-and-orange dress played a flute on a raised stage. A harlequin in a matching diamond-patterned tunic and orange, cross-gartered stockings waved a sword around. I laughed along with the rest of the crowd as he pretended to run himself through and leapt up, unharmed.

"And now," the harlequin shouted, "ladies and gentlemen, for your listening pleasure, the Singing Frogs from Beyond the Ken will perform everyone's favorite ditty, 'High Up On the Mountain.'"

The harlequin waved his hand, and a curtain behind him parted to reveal six large frogs seated on pedestals. The first frog opened its mouth and belched out a bass note. The second frog echoed with a tenor note as the two frogs at the end of the row pattered in alto counterpoint. The toads in the center tapped their feet with a steady rhythm. I'd never seen anything so ridiculous or amazing before.

"It's like magic," I said to Jack.

"It is magic," a woman standing behind us said. I turned around to see the pale blue dress with silver stitching that marked her as nobility. "But it's not very good."

"How can you tell?" Jack asked without looking at her. He stared at the stage, entranced, as the toads in the center puffed out their throats to the beat of the song.

"Harlequin over there is using a simple voice-throwing technique. That's not magic, but the amplification spell he's using to multiply the number of tones his voice can create is. If you look closely, you can see the corners of his mouth moving. It's a decent job, but I've seen better." The woman laughed, shaking the stones that floated across her forehead on a twinkling silver chain. "You have too—at my eighth birthday. Remember, Jack?"

Jack turned to her. "How do you know my—" His expression warmed. "Bess!"

I had heard the name enough in the last five years that I made the connection immediately. The Lady of the Vale laughed and threw her arms around him. I glanced around to see if anyone else noticed the scene she was making. A few curious heads turned our way, but most of the crowd's focus remained on the stage where the frogs started another song. My cheeks burned, even though I didn't know exactly what it was I found so embarrassing.

"I can't believe it's really you!" Lady Bess looked Jack up and down, grinning with approval. "You got tall."

Jack ran a hand through his hair. He looked flustered. I couldn't blame him. Even though Lady Bess's hair was so fair it was almost blue, she couldn't have been more than a few years older than we were. A thick, jagged scar climbed up the left side of her face from her neck to her cheekbone, but instead of marring her beauty, it only made her more intriguing to look at.

"What are you doing here?" Jack asked her.

"Shopping. I saw you in the grain aisle, and I thought I'd surprise you. Who's your friend?"

"Oh!" Jack's eyes lit up as if he were just remembering that I was there. "This is Nora. She works at the Runes with me. Nora, this is Bess, Sir Milton's daughter."

"It's nice to meet you." Bess smiled warmly at me.

"You too, miss," I mumbled, angry at how awkward I sounded. I wasn't used to talking to strange nobles, and I couldn't find a familiar tone.

"Oh, come now, none of that 'miss' nonsense," she said. "Jack's never called me 'miss,' and neither should you." She turned back to Jack. "So, tell me about the Runes!"

A few people standing nearby shushed her.

"Come on." Bess took Jack by the arm. I followed a few paces behind as they left the tent. An uncomfortable, new feeling had knotted itself into my chest.

"Wait until I tell Papa I ran into you!" Bess said once we were back among the bustle of the Market. "He'll never believe it!"

I quickened my pace to keep up with Bess's rapid stride, ducking to avoid being hit over the head by a broadsword that a large man dressed in mail carried over his shoulder. For a moment, I thought back to the day before, when we ran from the Castle guards. I looked at the back of Jack's collar, where I'd had to wipe off black tree rot once we were safely in the wagon, and I stumbled, almost tripping over a small dog that meandered down the aisle. It perked up its ears and darted away as its master sounded a sharp whistle.

In front of me, Jack asked, "How is Sir Milton?"

"Same as always," Bess said as we reached the end of the row. "He's barricaded in his study with Gideon—Gideon's his other apprentice. You'd like him. Papa's teaching us how to do songsmithing."

"Sir Milton singing?" Jack laughed. "That's something I'd have to see to believe."

"Not just singing. Songsmithing is—" Bess stopped, looking around. She waved off the rest of her sentence with a toss of her head and tucked a lock of her blue-white hair back behind her ear. "I'll tell you later."

A vendor walked by, carrying a basket filled with grapes over his shoulder. With a movement so quick I wasn't sure it was actually happening, Bess reached into the basket and plucked out three bunches of grapes, pulled out a copper five-lil piece, and tossed it over the heads of the people who were now between us and the fast-moving grape seller. The coin landed in his basket. Bess handed Jack and me each a bunch of grapes, keeping the third for herself.

"So, tell me about the Runes!" she said as though nothing had happened. She popped a grape in her mouth.

"Uh…" Jack faltered, looking after the grape seller, whom we could no longer see in the crowded aisle.

"Did you ride here?" Bess had her hand on Jack's arm again. The uncomfortable feeling in my chest tightened, making it hard to chew. I willed it down with the grapes. While they were common in hilly areas like the Summit, grapes were a delicacy in the Runes. I had only tried them a few times before, sneaking one or two when Greta wasn't looking.

"We took the wagon," Jack said. Bess raised an eyebrow as some unspoken vestige of their childhood together passed between them. "Yes," he went on, stressing the word, "I did learn to ride. One of the kitchen servants taught me."

Bess leaned toward me with a wink in her eye. "When he was little, he got thrown off my filly right before he left for the Runes. We all thought he was hurt, but he just wanted to get back on so he could be thrown off again."

"That's only because I saw you fall so many times that I thought horses were supposed to be ridden that way!"

She joined in Jack's laughter. "And your mother? How is she?"

Jack's face fell. He never wanted to talk about Liana, not even with me. He took a breath as though he were about to say something, but no sound came out. Bess's joyful expression faded to one of concern. Jack glanced at me, eyes pleading for help, for reprieve, or for a moment alone, I couldn't tell. He looked back at Bess and swallowed hard.

I was suddenly overcome with the feeling that I was taking up too much space, even here, crammed in at the end of the crowded Market aisle.

"I'm going to go," I said. "You two obviously have a lot of catching up to do, and we still have things to buy. Jack, can I have the ledger?"

"No, Nora, I don't—"

I held out my hand, waiting until he fished the ledger from his pocket and gave me the chalk from behind his ear.

"I'll find you," I said, smiling to reassure him—of what, I wasn't sure —and walked away, down the aisle opposite where they stood. I glanced back once, long enough to see Jack and Bess sitting down on a bench near the textile stalls, already deep in conversation.

∼

I asked the satin vendor where I could find the jewelry, and he directed me two aisles over. Colored stones glittered on either side of me, but every time I closed my eyes, I saw an image of Jack and Bess sitting together. I took a breath. They were old friends. They'd had many years with each other and with Liana. Of course he'd want to talk to her. Plus, Bess had already experienced the slow death of a parent. Jack had told me about how Bess's mother, Lady Celia, passed when Bess was a girl. It was a long illness, he said, just like Liana's. I could only hope that Liana's illness wouldn't end the same way. I fiddled with the tree in my pocket, pressing its pointed branches into my hand. I would give it to Jack tonight at supper, I decided. As Liana's son, it was only right that he should have it.

The list of jewelry for the ball was also in my pocket. I asked the nearest gemstone vendor where I could find Harold of the Summit and was directed to the back of the aisle. On Harold's table, a rainbow of gold, silver, and colored gems sparkled on top of a piece of black velvet. I touched a bracelet adorned with pale blue stones, imagining how it would look around my wrist.

"Can I help you?" Harold asked. I yanked my hand away from the table and handed him the list. He glanced over it and looked at me with narrowed eyes.

"Lady Portia sent you?" he asked. I nodded. "She's been one of my best customers ever since I started in the mines." He picked up emerald and pearl hairpins, a delicate necklace with the pearl doublets Annabelle had asked for, and a thick gold chain with a heavy emerald hanging off it.

"Stiffed me last time I came by the Runes, though." Harold furrowed his brow as he placed the jewelry into a blue velvet bag. "She said she gave me the whole lot, but there was fifty lil missing when I counted everything up." His sour expression changed back to a wide smile. "It sure got her goat when I sent a message asking about it. The coins must have dropped right out of my pocket, she said. Must have been my fault."

I didn't know what to say, so I just stood there, biting my lip.

Harold looked back at the paper I'd given him, then down at his table. He picked up a necklace with gold beads and pear-shaped emeralds that matched Siobhan's drawing.

"Who's this one for?" he asked.

"Her daughter," I said.

"Which one?"

"Siobhan."

"The one who looks like her?"

I nodded.

"Jewelry for the ball, I suppose," Harold said. "I suppose they'd be thrilled if Siobhan ended up marrying the prince."

"I suppose so," I said. I was itching to leave. This transaction had taken a strange turn. Harold put his loupe up to his eye, examined the stones on the necklace, and made a show of thinking about what he was going to say next.

"I'll give it to you for twenty lil," he said. "I'm having a special due to a surplus at the mines in the Summit. Any other day, I'd charge you eighty. It's a hundred and fifty for the others, and I'll throw in the hairpins for free."

I counted the coins in my bag and gave Harold 170 lil, more money than we'd spent on the satin for all three dresses. I marveled at how Portia could hand so much money over to be spent all at once.

Harold took the coins and dropped the last necklace into the bag.

"Nice doing business with you," he said. I put the bag in my pack. "Send my best to Lady Portia."

I murmured thank you, stepped away from the stand, and took out the ledger. I did the math once I'd recorded the purchase, subtracting from the amount we had before going into the entertainment tent. I did the math again. We bought everything on the list, and there were ten lil left over. Portia wouldn't have miscalculated; she would have given us exactly the amount we needed, without any lil left for yellow flowers. But even though Jack said we overpaid for a few items, he bartered with other vendors, and I got a discount on Siobhan's necklace. I did the math a third time. It couldn't be right, but it was. I took the extra coins, two five-lil pieces, out of my bag and weighed them in my hand.

No one said what to do if there was money left over. Portia wouldn't miss a few lil if she didn't expect them back in the first place. I looked back in the direction where Jack and Bess were seated, obscured by the crowd. Jack certainly didn't have anything else to get. He found what he wanted before I even started looking. I needed to find something that could be mine alone.

I walked down aisle after aisle until the crowd thinned out and the items on the tables began to change. Instead of finely cut and mounted stones, vendors displayed jewels with jagged edges and cloudy spots. Some advertised jewel dust, claiming that powdered rubies would help with knee pain or that gold dust would make old skin youthful again. Others sold oddly shaped bottles filled with colored liquid and candles that smelled when lit and gave off colored smoke.

Ahead of me, a woman haggled with a young man who was trying to sell her a large, nacre bowl edged with white stone. The vendor leaned heavily on the crutches under his arms as he extolled the bowl's virtues to the woman's evident skepticism. I watched, wide-eyed, as he scooped up peach-colored crystals in his palm and dropped them in the bowl. With a flick of his wrist, translucent mist rose from the bowl, swirling and forming into an image of a young girl and an older man reading a book together. The vendor swiped his hand again, and the image disappeared. Cowed, the woman placed her lil in his outstretched palm.

I didn't know whether to run out of the aisle or go farther in. There was magic here, real magic. Not kisses that would wake the dead or transmogrifying witches, like in Peter's stories. This was the kind of magic that was supposed to only be practiced in secret corners of Colandaria, in back rooms or under the cloak of darkness. There was nothing like this at the Runes market. The novelty was overwhelming. The candle salesman behind me lit wicks with the tips of his fingers. A customer at the booth with the cloudy gems watched as a spherical sapphire spun in the air above his hand.

I always pictured the Kindred as having a supernatural air about them. Maybe they glowed or had purple hair. I knew that Bess's family practiced. Jack had told me stories about Sir Milton conjuring a wall of mist to hide the Vale proper from intruders or about how his late wife, Lady Celia, could make raindrops glow so that it looked like tiny suns were falling from the sky. With her strange hair and the chain of stones across her forehead, Lady Bess looked like I would expect a sorceress to. But the vendors here, haggling with their customers? They looked just like everyone else.

It was all right here, only twelve or fifteen aisles away from where vendors sold fish and popped corn. And yet most customers were choosing to ignore it. The aisles weren't empty, but they didn't come close to matching the bustle of the rest of the Market.

Liana's voice popped into my head. If she were here, she would pull me out of this aisle, straight back to the food and textiles. I touched her tree in my pocket. Sorry, Liana. I had lil to spend.

I passed a stand with herbs I'd never heard of and was tempted to buy something for Greta, but I pressed on. At the end of the aisle, a thin, balding man with a goatee stood in front of a table that displayed books with yellowed pages and worn covers. I picked up one that looked remarkably like the nature book I'd made when I was a child. The pages were covered with detailed drawings of unfamiliar plants and words scrawled in a language I didn't recognize.

"It's Ionian," said the man behind the table. "You speak it?"

I shook my head and continued to flip through the pages. The back half of the book was filled with recipes, but I couldn't understand any of the directions.

"It comes from the Farlands," the vendor said. "Fifty lil and it's yours."

My mouth fell open. That was more than Siobhan's necklace cost.

"I don't have that much."

"So you'd best leave it, then," the vendor said, indicating with a disparaging nod for me to put the book back on the table. "No point getting something you can't even read."

I put the book down next to the other items on the table: several wooden boxes stacked on top of one another and a few dull crystals. The boxes were stunning. The details in the intricate carvings on their tops and sides glistened with oil. For the first time that day, I remembered the sheath at my side and reached for my knife. In a moment of panic, I worried it wouldn't be there and that I had been the victim of one of the pickpockets who had gotten to Jack the last time he was here. With relief, I pulled out the carved blade and held it up next to the boxes. The carvings on the handle weren't exactly the same, but they were similar. The hilt of the knife was made from the same type of wood as the boxes.

The vendor's eyes narrowed into slits.

"Can I see that?" He reached for my knife. I stepped back from the table and returned the blade to its sheath.

"Do I know you?" the vendor asked, tilting his head and stroking his goatee in a way that made the skin on the back of my neck crawl. "You look kind of familiar." His eyes traveled from my face down to my arms, where I had pushed my sleeves up in the heat. I clasped my arms behind my back, hiding my scars from his gaze. I didn't know what he was looking for, but I knew that I didn't like it.

"I suppose I don't," he said, answering his own question. "It's about time to buy something or get away from my shop. I have actual customers to deal with." He gestured behind me, and I turned around to find Lady Bess with her hands on her hips, meeting the vendor's annoyed glare with one of her own. Jack stood behind her, looking around, trying to take in every stand at once.

"Leave her be, Tyrus," Bess said.

"She a friend of yours?" the vendor asked.

"As a matter of fact, she is." Bess paged through one of the books on the table.

The haughty expression melted off Tyrus's face.

"Sorry, Bessie, I didn't know she was with you. She looks like a pretender with that—"

"There's a lot you don't know," she interrupted, shooting me a glance that asked me to play along. "And if you think you and your Handlers can just waltz into the Vale again without warning, you've got another thing coming."

Tyrus stammered an apology. I slunk back next to Jack.

"What's going on?" he whispered. All traces of his earlier sadness had evaporated.

"Your friend here seems to know everyone at the Market."

Bess continued to argue with Tyrus, who sank into his skin as she railed at him for whatever offence he'd committed at the Vale.

"Now, did you find the book I was looking for?" she asked when she finished with her tirade. Tyrus hunted around in his stacks and pulled out a small green volume.

"I only managed to track it down a week ago. Found it with some cave dweller up in the Fall." Tyrus sweetened. "Now don't you be going all reclusive on us, Bessie."

Bess rolled her eyes. "You don't have to worry about that. I'm quite happy where I am."

Tyrus handed her the book. At this point, I wasn't surprised when he didn't ask for payment in return.

"Was there something you wanted to buy?" she asked me.

Tyrus looked at me, and the sweetness he'd put on with Bess was gone. I thought about just walking away, but the ten lil weighed heavily in my pocket. Everyone was waiting for me to make a move. The boxes on the table were beautiful, but they certainly cost more than ten lil. Sunlight glinted off one of the clouded crystals. I picked it off the table and held it up. Light passed through the edges, but the center of the crystal was a dark, opaque red. It reminded me of the stonefruit Greta liked to cook with.

"How much for this?" I asked.

"You sure you're not a pretender?" Tyrus asked. Bess cleared her throat, and he said, "Twelve lil. But it's useless unless you got something to open."

I put the crystal down with a pang of disappointment. "I only have ten."

"Take it for ten, then, as long as you're a friend of Bessie's."

I handed him the coins and slipped the crystal into my pocket next to Liana's tree. I could hang it next to the window in the kitchen house. It would cast a nice light onto the floor when the sun hit it. Tyrus muttered something else about my being a pretender as we walked away.

"'Til next time, Bessie," he called, louder now. "Have I told you how beautiful your scar is?"

Bess shook her head. "Gross."

As soon as possible, I wanted to get out of this aisle and back to what was familiar. Bess stopped at the stand where the young man with crutches was selling his bowls. His eyes lit up when he saw her.

"Cort!" she exclaimed, embracing him. She looked back at Jack and me. "I'll just be a bit. I'll find you at your wagon." She made a series of rapid gestures. The vendor laughed, countering with his own hand movements, and I realized they were talking without words. My chest tightened even further.

"Bess is having dinner with us," Jack said as we made our way back to the Market entrance. "You know, if it's okay with you."

I bit back my disappointment. The Lady of the Vale seemed nice enough, but she was a lot to take in at once. Still, it would make Jack happy.

"Sure," I said, and the knot in my chest threatened to strangle me.

~

We stowed our purchases back at the camp. I looked over the fresh food piled in the wagon and sighed as I got out the half a loaf of bread that was left for dinner. There was no give when I squeezed it. I was sure that there would be an accounting of everything we bought once we got back to the Runes, and there would certainly be questions about anything that was missing. So, stale bread for dinner it was.

New faces sat around the fire pit. Bess joined us, bringing cheese and fruit from her wagon, which was hitched a few circles over. I spent most of dinner in silence as Jack and Bess reminisced about their childhood in the Vale. Jack would occasionally throw a comment or question my way, but I had nothing to add. Until now, my little life had been confined mainly to the Runes proper. Bess, it seemed, had traveled all over Colandaria, even to the border of the Farlands, before she was fourteen. From the way she talked, I got the sense that some of this traveling was done on her own. I couldn't even imagine having that kind of freedom.

The sky was dark by the time we finished eating, but it felt like Jack and Bess's conversation could keep going into the wee hours of the morning. The fire sparked, and an ember jumped out of the pit, landing on the edge of Bess's blanket and lighting it ablaze. I grabbed for my water skein, but before I could reach it, Bess had her hand above the fire. Blue-green mist curled down from her palm to calm the flames.

It took effort to keep my mouth from falling open. Here, away from the mystical Market aisle, the magic seemed even more real.

"Good catch," Jack said. His blasé attitude made me feel even more unworldly.

"Parlor tricks," Bess said, shaking her head. "I wouldn't do any of the real stuff here. You never know who might be watching." She turned to me. "Some particularly ignorant folks think every Kindred they see is a dark mage from the Farlands."

"What does your family practice?" I asked, even though I didn't think I would understand the answer. I knew from Peter's stories that there were different types of magic that were mostly practiced along family lines.

"Papa comes from a family of mist mages," Bess said. "My mother was a candlebearer. I can do both, but mist magic comes easier to me." She turned her palm over, and blue-green mist floated off it again. "I am my father's daughter after all." She closed her hand, and the mist disappeared.

"So all those vendors—Tyrus and the boy with the crutches—they're all Kindred too?"

Bess nodded. "Cort's family makes bowls for scrying. They've been doing it for generations. Tyrus is a potions master, but he's been hanging around with a group of Handlers recently, and—"

"What are Handlers?" My world was swiftly expanding beyond the kitchen house, and I was determined to learn as much as I could.

"Handling…" Bess's hand went to her chest, where a small gold key hung from a chain around her neck. She rolled it between her fingers. "Handling is one of the more unpleasant forms of magic. A lot of the dark mages from the Farlands are Handlers, but there are Kindred here in Colandaria who practice that way too. They use blood in their spells. Animal, sometimes. Human, too, more often, I think." She grimaced. "It's powerful magic, but we stay away from it."

I grimaced along with her. "They sacrifice people?"

"I don't think so. That seems too barbaric for any Kindred to consider. We don't really talk about it in our house, and I've only ever met a few Handlers myself. Papa sticks with the mist magic. Although now that he's apprenticing Gideon, we're studying songsmithing—using sounds to create energy." She looked over at Jack, who had been strangely silent since I perked up and joined the conversation. "Are you okay?"

I could see the wheels turning in his head.

"Ma and I left the Vale when you turned fourteen, right?"

Bess bit her lip. "Just after I apprenticed to Papa."

"We left because you were Kindred, didn't we?" In the firelight, his face was an angry mask. "Ma never said why we were leaving, but I knew she wouldn't have moved us for no reason. I always thought it was because my pa died and she needed a new start, but it wasn't, was it? It was because of the magic."

Bess's brow knotted. "I guess Liana thought I was a bad influence on you."

"But you were my friend!" Jack's eyes flashed.

Bess touched the scar that ran the length of her cheek. "I don't think it's any coincidence that Liana started looking for work right after I came home with this. I ran away, remember? Even if I meant well by doing it, I came back with a gift from a dark mage. If Papa taught me anything, it's to be respectful of what other people think. Your ma didn't want to be a part of something she didn't agree with, and after your pa was gone, she had no reason to stay in the Vale. Don't be mad at her." She reached over and squeezed his hand. "Not now."

Jack's brow creased as he looked into the fire. As much as I wanted to help, I didn't know what to do for him. And it seemed like I wasn't the one he needed right now. I faked a yawn.

"I'm going to sleep," I said. Bess whispered something in Jack's ear that cracked his sober expression, and his laughter followed me to where I lay down next to the wagon. The fire reflected off the silver threads in Bess's dress and the stones in her hair, giving her face a warm glow. I rested my head on my pack, but not before pulling my sleeves down to cover the shiny scars on my arms.

~

he Zephyr's call jolted me awake. I looked around through bleary eyes to see that I was alone. Everyone was either passing through the entrance gate or had packed up their wagons and left the Market.

"Oh, good, you're up."

Lady Bess stood behind me, holding a small loaf of bread and a piece of cheese. I sprang off the ground and grabbed my blanket, taking the food she offered.

"Where's Jack?"

"Here!" His hand shot up from behind the wagon where he was tying a rope around the cart to keep everything in place.

"Why didn't anyone wake me? I could have helped."

Bess shrugged. "Jack said to let you sleep."

"I could have helped," I grumbled, folding my blanket and throwing it on top of the wagon. Jack climbed over the seat.

"Did you eat?" he asked. "Bess and I had breakfast, but I didn't want to wake you. Oh," he added as an afterthought, "she brought over this amazing tea that you should try. Nettles and cinnamon, I think. From the Farlands. Wakes you right up."

"Mm-hmm," I said. The knot in my chest reasserted itself. "I'm going to get Honeycomb." I left the bread and cheese in the front of the wagon and went over to where the horses were grazing in their pen. My stomach growled in protest. I gave my name and Honeycomb's description to the groom. He went into the pen to find her. As I waited, I looked back at our wagon. Bess was pouring Jack another cup of

Farland tea, which he downed in a single gulp. She looked well rested, like she'd never slept on the ground a day in her life.

As I turned away, my gaze fell to my reflection in one of the troughs set out for the horses. The hair on the top of my head stuck up at an odd angle, and there was a dark purple stain on my shirt from some of the fruit Bess had shared with us at dinner. Strange gold eyes stared back at me, muddied by the brown water. A wave of anger rolled through me, and I had to stop myself from kicking the trough. Instead, when I got back to the wagon with Honeycomb, I thrust Jack's cap onto my head, stuffing as much of my hair underneath it as I could.

"Anytime you can get away to visit," Bess said, "we'd love to see you."

She hugged Jack goodbye, whispering something in his ear that brought color to his cheeks. He climbed onto the wagon seat. I trailed after him.

"Nora," Bess said, "it was so wonderful to meet you. We'd love to have you at the Vale too. I hope you'll visit."

"Thank you," I said. As much as I didn't want to admit it, it was hard not to like the Lady of the Vale.

"Be safe." She waved as Jack guided Honeycomb back onto the forest trail.

We rode without talking. I didn't like the silence, but I didn't know what to say. This was different from the rage I felt towards Alcander or the shame that Portia made me feel. I didn't have a name for the heaviness in my limbs, the knot in my chest, or the lump in my throat. But it felt like once again I had lost something essential.

We approached the Castle around lunchtime. In the two days since we had our glimpse of the Prince and Princess on the other side of the wall, everything had shifted. There was a Market and magic and Bess. I wanted to talk to Greta, but she was always too busy. Liana had too many of her own worries for me to burden her with my emptiness. At that moment, I felt a painful longing for my mother, Izella, whoever she might have been.

"What did you think of Bess?" Jack asked, breaking the silence.

"She was nice."

"You should come to the Vale with me," he said. "There are so many things I could show you. The kitchen, the grounds, the stream…"

"The stream where your father's spirit lives?"

"Yes," Jack said, acknowledging my gentle mockery. "That stream. I'm sure he'd love to meet you." He looked up, and the sunlight brightened his face. "There's this rosebush that grows near the main entrance to the house. It has flowers that are so white they're almost blue. When the sun is setting, they look silver. Sir Milton used to say that Bess was a flower he plucked off the bush, you know, because the roses were the same color as her hair." He laughed. "When we were little, Bess used to pick flowers off the bush and wait for them to sprout arms and legs and grow into a brother or a sister for her." He paused for a moment, shifting the reins in his hands. "She never treated me like one of the servants' children, probably because she didn't have many friends, either."

I nodded. I knew very well how loneliness could bring people together.

A flash of brown darted through the trees next to us.

"I wish some of those deer would come by the Runes," I said. "I'm getting sick of pheasant, and even they're a rare catch now."

The air became increasingly warm as late morning changed to afternoon. Jack took off his vest and rolled up his sleeves, and I hitched my skirt around my knees, swinging my bare legs back and forth with the movement of the wagon.

"How much did you know about the magic at the Vale?" I asked.

"Not much," Jack said. "Sir Milton would disappear into his back rooms a lot. We all knew that he was practicing in his study. Ma called it his 'knightly duties.' She always avoided talking about it. I never really thought about it at the time. She hated it, though. The magic. She must have wanted to get away as soon as she could. It really set her off when Bess disappeared. It was a few months after my pa died, and—"

The flash of brown appeared again between the trees. I peered into the woods, trying to see what it was. Our wagon bounced, and Honeycomb reared up with a frightened neigh. I braced my arms against the front of the wagon to avoid falling forwards out of my seat as something jolted against my hip.

"Nora?" Jack's voice was thin and pained, his eyes wide with fear. A muscular man stood behind him, perched on the edge of the cart with one arm tightly around his shoulders and the other pressing a knife to his throat.

My hand flew to my belt.

"Looking for this?" The man flexed the blade towards me so I could see the carvings on the handle. Jack cried out as the metal bit into his skin.

A voice from in front of our wagon: "Good afternoon, travelers."

A woman in deerskin pants and a dark brown tunic stepped onto the path, holding a crossbow. She had the whipcord pulled back so tightly that the bolt would fly out of its slot with just the slightest movement of her fingers.

"I see you've come from the Market," she said. "We'll be happy to take those purchases from you."

CHAPTER 10

The need to flee surged through me, but instead of leading me away from the wagon and the crossbow pointed at us, it froze me to my seat. Jack's fists clenched as though he were ready to jam an elbow into the gut of the man who held the knife, my knife, to his throat. But if he made a move, there would be more than just the trickle of blood already running down his neck.

The woman with the crossbow stepped forward with her arrow trained on Honeycomb. Her dark braid swung behind her like a tail.

"Either we take what's in the wagon," she said, "or I shoot your horse, then you, then we take what's in the wagon."

"It's just food," I stammered. I had a fleeting hope that the thieves would leave us alone if they thought there was nothing of value in the cart.

"Everyone has to eat." The woman lowered her crossbow, slung it over her back, and nodded towards the trees. Five more men appeared, each holding a knife or bow. One of the thieves cut the ropes that Jack had looped around the cart and began to paw through the packages. He tossed the woman the blue bag I'd tucked between crates of fruit. She opened the bag and poured out the jewelry. Emeralds glittered in her hand.

"This doesn't look like food," she said.

"Liar," the thief standing next to me barked, smacking me on the back of the head hard enough to knock off my cap. My head smarted from the blow. Jack made a small move forwards, but the large man behind him tightened his grip around his shoulders.

No one moved. The thieves looked at each other, then at the woman. She remained still, looking at me with eyes that held both recognition and confusion.

"Arelys," the man standing behind Jack said. "Are we taking the haul or what?"

The woman, Arelys, poured the jewelry back into the bag, yanked the drawstring shut, and hurled it at me. The bag smacked harmlessly into my chest. I picked it off my lap with shaking hands.

"No," she said. Then, to me: "Get on the ground." She raised her crossbow. I jumped off the wagon, wringing the bag between my hands.

"You come from the Runes proper?" Her expression reminded me of the look that Tyrus, the vendor, gave me when he was trying to get a closer view of my knife, like he knew me, even though we'd never met. I had the same feeling. Her name was familiar—I had a dim memory of seeing it written somewhere.

I nodded.

Arelys shifted her weight from one foot to the other. "Who are your parents?"

I returned her confused stare. "Why does it matter?"

The thief who hit me reached for his broadsword.

Arelys held up her hand. "Back off."

The thieves stowed their weapons. Only the man standing on the wagon stayed in place, knife to Jack's throat.

"I said back off, Roland."

Roland sighed and jumped off the cart. Jack's hands flew to his neck as blood seeped between his fingers. I watched, unable to stop him as Roland tossed my knife over our heads. Arelys palmed it out of the air, examined the hilt, and stuck it in her belt.

"You can't take that." I said lamely. "It was my mother's." Of all the things the thief could steal, this was the one I couldn't do without.

Arelys shrugged. "It seems only fair, Eleanor. Consider it a debt paid." She put her hand to her mouth and trilled a birdcall. The men disappeared back into the trees as Roland and Arelys turned down the path and slipped back into the woods.

"You didn't tell her your name," Jack croaked. His hand was still around his throat. Red spots peeked between his fingers. "How did she know your name?"

Then it hit me. I had seen her name five years before on the night of the banquet in the ledger in Alcander's study. If she recognized me, it was because I looked like someone she knew, someone who was alive when she worked at the Runes. Someone who Tyrus might have known too.

Izella.

I grabbed the reins and shouted for Honeycomb to go. Instead of continuing on the path to the Runes, I pulled hard to the left, leading Honeycomb into the woods, onto the narrow side route where Arelys and Roland walked. She turned around at the sound of the wagon wheels.

"Nora, what are you doing?" Jack hissed in my ear. "The knife isn't worth it."

"It's not the knife I want," I said.

Roland reached for his sword. Arelys put a hand up to stop him.

"You knew my name. You used to work at the Runes proper, didn't you?"

Arelys ran her tongue over her teeth, just looking at me long enough that I thought I'd made a mistake. Finally, she nodded.

"I've never had someone follow me after we've completed our business before," she said. "I have precautions in case anyone does." She nodded to the trees. I glanced up to see her men perched on the branches around us.

My jaw tightened. "You knew Izella. My mother."

"She was a good lady," Arelys said. "Never made us feel like any less because we were servants and she was Lady of the Runes."

The air warmed around me. Only in my wildest fantasies had Izella been a noblewoman. Most of the time, I imagined her as a servant with whom Alcander had a passionate affair. Why else would I have such a lowly status? Arelys's words were confirmation of everything I felt—that I deserved more than this lot in life, that Alcander had taken something essential from me.

Arelys went on, "It's only out of respect for her that I didn't take the wagon. Still, she did leave us in the lurch by dying like she did, so I figure she owes us one." She patted her belt, where she'd stored my knife. "You look like her," she said. "Almost. Same hair, same eyes, but she was put together. You look like someone ran you through a briar field."

It didn't matter whether she was talking about my hair or the scars that raked across my arms. The words hurt. I was supposed to be dressed in fine silks and satins, the daughter of the Lord and Lady of the Runes, with my skin pristine and my face impeccable.

"Yllianne will want to hear about this," Roland said to Arelys. "Tell her you saw Izella—it'll make her week, if she can remember it tomorrow."

Yllianne. Another name from Alcander's ledger.

Arelys glared at her partner. "Screw off, Roland."

"Could I talk to Yllianne?" The words were out of my mouth before I could stop them.

Jack nudged me with his elbow and talked through tight lips. "We need to go home. Now." He gestured at the men who looked down on us from the trees. I got off the wagon and walked towards Arelys. She raised her crossbow.

I took a wild guess. "Is Yllianne your mother?"

She gave the smallest of nods.

"I'm trying to find out about mine. All I had of hers is the knife that you took. If you or Yllianne could tell me anything about her…" I trailed off. I didn't know how to explain to this woman what it would mean to finally have a part of Izella I could hold on to.

Arelys stared me down with her arrow. Finally, she lowered the crossbow.

"Go back to the main path," she shouted to her men. "Watch for wagons." Before I could turn around to watch her do it, Arelys had brushed past me, jumped up on the wagon seat next to Jack, and grabbed the reins.

"Well?" she said. "Let's go."

∼

*B*y the time Arelys took the wagon off the side path and into the trees, Jack was looking at me over her shoulder. His eyes were wide with fear.

"If you try to jump off this wagon," Arelys said, "I'll call my men back. I don't think Roland will pause in slitting your throat this time."

Color drained out of Jack's face. The front of his shirt was spotted with blood.

We traveled through the forest in silence. My skin thrummed with anticipation. Each turn of the wagon's wheels brought us closer to someone who would have answers to the questions I'd carried inside me for years. I couldn't get over the fact that Portia had not been the first Lady of the Runes. She acted like the house had always been hers. That sense of ownership should have been mine.

Arelys led the wagon between the trees, making what felt like random turns. I ducked to avoid being hit by low-hanging branches. Finally, she stopped Honeycomb in front of a stand of oak trees behind which I could just make out the exterior of a small cottage.

"Stay here." She jumped off the wagon and disappeared into the house.

"We're going to get murdered." Jack reached for the reins. "This is her murder house. We need to go."

"Jack," I said, almost pleading. "The woman in that house knew my mother."

"In case you forgot," Jack said, "I have a mother too. One who is going to think I'm lying dead in a ditch somewhere if we're not home on time. And this won't help matters." He pointed to the cut on his throat. "She's never going to let me leave the Runes again."

I scanned the forest floor. When I saw what I needed, I leapt off the wagon.

"Nora!" Jack looked back at the house, panicked.

I pulled up a yellow-tipped fern from the ground, plucked off the leaves, and chewed them. When I had enough, I spat them onto my hand and climbed back up onto the wagon.

"Here. It's yellowtail weed. It will stop the bleeding." I pressed the leaves to his neck. "Hold that." I ripped a piece of cloth from one of the sheets in the cart and tied it around his neck to keep the leaves in place. He murmured a grudging thanks as Arelys came out of the cottage.

"You can talk to her," she said, "but I don't know how much she can tell you." She held the door open. "Upset her, and I'll see that neither of you ever talks again."

My feet quaked as I stepped into the house. Jack was close behind me. The cottage reminded me of one of Greta's old blankets, warm and fraying at the edges. A fire wheezed in the hearth. The room was divided by a curtain, which Arelys pushed aside to reveal an old woman sitting on a bed. Her short grey hair curled around her ears, just touching the blanket that wrapped around her frail shoulders. She looked at me with clouded eyes.

"Izella?" Her voice was paper-thin.

I knelt beside her. "Izella is my mother's name."

The old woman reached forwards and touched my face. She blinked, and the clouds in her eyes cleared away. "Eleanor?" she whispered. I nodded, and she placed her hand on top of mine. "You look just like your mother." Her hand was warm, like I imagined Izella's would be.

Arelys stared Jack down until he gave her his name. Then she introduced us. "Eleanor, Jack, this is Yllianne."

"You were a servant at the Runes proper," I said.

"A long time ago. Now my Arelys is a hunter," Yllianne said, gazing affectionately at her daughter. "She and her men sell what they catch at the Market."

Jack opened his mouth to speak, but Arelys's eyes flashed a warning. His hand went to his neck.

"I'm sure she's very good." He sounded strangled, and not by the bandage I'd tied around his throat.

"Izella?" Yllianne said. The cloudiness returned to her eyes. Arelys raised her chin at me. Play along.

"Yes?"

"I need you to know—" Yllianne coughed into the blanket. "I need you to know it's safe. I hid it before he could get it."

"Hid what?"

"I saved it from the fire." The old woman's voice faded, and her eyes lost their focus as she slumped into herself. I fought off frustration. I had searched the main house for remnants of Izella's life and had come up empty-handed. But they were here, locked up in this woman's memories.

"Her mind started to go last summer." Arelys sat down next to her mother. "She asks for Izella a lot. That's the only reason I agreed to bring you here. I thought maybe seeing you would give her some peace." She tucked Yllianne's hair back behind her ear. This was not the same woman who had given orders to the band of thieves. This was a daughter, the kind I wished I could have been.

"I hid it where no one would find it, not even Portia," Yllianne murmured.

"Portia?" What did she have to do with anything? I looked to Arelys.

"Izella's sister," she said.

I wished I could grind time to a halt and take in this new information. This revolting closeness to Alcander's wife—my aunt—made my stomach roll. But time marched on, and Yllianne started to speak again.

"Your necklace!" Yllianne pointed at my chest. "What did you do with it? I can't remember." Her head darted back and forth as she looked around the cottage. She started to rise off the bed. Arelys eased her back down.

"Mama, don't get upset. You rest. I'll look for the necklace." She gestured for me to get up, closed the curtain around the bed, and sank down at the kitchen table with her head in her hands. I sat next to her.

"I'm sorry," I said. "I didn't mean to upset her."

Arelys shook her head. "It's not you. She's always talking about that necklace."

I glanced at Jack, who hung back by the door, ready to make a quick exit. If there were a piece of Izella's jewelry tucked away somewhere at the Runes proper, I had to have it. It might not be much, but it would be something.

Arelys went on. "Izella always used to wear this glass pendant with a rose in it. It was some kind of good luck charm. Maybe she was right to be superstitious about it. It went missing just before she died."

"She died in childbirth," I said. Childbirth with me. My fault.

Arelys nodded. "Sir Milton couldn't save her."

"Sir Milton?" Jack came away from the door. "Don't you mean Sir Alcander?"

"No. Milton and his wife were always at the Runes. When Izella went into labor, Milton was the only one who could get her to stop tearing the house apart looking for that necklace."

This didn't make sense. Alcander and Milton were far from friendly with each other.

"Where was Alcander?"

"Gone to the Castle," Arelys said. "Official business for the King. No one expected you for another few weeks. Alcander came back home right after you were born and Izella passed. I don't know what happened. Milton wouldn't let anyone in the room while Izella was in labor, and Alcander wouldn't let anyone in afterwards. He banished Milton from the Runes right then and fired all of us a week later." Arelys snorted. "We should have expected it after the fire, but it still took us by surprise."

There it was: the darkness breathing down my neck. Black tendrils twisted at the edges of my vision. Arelys looked over to where Yllianne lay behind the curtain.

"My mother still has nightmares about it. The noise woke us up in the middle of the night. We couldn't see any smoke, but I remember feeling like something was wrong. One of the main house servants ran out screaming. We grabbed pots, buckets, anything we could, got water from the well, and ran in to put it out. We were lucky we got it before it spread past the one room."

"The room with no windows." My voice sounded wounded and strange.

"Izella's library. Alcander said it was an accident. He knocked over a candle, and the drapes caught fire, but that didn't made sense. Like you said, there were no windows. And it wasn't an accident that all of Izella's things were in the room when it lit up. Her portraits, her letters, her clothes. They all burned before we could put the fire out."

It was no wonder that I couldn't find anything of my mother's in the main house. Alcander destroyed it all. I hated him for this more than for his refusal to look at me, more than for the stony silences, more than for making me a servant. What had my mother done to deserve being erased from Alcander's life? From mine?

"And then he married Izella's sister?" Jack said. "Why would he do that?"

Arelys shrugged. "We were long gone by then. But he courted Portia before he even knew Izella, so I'm not surprised if she swooped in after Izella died. She never let go of the idea that Alcander was hers first. She and Izella had this big fight the day before Izella died. I didn't think that

Portia would come back to the Runes proper after that, but obviously she did."

I pressed my hands to my temples. Drumbeats echoed between my ears. It wasn't just Alcander. Portia had a hand in taking away my birthright too. If Izella won Alcander away from her sister, then it made sense why Portia hated her, and me, so much. I pictured her icy blue eyes and tightly laced corsets. There was no room to breathe in her. If I were going to be anywhere around the Runes proper, she would see to it that I was strangled too.

"Arelys?" Yllianne's voice came from behind the curtain. "Who are you talking to?"

"No one, Mama."

"Is that Eleanor? I thought I saw Eleanor all grown up."

Arelys pushed the curtain back. Yllianne was sitting up again, clear-eyed. She looked me over.

"You look so much like your mother," she said. "She was such a good girl. She never forgot us in the kitchen house." She looked at Jack. "Do you work in the kitchen house?"

He nodded.

"Well, Eleanor must come visit you too. Right, dear?"

Jack shook his head. "No, Nora is—"

"It's Eleanor," I interrupted. Then, to Yllianne, "Yes, of course I do."

Jack's face crumpled. "Of course she does," he murmured. "It's very kind of her to visit us in the kitchen house."

Yllianne smiled. "Just like her mother. I knew it."

Jack glared at me. I glared right back. Even though I was dressed in serving clothes, Yllianne never questioned my status. I was a lady like my mother before me. I just wished I could meet her expectations.

"Lady Eleanor." There was ice in Jack's voice. "We ought to be going home before your father starts to worry. You know how much he cares about your safety."

The pounding in my temples got stronger. If I didn't look at him, he couldn't see how much those words hurt.

"He's right," Arelys said. "Mama, they have to go. You need your rest."

The old woman reached for my hand. "Tell your mother I think of her often."

I nodded. "I will."

"You seem like a fine girl. I bet she's proud of you."

I doubted it.

~

Outside, one of Arelys's men was going through the purchases in the back of our wagon.

"Hey! That's enough," Arelys shouted, waving him away. "Get out."

He put down the package of satin that was meant for the ball and slunk back into the forest. Arelys took my knife out from her belt.

"You know, my mother was the one who saved this for you," she said. "She hid it in the kitchen right after Izella died." She handed it to me, hilt-first. "You ought to take better care of it. Your mother never would have let me nick it."

I took the blade from her, closing my eyes for a moment to savor the feeling of the wood against my skin. After today, it no longer had to be the only thing of Izella's that I had. There had once been a woman who looked like me who traveled between the kitchen house and the main house, staking claim to both. Now, there was so much more to find: a hidden necklace and the rest of her story.

"Do you know where Izella's ashes were scattered?" I asked Arelys.

"Under the hazel tree in the field behind the main house. It was my mother's idea."

My breath caught. Of course her ashes were under the hazel tree. My tree, the constant, comforting presence outside the kitchen house.

"Nora." Jack was already at the wagon.

"We should do something for them," I said. I searched through the cart until I found a sack of flour and a flagon of wine. I held them out to Arelys. She took them, nodded her thanks, and turned back to the cottage.

"Looks like you got what you wanted after all," Jack said to her. "Maybe next time try talking to people instead of threatening them with knives and arrows."

Arelys wheeled back around. "I do what I need to do to survive. And in case you haven't noticed, I'm pretty good at it. I don't need some lady and one of the servants who took my place looking down on me." She stormed back into the house, slamming the door behind her.

Jack shook with anger.

"She's not wrong," I said as I climbed up next to him.

"Not wrong? In case you forgot, she nearly had my throat slit." He jabbed a finger at the bandage around his neck. "Never mind. Lady Eleanor wouldn't care." He looked around, clenching the reins in frustration. "I don't even know where we're going. Maybe you can go back inside and get directions from your new friend."

"Jack—" I didn't know what to say. He had to know what this afternoon meant to me. Jack cracked the reins, and Honeycomb lunged forward.

"Couldn't tell them you were a kitchen servant, could you? Maybe you can grace us with your presence in the kitchen house tonight while we're making dinner."

I was stunned into silence.

"And since you're related now, maybe you'd care to explain to your loving Aunt Portia why half the food is missing."

I turned around to look in the cart. He was right. The piles of food were significantly smaller than when we left the Market. Arelys's men must have made short work of our wagon while we were in the house. Portia would be furious. So would Greta. But, I reasoned, we would make do. We always made do in the kitchen house. Portia would have to learn to do the same.

Jack guided Honeycomb through the forest, cursing every time he had to turn around and ignoring my suggestions of other paths to try. Finally, I stopped suggesting and turned my thoughts to what I'd do when we got home. I would go back through the main house room by room, searching every nook and cranny to find Izella's necklace. Maybe it would bring me good luck too. The more I thought about it, the more I felt ready to lift off my seat. There was something of my mother's that Alcander hadn't managed to turn to ashes. Soon, it would be mine.

The sun had begun to set by the time Jack found the main road.

"Ma's going to have a fit," he said. His anger seemed to have tempered, but he was quiet for the rest of the ride, only hissing at me to sit down when I stood up in my seat as the Runes proper came into view.

"Go ahead," I said. "I'll meet you in the kitchen house." I jumped off the wagon as we approached the hazel tree. Jack drove the wagon to the kitchen house entrance, where we could unload what was left of our purchases. I threw my arms around the trunk of the tree.

"Hello, Mother," was all I could get out before happy tears began to stream down my face. Izella had always been a part of my life, right outside my window as I sat at the kitchen table and under my feet as I sat in the tree, leaning my cheek against her smooth trunk.

A howl filled the field, shuddering the hazel branches. Fear rushed through me. We hadn't had wolves in the woods around the Runes in years. The noise sounded again. It came from the kitchen house.

I ran across the field and threw the door open. Greta and Peter stood next to the hearth with their arms locked tightly around each other. Greta's dusty face was streaked with the paths of her tears. I followed their gaze to where Jack knelt on the floor, holding one of his mother's hands as his cries subsided to a low moan. Liana looked like she was merely sleeping in front of the hearth. Searing hot tears sprang to my eyes and burned down my cheeks.

"What happened?" I choked out. Peter held out his hand and pulled me into his arms.

"She passed a few hours ago," Greta said. "There was nothing we could do."

"Nothing?" Jack snarled at her. "You're supposed to be a healer. Why didn't you help her?"

"I tried." Greta knelt down next to him. He shoved off the arm she tried to put around his shoulders. "She wouldn't let me help her, not as much as I could have. You know that."

"Jack—" I broke away from Peter and reached for him.

His eyes narrowed. "Don't," he said with much more venom than he had in the wagon. "If we hadn't stayed so long at that thief's house, I could have been here. I could have done something. I could have…"

"There was nothing anyone could do," Peter said. "She was too sick."

"Jack, I'm sorry," I said. It came out as a breath that I couldn't catch.

"What do you care, Lady Eleanor?" He spat the words at me. "She was just another kitchen servant."

I reeled back as though he hit me with his hand instead of his words and cried in the circle of Peter's arms.

For the rest of the evening, Jack didn't move from beside Liana's body. Greta and Peter hovered around him, trying to offer a comforting word or embrace. He refused their advances. I huddled uselessly in the corner, unable to push away the cold that crept through the room.

I pulled the crystal I bought at the Market out of my pocket. Its red center pulsed like a secret heart. I felt like I was betraying Liana by bringing it into the kitchen house. The crystal came from a world of floating pictures and colored smoke, of mist that came off of Lady Bess's skin and stories of people who used blood to cast spells. I didn't know what I was thinking when I bought it. Whether or not the crystal had any power, Liana would have hated it. I climbed up to the loft and stuffed it under my mattress.

Reaching back into my pocket, I took out Liana's last gift, the tree she carved from the hazel branch. Liana had been a master carver. She could have sold her work at the Market. Instead she chose to make her way here, as a servant. I looked down at where Jack sat by the hearth, still holding his mother's hand. Greta had covered her body with her favorite blanket. Even if Liana hadn't needed to come to the Runes, I was so grateful that she had.

I ran my thumb over the owl carved into the heart of the tree. Part of me still wanted to give it to Jack. But the carving came from Izella's hazel tree. Now that I knew it was a little part of my mother, I couldn't give it up. I put the carving under my mattress with the stone.

Greta threw together a late dinner for the main house. Sarah and Matthew came to fetch it, whispering condolences that came and went as fast as they did. Peter put a plate of dried meat and carrots that he took out of our stores in front of me. I choked it down, swallowing hard to push the food past the heavy lump in my throat. Peter motioned to Jack and handed me another plate.

I shuffled over to him. "You should eat."

He didn't look up from where his mother's pale, greying hand rested in his palm. It was only through the slight rise and fall of his shoulders that I could tell he was still here, present and alive. I put the plate down next to him, and my tears began to flow again.

The plate and Jack were both still there in the middle of the night when I peeked over the edge of the loft and looked down into the kitchen. He hadn't moved, hadn't made a sound as we got ready for bed.

Peter murmured something to Greta about making arrangements for Liana in the morning. I curled up on my mattress under the window. The space of two missing bodies in the loft felt heavy, like a pit that could never be filled.

~

*W*hen I woke up, Jack was gone from his place at Liana's side. A cracking sound came from outside. I climbed down from the loft and looked out the window in time to see a small tree keel over at the edge of the forest. A short while later, another followed.

My breath fogged the glass between us as Jack hauled the trees closer to the kitchen house and chopped them into pieces. I watched as Peter went out to help and Jack first silently refused his advances, then as they worked side-by-side to build Liana's funeral pyre. Greta came down and opened the windows, letting out the stench of death that permeated the kitchen.

I wondered who had built Izella's pyre, if Alcander had done it or if he had left it for the servants. A wave of grief crashed down on me, grief for the mother I'd never met and the father I'd never known. My shoulders shook as I cried, trying to stifle my sobs as I buried my head in my arms.

Jack was silent as we brought Liana outside and lifted her onto the pyre. She was wrapped in her blanket; the blue, green, and brown birds that she had embroidered on it would travel with her on the wind. Jack hung back, away from Greta and me, as Peter lit the logs and the fire began to blaze. The light of the flames was reflected in the tears that streamed down his face.

All through the ceremony and afterwards, as we were called into the main house and screamed at by Portia for the stolen items from the Market, Jack didn't say a word.

He had stopped talking completely.

CHAPTER 11

*I*n the month that followed, the kitchen house was haunted by two specters instead of one. Jack went about his chores with a listless expression, pale and silent. His hazel eyes turned a dull brown. I took his turns in the main house without asking. Peter and Greta shared worried conversations over dinner as Jack sat by the hearth, occasionally picking at his food. This sad, quiet man was not the Jack I knew. I kept my distance, afraid that if I did or said the wrong thing, my Jack might slip away forever.

Liana had carved her own urn out of a heavy piece of birch. None of us ever saw her work on it; Peter found the urn in the loft in a chest with Liana's belongings. The fact that she knew the end was coming somehow made everything even worse.

Tradition said that until someone took the urn out and set the ashes to the wind, the person's spirit would linger. Peter said we needed to leave the decision of when and where up to Jack. Until then, the urn sat on a shelf by the door, and Liana's spirit hung over the kitchen house. I didn't know if I believed the teachings about the World Apart, but I did know that with the urn just a hand's distance away every time we entered or exited, there was no getting away from our loss. I entertained thoughts of the urn mysteriously disappearing and Jack's burden lifting.

Each night, I brought out Liana's tree and the red crystal from under my mattress and held them so tightly that my fingers ached. The red marks the tiny hazel branches made as they poked into my palm were painful reminders that I was still here, that this version of the kitchen house, this sullen place that was so different from the warm home I was used to, wasn't a dream. Watching the marks fade was reassurance that something might change.

In the dark of the loft, I imagined a rose trapped in the bloodred core of the crystal. A tiny rose, just like the one in the necklace that existed only in my imagination and the memory of an addled old woman.

I approached the only person in the main house who might be able to give me an idea of where to start my search for Yllianne's hiding place.

"I know there was a fire here after I was born," I said to Robert. His frown appeared as soon as I started talking. "A lot of my mother's things were lost, but was there anything left? Any letters or pictures?"

Robert's frown deepened.

"Or any jewelry?"

He glanced back at the dining room where Alcander and his family were eating. Their voices drowned out our whispered conversation.

"I don't want to know how you found out about the fire," he said, "but you need to let it be."

"Why? Alcander might not want anything that belonged to my mother, but I do."

"The less you have of that woman, the better." Robert walked away, leaving me slack-jawed in the middle of the hall. I understood why Alcander kept him on even when he'd fired all of the other servants. Robert was loyal to a fault.

That night, when everyone in the kitchen house was asleep, I crept out of the loft. I stepped over Jack, lingering briefly to look at his face, brightened by the moonlight that shined from my window. He only looked like his old self when he slept.

Taking a candle from the kitchen, I let myself into the main house through the back entrance. I started at the far end and made my way through the rooms, scouring shelves for hidden compartments and walls for crevices that might contain Izella's necklace. Though I discovered half-eaten cookies, dropped quills, and a stash of letters addressed to

Annabelle from a son of a neighboring lord hidden in the metronome in the music room, the necklace was nowhere to be found.

I placed Annabelle's letters back inside the metronome before holding my candle over Siobhan's sheet music and obliterating the notes with splashes of yellow wax.

I took out the rest of my frustration in Alcander's study. I switched the labels on his ink jars so that he would dip his quill into the red container when he meant to use blue and would get black when he reached for green. I switched the order of the books on his shelves. I knew that these were childish aggressions, that the most I would do was annoy him. But it made me feel better to picture Alcander yelling in frustration over a map that was destroyed by the wrong ink. It was too bad I wouldn't be there to see it.

I took out his logbook and grabbed a quill, about to write in all the back pay he owed me, but I stopped. As much anger as I had, I was more afraid of what would happen if I were caught.

⁓

In the kitchen house, I was learning that loneliness can be so much worse when someone else is with you. With Liana gone, Greta threw herself into her work, no longer humming as she mixed ingredients and kneaded dough. We talked only when we needed to. Peter busied himself outside, always finding something new that needed fixing. Even meals were sadder without Liana's whimsical carved fruits and vegetables to decorate the plates. We existed in three different kitchen houses. Jack shut everyone out of his, and I was ready to close the door on mine. Greta and Peter made attempts to bring us back together, but the gulf created years ago when I found out where I came from was becoming too hard to traverse. They wanted to be my parents, and even though I didn't want to, I kept pushing them away.

As the days went on, I thought about setting out on the forest path and saying goodbye to the Runes proper for good. I had already left the province once. Surely I could do it again. I imagined walking over the mountains and into the Farlands, where the stories were born. I would become one of those stories, living among people who could see the future and shoot sparks from their fingers. I'd have a different name in the tales that would be told about me, and Alcander and Portia would never know that I was the one doing the wonderful things that would become the talk of Colandaria.

Inevitably, thoughts of Greta and Peter, and Jack, whom I already missed terribly, ripped at the pages of those dreams. I had to repair what was broken and get the kitchen house back to the way it was. And now Izella tied me to the Runes proper. Until I found what was hidden in the main house, I couldn't leave.

I stared at Jack across the room as he sat on a stool, cutting up a loaf of bread. His hair fell limply over his forehead, and he regarded his work with little interest. He looked at me for only a moment when I took the bread for the dinner plates. There was no light in his eyes. Liana said that Jack didn't talk for almost a year after his father died. The thought that this could go on for that long was unbearable.

It was Jack's turn to take dinner into the main house, but I went for the cart instead. Jack pushed past me, shaking his head and wheeling the cart outside.

"Let me do it," I insisted, running out the door to catch him. "I don't mind."

He looked at me, coming to life for the barest moment. His chin twitched in an expression that told me he knew better. It was gone as soon as it appeared. He continued across the field.

"Fine, you're right, I do mind," I said, trailing after him. "But let me do it. You don't have to." I could only imagine what Siobhan or Portia might say to him.

Jack pressed on inside and to the dining room. I wanted to protect him from whatever might wait in the halls, from the nauseated feeling I still got every time I stepped inside, from the dark that had already stolen the light from his eyes.

Everyone was already seated at the table. I curtseyed, and Jack gave a half-hearted bow in the doorway. Alcander waved us in. Siobhan hooted under her breath as I walked by.

"You're late," she said. "Did someone else die?"

Alcander's gaze flitted over me before focusing on Jack. He coughed into his napkin.

"I'm sorry about your mother," he said. Jack gave a curt nod.

Alcander's belated condolences hardly seemed enough. He rose from the table.

"I'll take dinner in my study."

"But, Papa—" Annabelle pouted.

"I have work to do." He left before she could say anything else.

We continued around the table. Jack put down plates of roasted chicken, and I poured the wine. Siobhan jerked her cup aside so that some of the wine from my pitcher spilled onto the table. Portia clucked her tongue in disapproval.

"I'm sorry about your mother too," Siobhan said to Jack. "But it must be a relief that she won't have to look at Owl Eyes's ugly face anymore."

I fought the urge to pour the rest of the wine into her lap. Jack was silent, putting Annabelle's plate down as if he hadn't heard. Annabelle murmured a quiet thank-you and fiddled with something in her lap.

"Ugh," Siobhan stabbed the chicken with her fork. "I think this cooking might have killed her. Did you drop this on the floor before you brought it in here?"

"I wish," I muttered.

"Siobhan," Portia snapped. "Grow up. Have a little more respect for the dead." I was so surprised that I almost spilled Annabelle's drink. Portia went on. "And for goodness sake, you're old enough to know that it's not worth talking to the servants."

Annabelle's cheeks reddened. Standing behind her, I could see her squeezing a small piece of paper in her hands. She looked up at me, and I could have sworn she mouthed *Sorry*.

Siobhan rolled her eyes. "It's hardly talking when one of them has gone mute." She poked Jack with her fork. His jaw tensed. "Aren't you going to say anything? It's like talking to a wall."

I slammed the pitcher down on the table. "Shut up. Leave him alone."

Portia's eyes flashed. "Eleanor. Leave. This instant."

I stomped out of the room. Jack followed with the dinner cart.

"I hate them," I seethed as soon as we were in the hallway. "I hate them so much." I rubbed at my arms as though I could get the stink of the blood we shared out from under my skin. As I turned on Jack, about to admonish him for not standing up for himself, I saw the last plate still on the cart.

"Alcander." I sighed. Jack turned the cart towards Alcander's study. I ran around the other side and stopped him. "No. I'll do it."

For a moment, he looked unsure. I had the sudden urge to throw my arms around him and press my lips to his, as though I could bring him back with a single kiss. The thought frightened me, and I took a step back.

"I'll do it," I said again. Jack held his hands up, relinquishing the cart. After he left, I stood alone and regrouped. The handle of the cart was still warm where his hands had been.

I wheeled the cart down the hall until I stood at the entrance to Alcander's study. The door was open. Alcander sat at his desk.

"Sir?" I said. Fear washed over me as he raised his eyes to meet mine. Did Robert tell him I was asking about Izella? Did he know I had searched his study? I suddenly regretted my childish acts of revenge.

Discomfort blinked on Alcander's face for an instant before his expression hardened to apathy. Anger raged through me. I would rather he punish me for entering his room and messing up his inks and books. Scream at me for taking too long with his dinner. Fear me like the vengeful ghost of my mother I was afraid I was becoming. Anything other than looking at me like I was just another servant to ignore.

I put the plate down on the small table next to his desk and turned to leave.

"Eleanor."

"Sir?" Hope—of screams, embraces, anything—surged through me.

He held out an empty plate. "Take this back to the kitchen house. No one came to clean it up yesterday."

Hope crashed at my feet. I took the plate. "Yes, sir."

"The servants need to be better about keeping this room clean. I don't want rats eating my work."

I wanted to argue that it was the house servants' job to keep the room clean, but Alcander had already returned to his work. His quill *skritch*ed across the parchment, mapping far-away places I'd never see.

"Well?" he said without looking up. "Are you waiting for something?"

"No, sir." As I turned away, my eyes fell on the keys hanging on a hook by the door. I glanced back to make sure Alcander wasn't looking before grabbing the ring and shoving it in my pocket.

There was one room I had yet to search.

~

*E*very time I went into the main house, I skirted past the room with no windows. The door waited innocently in the middle of the hall between Portia and Alcander's quarters and the dining room, just another door in a house full of them. It was the only door in the main house that was always locked, the only one under which no light ever shined. Izella's library was condemned to darkness. It was the fear of my childhood, the fear of my actually finding what I was looking for in the dim memory of a stone that could be pried from its moorings. And it was the only room in the main house I hadn't searched.

Night never fell more slowly than it did as I tidied up the kitchen house and urged Jack, Greta, and Peter to go to bed early. Jack acquiesced without a word, but Peter and Greta insisted on staying up with me until the last dish was clean and the evening dough was covered with cheesecloth and put away to rise until morning.

"I've got it, really," I said. If I could have pushed them up the ladder to the loft, I would have.

Greta's face hardened. "You don't seem to need us for anything anymore, do you?"

Peter turned to look at her. I froze with my mouth open. I didn't know what to say. I thought of throwing myself into her arms, but I had never called her "Mother." I didn't feel like I could start now. Greta climbed into the loft without waiting for my response. I sat at the table and put my head in my hands. Peter sat next to me.

"I kind of want to be alone," I said. Then, seeing the hurt on his face, I added, "I'm sorry."

Peter left for the loft without another word. I rested my forehead against the table, willing the throbbing between my ears to stop.

I woke with a start. The table was wet, and I wiped moisture from my cheeks with the backs of my hands as I looked out the window. The moon peeked out, a sliver of white above the main house. No sound came from the loft.

I slipped out of the kitchen house with only the weak moonlight to guide me. Somehow, the prospect of using a candle to see inside the room with no windows was more terrifying than going in in the dark. I darted across the field and let myself into the main house, feeling my way along the walls as my eyes adjusted to the darkness in the hall.

Voices came from the music room. I peeked inside to see Siobhan and Annabelle dancing a slow waltz. Annabelle led with her arm around Siobhan's back. They swept jerkily around the room a few times before Annabelle threw her hands down in frustration.

"You can't lead," she said. "You have to let the man lead!"

Siobhan stomped her foot. "So lead better!"

"I'm leading fine. You need to follow." Annabelle went over to the metronome, which clacked along at an even pace. "I'll slow it down so you can get it."

Siobhan leapt in front of her, getting to the metronome first and pulling out the stash of letters I found weeks before. She stood on her tiptoes and waved them in the air, out of Annabelle's reach.

"It's not fair that you're better at this when you're not even trying to impress Prince Edward. You'll just go off with your Daniel while the rest of us are fighting for a dance. Maybe I should deliver these to Mother. She'd love to read about Daniel's 'undying adoration' for you."

"No!" Annabelle jumped for the letters. Siobhan took off across the room. While they were distracted, I hurried past the door.

I passed the dining room, and there it was: the door to the room with no windows. Even in the dark, I could make out the charring around its edges. It was a wonder that I'd never noticed it before. The doorknob was cold. I fished Alcander's keys out of my pocket and began trying them in the lock. After three failures, I wondered if he even had a key to Izella's library. He'd finished his work there years before. What reason would he have to go in now?

The fourth key slid into the lock. I turned it, and the door creaked open.

The room was darker than the hallway. My temples began to throb again, and I hesitated to step inside. This was it, the nightmare of my childhood. If I entered, I would be right back there, twelve and terrified, about to be consumed by the void. I instantly regretted not bringing a candle from the kitchen.

I shook my head. I was not twelve anymore, and I would not be terrified. I crossed the threshold.

The room blazed with light. Unease crept through me. The walls were covered with book-lined shelves. There was a handsome wooden table in the center of the room and a comfortable chair in the corner.

I took a halting step backwards and peeked out of the room. Down the hall, light from the music room spilled onto the floor. I could still hear Siobhan and Annabelle. The metronome was going again, and Annabelle was counting steps. In Izella's library, the light from the torches on the wall stopped in a sharp, defined line at the door. Just outside the room, the hallway was dark. The pit in my stomach deepened.

There was a pieced rug on the floor made from scraps of fur, heavy satin, and wool. I ran my hand over it, feeling each texture. It seemed as real as everything else in the room. Air moved behind me, and I jumped up, half expecting to see Izella standing there, ready to tell me that my entire life was a fever dream just like this was.

Darkness descended, coming off the ceiling and from the walls as the room crumpled in on itself. The candles disappeared, and the room plunged back to black. My unease turned to cold, sharp terror. I wheeled around to make sure the door was still there. Faint light from the hall illuminated the entrance to the dark room. I had to get out of there. I threw myself at the walls, pawing for a loose stone I feared was just another dream.

Footsteps sounded from the hall as I moved wildly, hands scrabbling over the stone. The walls were tightly sealed. I moved to the corner of the room. Cold breath blew onto my neck, and I wheeled around, smashing my face into the wall next to me. A bright flare of pain burst around my nose. I tried to catch myself before I fell, but I hit the ground hard, my palms smarting against the ashy floor.

I rose on shaking legs, unsure that what I felt was real. One of the stones had moved in my hand as I went down. I felt along the wall again and moved the stone back and forth in its slot until it fell out, landing at my feet. I closed my eyes—the darkness behind my lids was somehow more hopeful than the darkness in the room—and reached into the hole.

My hands closed around a wooden box, which I pulled out and clutched to my chest. I turned from the depths of the room, dashed to the safety of the hallway, and slammed the library door shut. Just before it clicked back into place, I was sure I saw candles blazing inside again.

～

I tossed Alcander's keys on the floor in front of his study so that he would think he had dropped them on his way out. A minute later, I was back outside, gasping in the night air. I let myself back into the kitchen house, wincing when the hinges creaked as I closed the door. Greta's snores sounded from the loft.

I lit a candle and sat down to examine my prize. The box was flat, roughly the size of a loaf of bread. The top and sides were carved with whorls and loops just like the boxes I'd seen at Tyrus's stand at the Market, just like the whorls and loops on the knife that was tucked under my mattress. I pulled the top of the box, but it wouldn't budge. I looked closer at the carvings. There was a hole in the middle of the patterns on the front of the box. I cursed under my breath. I had grabbed the box and run out without thinking to look for a key.

I looked around for something I could use to pick the lock. I stuck one of Greta's hairpins into the keyhole, jiggling it and listening for a click of release. My impatience grew along with the throbbing in my face. It hurt to blink; I could feel the flesh around my eyes and nose swelling as I climbed up to the loft. Perhaps the blade of my knife was thin enough to stick under the top of the box. If I used the right amount of pressure, I might be able to force the lid open.

Greta and Peter were asleep by the back wall. I stepped over Jack, who had moved his mattress to the middle of the loft, an arm's length from my window, a few weeks before. If she were alive, Liana would have made Jack drag his mattress back to the other side of the loft and given a him lecture about rules of propriety for young men. But she wasn't there, and Greta and Peter hadn't said a word. I couldn't blame Jack for wanting to be closer to the light.

As I reached under my mattress, my hand brushed the red crystal. I almost let it be, but the memory of Tyrus's stand rushed back to me. The stones had been placed next to the boxes on the table like they were supposed to go together. And then there were Tyrus's words: *It's useless unless you got something to open.* Excitement muted the pain in my face. I grabbed the crystal and my knife and dashed back to the ladder.

"Ow!" Jack yelped in pain, sitting up straight and awake. I'd stepped on his hand in my rush to get back to the kitchen.

"Sorry," I whispered, glancing over to make sure that Greta and Peter hadn't woken up too.

Jack rubbed his eyes. "You're bleeding."

"Go back to sleep," I said and climbed down into the kitchen.

I put the knife and the stone on the table next to the box as Jack stumbled down the ladder.

"What are you doing?" I stood in front of the table in a feeble attempt to hide the box.

"I think I'm the one who needs to ask you that," he said.

It was only then that I realized: "You're talking."

He shrugged. "You're bleeding."

I wasn't sure if it was an explanation or an observation. I looked in the glass that hung on the wall. Blood from my nose covered the lower half of my face, dripping onto my neck.

"Ugh," I murmured, wiping the blood away. My nose smarted when I bumped it with my hand. I peered at my reflection. My nose didn't look broken, but there was a deep cut on the bridge. Puffy, dark circles rimmed my eyes.

"Here." Jack held out a cloth. I waved him off and went back to the table. He pointed to the box. "What's that?"

Given his reactions in Yllianne's cottage, I wasn't sure I wanted to share this with him. But here he was, talking again. I couldn't lose that.

"I think it was my mother's," I said. "It was in the main house." I wasn't ready to talk about the dark room and how, for a moment, it wasn't dark at all.

Understanding dawned on Jack's face. "It's what Yllianne hid. Can I?"

I nodded. He pulled at the lid of the box. It wouldn't open for him either. I picked up the crystal. Blood from my fingers smeared the surface, disappearing into the deep red at the center of the stone.

"I think this might open it," I said. I held the stone up to the candlelight, expecting that I would have to clean it off before I figured out how to use it. The flame shined through the stone, and the surface was as smooth and clean, as though my blood never touched it. The center of the crystal seemed redder than before. I swore I could see it pulsing in time with the rapid beat of my heart. When I moved it away from the light to show Jack, the candle went out. Smoke trailed up from the wick. The only light in the room came from the crystal as the stolen flame danced inside.

The crystal brightened, and its surface began to warm. I dropped it on the table. Acrid smoke filled the air as the crystal melted, contorting into a twisted black key. Jack put a hand on my shoulder. I put my hand on top of his to reassure myself that we were both seeing the same thing. For the first time, there was magic in the kitchen house.

"I think Izella was Kindred," I said, feeling foolish for not having realized it before. Why else would she have a box that could only be opened using a magic charm? Why else would Tyrus have thought he knew me?

I needed to know everything. Did my mother mix potions in a bubbling cauldron? Could she talk to animals or whisper with the wind? Did she use magic in subtle ways or with grand, sweeping gestures? If she had been alive, would she have taught me? After all, this meant I was Kindred too.

Jack lit the candle again and looked on, dumbfounded, as I picked up the key. The metal was still warm. I slid it into the hole in the front of the box, turned it, and heard the click of the lock. The box creaked open, and the scent of roses filled the room. I felt for the necklace, fishing between the dried petals that spilled out of the box in dusky pinks, dark reds, pale yellows, and faded brown-whites. Instead of a chain, I pulled out a small, leather-bound book. The pages were edged in gold leaf that flaked onto my hands. I dumped the rest of the petals onto the table, waiting to hear the clink of the necklace landing on the wood, but I was only rewarded with the gentle ruffling of the flowers.

I bit back my disappointment and turned my attention to the book. A list of names was written on the first page: Elora, Adele, Frances, Justina, all the way down, ending with Jane and Izella. My breath quickened as I turned the fragile pages. There was nothing left in the room but this book and me. Even the pain in my face disappeared.

Written on each page were instructions for a spell: getting a garden to grow, making dough rise faster, cleaning a house in moments, enchanting a looking glass so the viewer could see a loved one from far away. The words blurred as tears sprang to my eyes. When Alcander took Izella away, he took her magic too. Now, my birthright was here at my fingertips.

Back on the first page, there was an empty space below Izella's name, space that I could fill with my own. I got up and looked through the shelves for ink and a quill.

"What is it?" Jack asked.

"Izella's spellbook." Saying the words out loud felt both right and absurd.

Greta's inkpot was on the herb shelf. When I turned back to the table, Jack was paging through the book. My elation was absent from his face. He looked up at me and spoke in a measured tone.

"Nora, I'm not sure you want to—"

I held out my hand. "Give it to me."

"But did you see the—"

"I said give it to me!" I didn't want Izella kept from me a moment longer.

Jack held the book fast. "Do you remember what Bess said about Tyrus?"

"I don't care about Bess." I wrestled the book out of his hands. One of the pages tore under my thumb.

Jack spoke quickly, before I had a chance to look at the book again. "Nora, your mother was a Handler."

I flipped through the pages. The spells called for herbs, salts, soils, feathers, and stones. But every spell had one ingredient in common, one ingredient that took all my strength away.

"Blood magic."

The book fell out of my hands, landing open to a page with the word *Glamour* written at the top. Below it: *To Conceal that which you wish to remain Hidden.* The last ingredient was *Blood, with Intent, from the Heart.*

"No." It was a plea that would never be answered. My eyes dropped to my hands, covered in the blood from my nose, the same blood that had disappeared into the opening charm before it turned into a key. It was dark and wild as my hair. A tacky crust crumbled between my fingers as I wrung my hands together. My stomach heaved, and bile rose to my throat. Without realizing it, I'd already performed blood magic.

There was no water left to wash off my hands. I scraped them against my skirt as hard as I could.

Jack picked my knife off the table and held it up, comparing it to the cover of the book. He looked at me. He didn't have to say it. The patterns on the handle of the knife, the ones I'd found comfort in rubbing against my fingers as a child, matched the design etched into the leather that covered the book. The book, the box, and the knife all went together, all artifacts of Izella's practice. I pictured the blade slicing across the neck of a doe, a bowl underneath to catch the syrupy blood. I had used the knife that way myself plenty of times, cutting the heads off chickens or slicing up meat from animals we caught in the woods. There was something much darker about causing that suffering in order to clean a room or make flowers grow.

Then I remembered something else Lady Bess said about Handlers as we sat around the fire outside the Market. It seemed so long ago, when Liana was alive and Izella only a wish. Now, Liana was an urn on a shelf, Izella was an invocation I wished I had never uttered, and I was picturing her dragging the point of my knife across her chest, her dark lips forming a triumphant smile as blood waterfalled down.

I felt like I had been doused with a bucket of cold water. I sputtered, drowning in the air, threw the book back in the box, and closed the lid. The box and key were in my hands when I started for the ladder.

Jack followed me. "What are you doing?"

"I'm not this," I said. "I can't be this." My face pulsed with pain. Yellow flashes mingled with swirls of the darkest black in front of my eyes. I clutched the ladder to stay upright.

"I can't be this," I repeated, needing to hear the words again. Jack offered me the cloth again, and I took it, wincing as I wiped my face.

Moments ago, when Izella was just one of the Kindred, a thousand thoughts ran through my head, all beautiful like the pictures that rose out the bowl the man with crutches sold at the Market or the way Lady Bess described making magic through song. For a few minutes, all of Colandaria had opened up to me. It was no longer just the Runes or the kitchen house—it was anywhere the birds could fly because I could fly too. But now, instead of freedom, I felt ugliness growing beneath my skin, trapped within my blood. If Izella hadn't died, I might have always been using my knife to release it.

I buried the box and key under a pile of hay in the corner of the loft. In my haste, I forgot to put away the quill and inkpot I'd taken off the shelf. I looked down into the kitchen to find Jack cleaning up. He leaned over the table and blew out the candle, plunging the room back into darkness.

"I'm sorry," he said once he climbed back into the loft. He handed me my knife. I stuffed it under my mattress. I didn't want to hold it, didn't want to touch the carvings that connected me to my bloodstained inheritance. I lay down on top of it, closing my eyes and clenching my jaw against the feeling of the knife dripping beneath me. I felt like I might float away on its tide.

"Nora?" Jack said. I turned over to look at him. He lay on his mattress, wide-eyed, looking at me with questions he decided not to ask. He reached his arm across the space between us. I reached mine out to meet his, and we met in the middle, pressing fingertip to fingertip in an old gesture, a reminder that we were both here. My breath evened out as the contact sent a warm sensation up my arm.

"I'm sorry for what I said to you after my mother passed," he said.

"You don't have to be," I said, "but thank you. I'm sorry we weren't there for her. That was my fault."

Jack rolled on his back without letting go of my hand. My fingers moved of their own volition, running over the lines of his palm.

"She didn't want me to be there," he said. "That's all I've been thinking about for the last month, just replaying that last conversation over and over in my head. She was getting worse. I wanted to stay with her instead of going to the Market, but she made me go. She practically pushed me out the door. She said, 'I don't want that to be the way you remember me.'"

He turned back over to look at me. "She knew she was dying, Nora. And she didn't want me there. I want to respect that, but it's hard." Moonlight flickered in his eyes. "I would have been there for her."

"I know," I said.

He offered a small, sad smile. "Good night."

"Goddess keep you," I said.

When I woke in the morning, my shoulder was sore, and my hand was still clasped in his.

CHAPTER 12

*J*ack made his announcement as we cleaned up from dinner. "I'm going to the Vale. I want to scatter Ma's ashes in the same river where we put my pa's."

"I think she'd like that." Peter poured the bucket of dishwater over a cheesecloth that Greta stretched over one of the large bowls we usually reserved for dough. The cheesecloth was stained a nauseating tone of grey-brown. We'd been straining the dishwater for a week already. The well was almost dry.

"When are you going?" Greta asked.

"Tomorrow," Jack said, "if Alcander gives me permission."

Two weeks had passed since I found Izella's box. I had yet to unearth it from the pile of hay under which it was buried. Even though Jack was speaking again, his hazel eyes still hadn't regained their luster. I would often look across the room and see him with his shoulders slumped, staring into space. I would call out to him, and he would snap back into the kitchen house. Perhaps when Liana's ashes were scattered, some of his magic would come back.

"Do you want company?" I asked and immediately felt guilty. I wasn't asking just because I wanted to be there for him or to say a final good-bye to Liana. I needed the Vale for my own selfish reasons.

Izella's knife—I didn't want to think of it as mine anymore—was still under my mattress. Greta had noticed me using a regular kitchen blade.

"Where's yours?" she asked. The question was so brusque that I couldn't give her the real answer.

"The blade is dull," I said without pausing in my chopping. "I haven't had a chance to sharpen it."

"You know where the whetstone is."

I wanted to repair whatever was broken between us, but I didn't know how. I tried going out to gather herbs, hoping I could find something rare that would make Greta happy, but even common herbs were dead and gone with the drought.

Ever since I found out about Izella's magic, I could feel my blood pulsing under my skin, hot and urgent. I felt it burn when I thought about the knife that was not dull at all, as I watched Alcander eating dinner with his children, and as I sailed to the floor when Siobhan stuck out her foot and tripped me on my way out of the dining room. That blood flowed beneath the purple bruises on my knees and the ones under my eyes that finally faded to ochre. It felt powerful. I wasn't sure I liked the feeling.

According to Arelys and Yllianne, Sir Milton had been at the Runes when Izella died. Milton, not Alcander, was there when she needed someone. He could fill in the gaps in Izella's story. If I could just understand her, perhaps it would temper the burning in my veins.

Still, when I asked Jack if he wanted me to go to the Vale with him, part of me hoped he would say no.

Instead, he nodded and smiled a smile I hadn't seen for more than a month.

~

*J*ack decided to broach the topic of going to the Vale when we brought dessert to Portia and Alcander. The Harvest Moon Ball was only two weeks away, and during the day the house was a whirlwind of dance teachers working with Siobhan and dressmakers running back and forth with pins in their mouths and bolts of fabric in their arms. Now, Siobhan and Annabelle had retreated to their quarters, and the dance instructors and dressmakers had gone home. Portia and Alcander were in the parlor, a room adorned with deep green curtains and gold chairs. A few books sat on a shelf as though it had been ages since anyone noticed they were there. Portia was dictating a list to Sarah, who stood next to her, quill in hand.

"Good, you're here," she said as we entered the room. She nodded to Sarah, who handed me the paper. Jack put the tray of pastries on the table between Portia's and Alcander's chairs.

"The menu for the next two weeks," Portia said. "Make sure you actually follow it this time."

I scanned the list of meals and knew that when I gave it to Greta, it would end up as kindling in the hearth. At this point, most of the meals Portia wanted were impossible to make. The deer had gone elsewhere in the forest in search of water, so we couldn't serve venison, and even Jack had given up on the limp heads of lettuce in the garden.

"Sir Alcander," Jack said. Alcander looked up from the map he was studying. "With your permission, I'd like to scatter my mother's ashes tomorrow in the Vale."

Alcander nodded. "Give her spirit a proper send-off. Just don't be gone long."

"Thank you, sir," Jack said. We turned to go. Out of the corner of my eye, I saw Alcander glance at Portia. His jaw hardened.

"Jack," he said. "Eleanor is not to go with you."

His steely eyes shackled me to the floor. I knew there was no use protesting, but I did it anyway.

"Liana was important to me. I'd like to be there for her Final Rites."

Thin lines appeared at the corners of Alcander's eyes. "I was not speaking to you. Liana was not your mother. You have no need to be there."

We might not have been related, but that didn't mean Liana hadn't been important to me. She was the one who helped me perfect my knife skills. If Izella were alive, I would have learned an entirely different set of uses for my blade. I far preferred Liana's teachings. And Alcander was ready to deny her to me just like he did my mother.

Alcander went on. "I was speaking to Jack, who must understand me when I say that you are not to travel with him to the Vale." He stood, rising to his full, imposing height. Since I rarely saw him outside the dining room or his study, it was easy to forget that he cut a powerful figure, one with the power to throw people away or hold them fast.

"Now, Eleanor, I am speaking to you. Tomorrow, you are to stay with my daughters. They have a ball to prepare for. You will be there for whatever they need. Am I understood?"

There was no chance I could sneak out to go with Jack now. Siobhan, rat that she was, would tell on me in a heartbeat.

"Yes, sir," Jack said when I didn't respond. He put a hand on my arm to lead me out of the room.

"You forgot to curtsey," Portia called after me.

Without looking back, I pushed over an ornamental vase that sat on a pedestal by the door. It shattered into tiny pieces on the floor.

"You could take that out of my wages," I said, "if you paid me."

I rushed down the hall with Jack at my heels. No one followed from the parlor.

~

I knew there would be suspicious eyes watching from the main house the next morning. Jack seemed to be delaying leaving as long as he could. He hadn't even gone to get the saddle to put on Honeycomb when I saw Robert walking across the field.

"Here he comes," I said. We sat at the table by the window, finishing our small breakfast. There was no water to waste on tea. Jack yawned.

Robert knocked on the door. He gave me a pointed look as Greta let him in.

"You're needed in the main house," he said. Then, to Jack, "I'm surprised you haven't left yet," he said. "At this rate, you won't make it to the Vale until the middle of the afternoon."

Jack shrugged. "It's only a half day's ride to the Vale when you don't know where you're going." He fiddled with the lid on Liana's urn. I knew he was worried about it spilling open as he rode down the forest path.

Robert looked back at me. "Nora?"

With reluctance, I said goodbye to Jack and followed Robert to the main house. I felt his eyes on the back of my head as he followed me down the hall. Alcander must have ordered him not to let me out of his sight. I felt a certain delight in the fact that Alcander didn't trust me. He shouldn't.

Robert gestured for me to go into the music room. Siobhan and Annabelle were promenading around as a violinist played in the corner. This time, Siobhan wore shiny gold shoes, and Annabelle wore exasperation on her face. They whirled around the room with Annabelle dragging Siobhan along.

"Wait," Siobhan said, breathless, as they whipped by where I stood awkwardly in the corner with the violinist. Annabelle yelped as Siobhan stepped on her foot. She stomped on Siobhan's toes in return and threw her arms up in frustration. Siobhan screamed, hopping around on one foot. The violinist stopped playing.

"I'm going to find a drink," he said to no one in particular and walked out of the room.

"That's it!" Annabelle said. "I don't care what Mother says. I can't do this anymore. If you don't have it now, you're not going to get it before the ball."

Siobhan sat on the piano bench and took off her shoes. "It's these stupid things she's making me wear. They're scrunching my toes. She said they'd stretch out if I wore them long enough, but they haven't." She rubbed her feet as she looked in the shoes. "Ugh, there's blood in here."

I coughed. Better they acknowledge me now than realize later that I had been there the whole time. Siobhan stared daggers at me.

"What are you doing here?"

"Your father says I'm supposed to stay with you today," I said. "I suppose he thinks you need help too."

Annabelle hid her laughter behind the hand that covered her face.

"It's not funny," Siobhan wailed. "I'm practicing from sunup to sundown, and I'm still going to make a complete fool of myself in front of the Prince. Mother is going to be furious!" She looked menacingly at Annabelle. "And she's going to be furious with you when you don't dance with him at all. Maybe I will tell her about you and Daniel. If he's going to ask for your hand, shouldn't she and Father know?"

Annabelle flew to Siobhan's feet. "No, you can't! Not until after the ball. You promised! Daniel and I are going to tell them together. They wouldn't let me leave the house if they knew."

I took a tentative step forwards. "They don't like Daniel?"

Siobhan answered for Annabelle. "They don't even know him. His family is barely considered nobility."

"He's noble enough to go to the ball," Annabelle muttered, crossing her arms and walking over to the window. She peered outside. "Where is he going?"

I moved to see what she was talking about. Jack was saying goodbye to Greta and Peter. He had Liana's urn in a pack slung over his back. Honeycomb tossed her mane as he stepped into the stirrup and swung up onto the saddle.

"To the Vale to scatter his mother's ashes," I said. Jack glanced back at the main house before starting off into the woods. I sighed.

"Why aren't you going with him?"

"I can't," I said. "I'm supposed to spend the day with you."

"Hm." Annabelle held my gaze for longer than was necessary before turning back to Siobhan. "You're right. You can't hobble around when you're dancing with Edward. Nora, do you have anything in the kitchen house that would help sore feet?"

She called me Nora. Not Owl Eyes, not Eleanor.

"Not really," I said. "This is a bad year for plants." I pictured Greta's herb shelf. "There might be some calendula, but it wouldn't be enough to make a poultice."

"So go get more," Siobhan said without looking at me as she rubbed her feet.

I shook my head. "There isn't any around here. If it ever grew this summer, it's all dried up now."

"Maybe farther out in the forest?" Annabelle gave me a significant glance, gesturing with her eyes towards the path down which Jack had just disappeared.

I spoke tentatively, not sure I was understanding her correctly. "I guess I could go look."

Annabelle nodded. "If Robert comes looking for you, I'll tell him we sent you to find the calendula."

"It might take all day," I said, still measuring my words. "I'll see what I can do."

"Stop talking about it and go already," Siobhan said. Then, to Annabelle, "Thanks."

Annabelle looked at me, not Siobhan, when she said, "That's what sisters are for."

She knew. Suddenly, the connection between us didn't seem so bad.

I grinned and ran out of the room.

~

*J*ack had a head start on me, and I knew I'd have a hard time catching him on foot. I ran down the forest path, away from the Runes. When it forked, I turned west but eventually slowed to a walk. Jack knew a shortcut to the Vale. He'd probably turned down some side path and was long gone by now.

I might as well actually try to find the calendula, I thought. It would do me no good to come back without it. I stepped off the path, scanning the ground for the orange-yellow flower. The plants on the forest floor had begun to die off almost a month ago—only scrub was left. I made my way through the woods, stepping over fallen branches and around rocks that were once covered in dark green moss.

I heard voices and looked around, eyeing the treetops in case Arelys and her men were nearby. I didn't know how much of the forest they claimed as their territory. I climbed over a fallen tree, and there it was: a bright patch of calendula, and next to it, Jack, who was tearing up the herb and stuffing it into the underside of Honeycomb's hind left hoof.

"You couldn't have waited until the way home before you stepped on that rock?" he said to her. A sharp stone lay on the ground next to them. Jack must have pried it from the pony's hoof.

"Well, I can't say you didn't learn anything from me or Greta," I said.

Jack turned around. When he saw me, he grinned, and his face lit up with the sky.

CHAPTER 13

$\mathcal{W}$ispy tendrils of mist lapped at the bottoms of the trees and rose up in a thick mass around us. Even with Honeycomb's injured foot, we made good time through the forest as Jack led her down side paths that I wasn't sure were paths at all. For the first time since we were on the Castle grounds, we saw green as we entered the Vale.

I untangled my arms from around Jack's waist and plucked a large leaf off a low-hanging branch. It left bronze powder on my hands as I let it go, spiraling in the air behind us. Jack had given me the pack with Liana's urn, and I reached back to make sure that it had not also blown away. Satisfied that it was still there and closed, I leaned my chin on Jack's shoulder. His hair brushed the side of my face. This was far better than spending the day stuck in the music room, watching Siobhan and Annabelle prance around. I would have to do something nice for Annabelle to thank her for saving me from that fate.

"So, how long does it take to find calendula?" Jack asked.

"All day, apparently." I said. "I might have to go all the way to the Vale, since it's the only place where anything is growing these days."

"Sir Milton takes care of his own." Jack turned Honeycomb down yet another narrow path between the trees. "He wouldn't let the Vale die out."

Sir Milton's name sparked my nerves. Would he consider me a friend? Or had whatever happened between him and Alcander so poisoned the relationship between the Vale and the Runes that he would refuse to help me?

The sound of rushing water welcomed us to the Vale proper, and the stream came into view. The great house, so called because it included the kitchen inside it, sat a short distance away. Jack pulled back on the reins, slowing Honeycomb to a stop next to the water, and dismounted. I gave him the pack from my back.

"It's beautiful here." I looked around, trying to take everything in at once. From Jack's stories about the Vale, I expected the stream to be much larger. He and I could lie head-to-foot across the span and just be able to touch the shore on either side. Water ran swiftly over the riverbed, swirling in eddies that sparkled gold and silver at the banks. Mossy rocks peeked out from the middle of the stream. If only we could barter for water with the Vale instead of going to neighboring estates in the Runes where the wells were just as dry as ours. If only Sir Alcander and Sir Milton had remained friends, I might have spent time at the Vale as a child, playing hide-and-seek with Bess in the mist. There were a lot of "if onlys."

"Hi there, Pa," Jack said.

I stepped back in surprise as the water burbled back at him with a cadence that was almost human.

"I know." Jack knelt at the edge of the stream. He set the urn on the grass beside him and ran his hand over the top of the water. "I missed you too. I'm sorry I've been away so long."

For a moment, he looked very young and very alone. I could see him as a boy, sitting in this same spot with his knees hugged to his chest, listening for his father in the music of the water rushing over the rocks.

"Ma?" he said in answer to an unasked question. "Well, yes, she's with me, but—" Tears glistened in his eyes as he looked up at me. "I don't know how to tell him."

The stream murmured its response. Tradition said that though spirits moved on to the World Apart after their ashes were scattered, a small part of the spirit remained here to watch over those who performed the Final Rites. If that were true, Jack's father had been with him all along.

"I think he knows," I said.

He nodded. "Pa, I know you and Ma would want to be together, so I brought her with me. I think she'll be happy here with you."

He picked up the jar, pried out the cork, and stared inside for a moment before tipping out the ashes.

"Liana," he said, beginning the prayer for Final Rites. I joined in as he continued. "Goddess grant safe journey to the World Apart. May the tether that ties you to this world be unbound. Though your footsteps no longer fall upon the ground, we carry their echoes in us."

"Goodbye, Ma," he finished. "I love you."

Liana's ashes fell into the water, some settling at the bottom of the stream, some carried away by the current. A light breeze blew the last of the dust in the air, sending it floating into the forest of the Vale.

"She would have liked that," I said. Jack wiped at the tears on his cheeks. I put my arms around him, and we sat at the edge of the stream, watching as the water carried bronze-dusted leaves and Liana's ashes into the distance.

"Who is that?" The loud voice carried all the way from the great house.

Jack picked up his head from where it rested against mine. The space it left was palpable somehow.

"Bertram?" he called back. "It's Jack!"

"Liana's Jack?" A man stuck his head out a window on the first floor of the great house. From where we sat, all I could make out was a gigantic moustache. "Stay right there," he yelled. "Sally, Jack's here!"

Jack stood, brushing off the seat of his pants, and offered his hand to help me up.

"Bertram runs the kitchen," he said. "He's like the Greta of the Vale, only louder."

Bertram came out a side door and ran towards us much faster than I would have thought possible for a man his size. He towered over Jack as he swept him into a bear hug, picking him clear off the ground. A girl of twelve or thirteen followed behind him. She smiled shyly at me and went to pet Honeycomb.

"It's good to see you," Jack said, rubbing his side when Bertram put him down. "I think you bruised a few ribs there, Bert."

"Aw, you can take it." Bertram stroked his moustache. "Are you back for a visit? Or has your ma finally regained her senses and decided to come home?"

"Actually—" Jack picked the urn off the ground.

Bertram's expression sobered. "Your ma was a fine lady," he said. "Goddess grant her safe journey to the World Apart."

"Thanks." Jack glanced back at me. "Bert, this is Nora. She's my—"

"Oh, I heard all about you from Bessie after she saw the two of you at the Market."

"You did?" I said. I wasn't sure I made the most positive impression on Lady Bess.

"Bert cooks the best roast you've ever tasted," Jack said, cocking his thumb at the larger man. "If he'd give us his recipe, Alcander would triple our wages."

I was about to say, "So I could make three times nothing?" but it didn't seem like the time.

"Cook's secrets," Bertram said. "I'll give the recipe to Sally when I'm on my deathbed and not a moment before. Does Milton know you're here?" Jack shook his head. Bertram grinned. "Well, come on in, then! You can surprise him." He clapped a meaty hand on Jack's back, almost knocking him over.

"They must not feed you enough at the Runes," Bertram said as we made our way up to the house. Sally trailed behind us, leading Honeycomb by the reins. "You're too skinny, the both of you." He laughed. "I knew it was you down there. Who else would spend an hour just sitting by the water?"

"An hour?" I looked at Jack, alarmed. Being able to spend the day pretending to look for calendula was a gift from Annabelle. I didn't want to take advantage of it.

Inside the great house, rich velvet in royal and sky blues hung from the walls. Sunlight filtered through the windows and rippled across the fabric, making it flow like water from ceiling to floor. Fire opals glittered under our feet as white candles in sconces lining the halls dripped rosy pink wax that smelled of wildflowers. If the Runes were built on the earth, I thought, then surely the Vale must have come down from the sky.

Bertram walked ahead of us, updating Jack about what had gone on at the Vale since he left. I tuned out his excited stories about the new stove in the kitchen and turned my attention to the sounds coming from farther down the hall, where four voices sang in close harmony. I could distinguish a rich, full-barreled bass, a reedy, lilting tenor, and a soft, lyric alto. The fourth note sounded high above them as though it were coming from the walls themselves. The music made the hair on my arms stand on end.

Bertram stopped in front of an open door across from a wall of portraits just like the one at the Runes. He held a finger to his lips and nodded towards the room. Jack and I peeked around him to see inside. Sir Milton, Bess, and a man I didn't recognize stood around a small, round table by the window, singing. My eyes were drawn to the form that floated up from the shallow bowl on the table. It looked like a patch of night sky had been brought into the room. Bright stars twinkled within the form. It was those sparkling lights that made the fourth note I heard. They pulsed in time with the rhythm of the song. This was far more intense than anything I'd seen during my limited exposure to the Kindred at the Market. I wanted to run back to the safety of the Runes just as much as I wanted to join in their song.

Bess noticed us and stopped singing. The lights winked out, and the patch of night folded into the bowl.

"Jack! Nora!" She bounded over to the door. Jack's face brightened, and I fought to hide the frown that itched at my brow. She gave him an enthusiastic hug and whispered condolences in his ear. He didn't ask how she knew of Liana's passing.

I looked back into the room. There were no traces of whatever had been floating above the table. Sir Milton wore an expression of amused annoyance as he tossed a fine white sand into the bowl. The other man closed a large, heavy book and came over to meet us. Sir Milton followed. He had aged since I saw him at Portia's banquet five years before. The only hair he had left was a grey halo that went around the back of his head, making his prominent nose seem even larger than before. He met my eyes with the same look I'd seen when I was twelve, that of someone who knew me better than I knew myself.

Bess introduced the young man as Gideon, Sir Milton's apprentice. I nodded in his direction without really seeing him. My attention was fixed on the knight as he came out of the room. The last two fingers of the hand he offered to Jack were bent and immobile.

"I feel terrible about your mother. It's such a tragic loss," he said as Jack shook his hand.

"Thank you, sir. She's with Pa in the river now. We performed her Final Rites there."

"Did you have a nice conversation with your father?"

Jack laughed as if acknowledging a joke between them. "I did. Sir Milton, I don't know if you remember Nora—"

The knight turned to me. I curtseyed and immediately felt ridiculous. Formality was expected at the Runes, but I wasn't a servant at the Vale. I didn't know what I was here.

"I'm sorry we interrupted your singing," I said.

"We can finish later," Bess said. "It's so nice to have guests! You're staying until tomorrow, aren't you? I'd love to dig up some of our old haunts to show Nora and Gideon."

Jack shook his head. "We have to leave soon. Nora isn't exactly supposed to be here with me."

I let the frown take over my face. If I hadn't come, Jack could take all the time he wanted. I felt like a burden for keeping him from it, but I needed the Vale too.

"You were forbidden to come," Sir Milton said. It was a statement, not a question. I nodded, and the knight bristled. "Bess," he said, "Take the boys and have Bertram scare up some food in the kitchen for our visitors to take home with them. I'll wait here with Nora."

Bess nodded, whispered something in Jack's ear, and sprinted down the hall. He squeezed my hand for a second before letting go and following. Bertram and Gideon trailed behind them.

The hall felt larger, too large, even, as I stood alone with the knight. He was waiting for me to speak, but I didn't know where to begin. Sir Milton might have been Kindred like my mother—like me—but he was still a lord, and I was still Alcander's servant. I longed for the music that filled the halls just minutes before and for the glow of that patch of night that reminded me of the view from my window in the loft of the kitchen house.

"Is Jack's father really in the river?" I said, finally.

Sir Milton laughed, and I felt my face warm at the stupidity of the question.

"When Jack stopped talking after his father passed, we did

everything we could to help him," he said. "I enchanted the stream to respond when he was around. I hope it gave him some comfort. For a while, I think he actually believed it was his father talking to him. Bess was the one who finally got him going again." His expression darkened as he touched his hand to his face in the same place where Bess's scar was. There was some connection between Jack coming out of his silence and whatever had happened to Bess, but Milton dropped the subject. I pictured Jack yelling in alarm as Bess came home with her face flayed open, but the image changed to me sneaking around in the loft with blood dripping from my nose onto my chin. Jack had started talking then too.

Silence descended on the hallway. I let my eyes wander over the paintings on the walls. Milton's likeness was at the end of the row in a portrait with a slight, pale-haired woman who must have been his wife. She wore a gold key on a chain around her neck. The same key appeared in two other paintings, the first of which showed a woman with large green eyes sitting next to a man with blue-black hair.

"Is that the necklace that Bess wears?" I asked.

"The key belonged to my grandfather," Milton said, indicating the inky-haired gentleman. "He gave it to my grandmother, and it's been passed down ever since. I gave it to Celia, and Bess will give it to her beloved when she is betrothed."

"That's nice." I sensed a way into a more important conversation. "My mother had a necklace too. Maybe she would have given it to me if she were alive."

I held my breath, waiting for Milton's response. He narrowed his eyes at me as though assessing my fitness for what he was about to say.

"No. She wouldn't have."

He went back into his study. Even though he hadn't asked me to, I followed him.

"You knew my mother," I said. "And you knew who I was years ago when you saw me at Alcander's banquet."

"Nora," Milton said. He still wasn't looking at me. "My relationship with your father is strained at best. He wouldn't like me talking to you."

"I know. That's why I came. You've already told me more about myself than Alcander ever did. I didn't even know he was my father until

I heard you say it in his study." I didn't know what else to say. I had no leverage here. "Please."

When Milton turned around, he was smiling.

"You sound just like Izella."

Relief overwhelmed me. I jumped in headfirst. "I found her spellbook hidden in the wall in her library. I know she was a Handler." Milton's face fell, but I went on anyway. "What can you tell me about Handling?"

The knight turned back to his shelves and began to fit corks into bottles of sand and crystals. Above him, small bowls were evenly spaced across the top shelf. Misty orbs hovered over each bowl. Where one orb glowed like a miniature sun, the one next to it appeared to be raining into its bowl. A third sounded quiet bursts of thunder as lightning crackled on its surface. Yet another orb was in flux, twisting as hands reached out and mouths opened in silent screams within. I had the feeling of being watched. My skin prickled as the orb rotated and an unblinking eye stared in my direction. I turned away, rubbing my arms as Milton started talking.

"Magic hinges on willpower. Whatever you're doing, whether it's mixing a potion, reciting an incantation, manipulating the mists"—he waved his hand, and the sun-like orb floated over to where he stood. The mist unfurled into a glowing ribbon that twisted around the room, following the motion of his fingers—"you have to want it with every fiber of your being. The moment you don't"—the ribbon of mist disappeared with a bright flash—"the magic will fail."

The orb slowly reformed up on the shelf as whatever was in the bowl below it was sucked into the air.

Sir Milton went on. "It wasn't always the case that magic was frowned upon in Colandaria. But especially after the Border Wars, the Kindred needed protection from people who thought they meant only harm. I keep the Kindred in the Vale safe with the mists."

He was avoiding my question. I held my tongue, waiting for him to get to his point.

"If there is no magic without a will behind it, imagine the will it must take to not only perform that magic but also to hide it from everyone, even those closest to you. Your mother had the strongest will of anyone I knew."

I looked at the last orb, the one that stretched and screamed. It wouldn't have looked good for one of the heroes of the Border Wars to be married to a Handler. Izella must have hidden her practice, maybe even from Alcander. If she used her own blood for her spells, she would have been covered in scars.

"The glamour," I said. "I saw it in her spellbook. The glamour 'to hide that which you wish to be hidden.'"

Izella must have worn a glamour all the time to hide her Handling. I gasped as another thought came to me. Arelys said that the room with no windows was Izella's library. If she used that room for her practice, it must have been littered with the tools of her magic. One glance inside would have let everyone know what she was. She would have had to cast a glamour on her study as well if she wanted to keep her Handling secret. I had seen a remnant of that glamour when I got her box from its hiding place. Izella's will must have been enormous to keep the spell up, even in a flickering state, so long after her death.

Milton nodded. "Glamours are based partly on mist magic, so I can see past them. When Alcander brought me to meet Izella for the first time, it was like seeing two different people. On the surface, there was a woman who looked like she spent hours in front of the mirror. But the image was laid over that of a second woman, one whose whole body was covered with the marks of her practice."

I clasped my forearms, pulling and pushing at the skin until the burn scars were distorted. My mother and I were alike in many ways; even our skin was similar. I just didn't know whose scars went deeper.

Milton came closer to me, offering a comforting hand that never quite made its way up to touch my shoulder. "Handling has been misconstrued since the Border Wars," he said. "It's dangerous, powerful magic, but that doesn't mean that it is evil."

"What was she using Handling for?" I asked, still rubbing my arms. At least, if there were some sort of larger purpose for her magic, maybe I could understand what she did.

Milton shook his head. "If you've seen her spellbook, you know. I tried to show her another way. I would have taught her mist magic, or Celia could have apprenticed her as a candlebearer. Either way, she wasn't interested. Handling was in her blood. Her mother practiced, as did her mother before her."

As did I, I thought. Whether I'd intended to or not, I used my blood to open the box with Izella's spellbook. I always hoped that if Izella were alive, I'd be just as pristine and privileged as Siobhan and Annabelle were now. Now I knew that my arms would still be covered with scars, just of a different nature.

The spells in Izella's book were for everyday tasks. There was no larger purpose. There was no reason. It felt like the blood had drained right out of me.

"Alcander didn't know that Izella practiced," I said. Milton nodded. "Why didn't you tell him?"

"She made me swear not to, and Kindred protect our kind. I don't think anyone other than her mother knew when she was a child. Not her father, not Portia—"

"Portia is Kindred too?" I shook my head. Of course she was, if magic traveled along family lines.

Milton laughed. It was a harsh sound, full of derision. "There are plenty of Kindred who never practice. Portia never had the disposition for magic. I doubt her mother ever tried to train her."

"Alcander couldn't have hated the Kindred," I said. "Not if he were friends with you."

"My practice was no secret," Milton said. "All the soldiers in King Philip's regiment saw me use it a hundred times during the war. But they saw a big difference between my practice and that of the Handlers who allied with the Farland Army. When Alcander found out about Izella's Handling, it changed him. He didn't hate the Kindred before, but he certainly did afterwards."

For Alcander, seeing me was a daily reminder of Izella's deception. Whether I deserved it or not, for just a moment, I could understand why he gave me away.

"How did he find out?" I asked, not sure I wanted to hear the answer.

"Alcander was away when Izella went into labor. Her dark days were beginning, and she knew she needed help, so she sent a messenger here to the Vale. By the time I got there, she was a wreck. I could hardly get her to stand still. She was in labor for so long, and her necklace was missing, and…"

There it was again: the missing necklace.

"There was nothing I could do."

I wanted to get back to the necklace, but another phrase that Milton used stuck in my head.

"What are the dark days?"

"Some Handlers use charms to ward off the pain from their spellwork," Milton said, "but that kind of magic always has a price. For a few days each season, those Handlers receive all that pain, whether they want it or not. It weakens them terribly. We turned the tide in the Border Wars by attacking on the dark days. The protective charms help, but the pain is still devastating, much worse than if they hadn't used the charms in the first place."

"Her necklace was her charm." I went on for him as I put the pieces together. "She lost it, so she wasn't protected, and the pain of the dark days combined with the pain of having me—" I choked on my words.

"It killed her," Milton finished. "I don't know how she lost the necklace. I don't know how she could have when she never took it off."

"The necklace," I said, "it had a rose in it?" If I didn't know before why I was so fixated on the charm, I did now. It could have saved Izella's life. If I could get my hands on it, perhaps it could save mine.

"A white rose," Milton said, "dotted with Izella's blood and fixed in a round piece of glass. It would have only worked for her. It's a common Handler's charm. It would have clearly marked what she was to anyone familiar with the practice." He shook his head. I could see that these were painful memories for him to recall, but I didn't want him to stop. "Alcander came home just after she passed. After everything that went on, I wasn't thinking straight. I had you in my arms, and I needed to get you to your father and tell him that Izella had passed. As soon as I found him in the hall, the servant who was in the room with the body started screaming. Then I realized—when Izella died, her glamour disappeared. I ran back to the room and was trying to cast another spell so Alcander wouldn't have to see her…like that. But it was too late. He was right behind me. He'd already seen. I'll never forget the look on his face, like he didn't recognize the body as Izella's."

"So you told him," I said as thudding finality slammed into the room.

"I had to. He told me to leave the Runes and never come back."

"And when Alcander saw what her library looked like without its glamour, he lit a match and burned it all," I said. That was it, the end of my mother in everything except her box, her knife, and my countenance.

Milton's face filled with regret. I wanted to tell him that it wasn't his fault. As much as I would have loved to blame him for what happened on the day I was born, I couldn't. He had only tried to help. I looked past him into the mirror that hung on the wall and saw my mother's face reflected back at me. This was the face that was to blame for everything that happened, this face that I now wore. How I wished I could burn it away with a glamour of my own.

Someone cleared their throat in the hallway behind us. I turned around to see Bess, Jack, and Gideon.

"Scones?" Bess said, awkwardly holding up a bulky cloth tied with twine. Jack wouldn't meet my eyes.

"You need to get going." Milton ushered me out of his study. I was weighed down with new knowledge, and it took effort to put one foot in front of the other. Before I knew what I was doing, I turned and threw my arms around the knight.

"Thank you," I said.

He gave me a somber nod. "We should have had this conversation a long time ago. If you ever need anything"—he looked past me, at Jack —"either of you, the Vale is always here."

Jack bid his farewells as we walked outside with Bess and Gideon. Sally brought Honeycomb back around to us as Bess left me with a hug. I stood there stiffly, unsure whether to return the gesture.

"It was good to see you again," she said. "Maybe next time we can spend some time together. Talk about things we can't discuss with the boys around."

"Maybe," I murmured, even though I didn't know what she meant.

≈

"How much did you hear?" I asked Jack once we were on our way back to the Runes. I sat in front of him on Honeycomb's back, barely feeling his arms around my waist as he directed me through the forest.

"Enough," he said. "You know, you aren't your mother. She might have done some things that were—" He paused. "Not bad, but not good, either. But that was her. Not you."

I didn't say what I was thinking, not then, not as we returned to the Runes and I went back in the main house to deliver the calendula for Siobhan to rub on her feet, not as I stood there into the evening, watching my sisters get ready for a ball to which I was not invited. No, I was not my mother. But part of me wished I were.

CHAPTER 14

The day of the Harvest Moon Ball, the kitchen house and the main house could not have felt farther apart. In the main house, Portia and Siobhan radiated nervous energy down the halls. Greta and Peter were sent to barter for water, so they were not there to see the meals that were sent back because Siobhan claimed her stomach was too upset for her to eat. Portia did not even come to the breakfast table.

Since I returned from the Vale, something had shifted, and the kitchen house no longer felt like home. I noticed imperfections where I hadn't before, in the uneven boards on the floor, the crack in the mirror that hung on the wall next to Greta's herb shelf, and the lumpiness of the bread I took out of the oven each morning.

I tried to avoid looking in the mirror, but I would always catch it in the corner of my eye as I walked by. Izella's face. My face, the one that was so hated in the house just across the field. A mix of shame and entitlement burned beneath my skin. I was not Izella, so why should I be punished for her sins? I was not Izella, so why must I wear her face? My skin practically crawled with my desire to get out of it. As I cut up the flank of a deer that had miraculously wandered into one of our pit traps, I imagined the blood that slicked my cutting board creeping over the windowsill and going outside, flowing in surreptitious veins that made their way over to infect the main house.

I wished Jack hadn't gone foraging in the woods. He would inevitably come back empty-handed, and I didn't like being left alone with my thoughts.

Robert let himself into the kitchen without knocking. I wasn't sure I heard him correctly when he said that Alcander wanted to see me. Never in all my life had the man requested my presence, alone, in front of him. Well, he'd have me exactly as he made me. I wiped my hands on my apron, adding streaks of red to the mess that was already there, and tied it even tighter around my waist.

Robert led the way into the main house, leaving me at the door to Alcander's study. Inside, my father sat with the barest hint of a smile on his face. His eyes narrowed when I entered, and I knew that I had not been called in to clear away dishes.

"Do you think I'm stupid?" He leaned back in his chair. It was the casualness with which he asked the question that set my hair on end.

"S-sir?"

"You think you're crafty, don't you?"

I clenched my damp apron in my hands, but the deer's blood could not protect me from what Alcander said next.

"Did you think I wouldn't know you went to the Vale?"

I opened my mouth and closed it without saying anything. Had Annabelle betrayed me? Was her kindness just an act? Or was it Siobhan who realized I'd been gone too long?

"You rode back into the Runes like you were queen of the damned place. I didn't even need Robert to tell me what you were doing—I could see it myself. Just who do you think you are?"

I wanted to slap myself. I had been so wrapped up in what I learned at the Vale that I didn't even think of making it look like Jack and I were coming from separate places when we got back to the Runes. I felt like I was breathing through a pinhole. Darkness swam in the corners of the room. This was it: the punishment I thought I had escaped. I would be relegated to the kitchen house forever, unable to leave even to go to the Market. Or Alcander would take his punishment out on Jack. It would be especially cruel to leave me without my greatest ally in the house.

Alcander sat up. He was dressed for the ball, clad in a dark green tunic with bronze detailing. His finery next to my serving clothes, my hands and apron crusted with his dinner, made me feel like a piece of dirt to be brushed away. And brush was exactly what he intended to do.

He repeated, "I said, who do you think you are?"

"I'm Lady Izella's daughter." I stared at him, refusing to break eye contact.

Alcander slammed his fist down on the table. His mask was off.

"You would do well to remember that you are my daughter too. And as both your father and your lord, I can do with you what I please. You will leave the Runes in one week's time. A carriage will take you to the Fall where you will be married to Sir Reginald's valet."

It was all I could do to stay there in the room with him. The Fall was the northernmost province in the mountains of Colandaria and the farthest one from the Runes. It would have taken Alcander the entire fortnight since I returned from the Vale to make this arrangement, with all the messages that would have needed to go back and forth.

By marrying me off to a valet in the Fall, Alcander was not only sending me to a place as far from the Runes as he could, he was also sentencing me to a life of servitude. At the Runes, there was a slim chance that something might change. The moment I became the wife of a servant I didn't even know, any chance of getting the life and title Alcander owed me would vanish.

"No," I said. "I won't. I won't go."

Alcander leaned towards me. "You will be on that carriage if I have to put you on it myself. I cannot stand to look at you for a minute longer. We're done here." He walked out of the room, leaving me alone.

Every bone in my body said to run, to grab Honeycomb and ride far away so that while I wouldn't be in the Runes anymore, I would still have control of my fate. I gasped ragged breaths as I tilted my head up to the ceiling, where I saw the hollow moon shining down on me between the tree branches. I was right back where I was when I was twelve, standing on a path I couldn't traverse alone. I wanted to flee. I wanted to stay. I wanted home, and all I knew was that the Fall could never be it.

Without realizing it, I had walked back into the hallway. I had almost reached the door to get outside when I heard my name being called. I stopped in my tracks, feeling like a piece of twine being pulled from both ends. My middle was fraying.

"Eleanor!" Portia's voice thundered off the walls.

I closed my eyes. I would not go to her. I would get out of the main house, go somewhere. Anywhere.

Portia clacked across the floor with steps as urgent and even as Anabelle's metronome. When I opened my eyes, I found that she had come to me.

"With me. Now." She swept down the hall in a mass of green satin and gold lace, looking back to make sure I followed. When she saw that I wasn't moving, she came back, grabbed my wrist, and yanked. I didn't budge.

"Eleanor," she snarled, like I was an animal that had displeased her. "Get."

I gave up. I got.

I followed her to the dressing room where Siobhan and Annabelle were finishing their preparations for the ball. Annabelle sat in front of the mirror, sticking pins in her hair, which was bound up in a series of shining curls. Her excitement was a stark contrast to Siobhan's expression as she paced back and forth, pinching her cheeks to get more color into a complexion that was white with nerves. Every few seconds, she stopped in front of the mirror to look over Annabelle's head and check her face. Even in her nervous state, she was stunning in her jade green dress. The gold-and-emerald necklace that I bought at the Market was looped around her wrist.

"Give it," Portia said. Siobhan threw the necklace at her and continued to pace.

"Imbecile!"

Annabelle turned around, alarmed, as Portia thrust the necklace at me.

"What do you have to say for yourself?"

I had nothing to say.

"It's glass!" She dashed the necklace against the floor, where it broke into pieces. Beads scattered across the room and into the fireplace.

Annabelle jumped up from her seat. "Mother!"

Portia stood nose to nose with me, speaking in a low voice that only I could hear. "I should have known that you would try to sabotage this, Eleanor. It's in your blood." Then, louder, "Siobhan will have a hard enough time attracting the Prince without the costume jewelry. She doesn't need you squashing what little chance she has."

Siobhan buried her face in her hands. I couldn't tell what upset her more, the ball or her mother's words. At that moment, it didn't matter. Portia's hand twitched. She was close to slapping me.

I shook my head. This was not my fault. It must have been the vendor. He must have wanted to pay Portia back for stiffing him the last time she bought jewelry. There was no way for me to know the gems weren't real. Not my fault.

"I didn't know," I said in a dull voice. "How was I supposed to know?"

"No," Portia spat, "you're a servant. That blood of yours isn't good enough to know." She kicked one of the glass emeralds at me. "Now pick those up."

"No." I was done being ordered around.

"Pick up the stones, or I swear I will put you back in the cinder room until someone from the Fall comes to get you out."

Fear betrayed what little willpower I had left. While Alcander pretended Izella's library didn't exist, Portia knew well the power the room had over me, and she was prepared to use it.

Annabelle ran to Portia's side, looking like she was ready to protest. I desperately needed an ally right then. One glance from Portia made her step back. I burned with shame as I knelt to pick up the closest stone.

"Mother," Annabelle said, getting between Portia and her sister, "Siobhan can wear one of my necklaces. I have that green pendant that Father gave me for—"

I picked up a gold bead.

"Hush up," Portia said to her. She looked Siobhan over, assessing her dress, her hair, and her posture before poking her in the back. "Stand up straight."

I fished another gold bead out from the ashes in the fireplace.

Portia unhooked her own necklace and placed it in Siobhan's hand.

Green glass, dug out from against the wall.

"Wear this," she said.

Another gold bead.

Siobhan, surprised: "But, Mother, this is yours."

Another piece of glass.

Portia's voice dripped with honey. "I have other jewelry to wear. You have it now, dear." She looked at where I knelt on the floor, picking up yet another gold bead, and sent her stingers flying.

"It's a mother's duty to give things like this to her firstborn daughter."

"Maybe the necklace will get you a dance with Edward," Annabelle said. "It always brought Mother good luck."

My gaze flicked to the chain, fine as one of Annabelle's golden hairs, that Siobhan hooked around her neck. Clutching the beads in my hand, I leapt up and rushed to where she stood, admiring the necklace in the mirror. She shoved me back with a rough hand to the chest, but I had already seen it.

The charm that hung off the chain was large and round. In the center was a tiny white rose, marred by one drop of red.

Izella's necklace.

The beads fell from my hand, clattering to the floor.

"Eleanor! Pick those up." Portia's smile was thin, almost a smirk.

I ran out of the dressing room.

The kitchen house was empty. I shuttered the windows so that only hints of sunlight peeked through. Blood rushed in my ears as I got Izella's spellbook and knife from the loft. I knew what I needed, what I had wanted for ages, even if the thoughts had not crystallized before. Now, it was there, pulsing in front of me like a living thing.

I opened the spellbook and found the page with the instructions for a glamour. If willpower alone could give life to the spell, I would already be covered in a magical veneer. I glanced over the list of ingredients.

Dried lavender was on the herb shelf.

Honey, from a jar behind the salt.

Rose petals came from Izella's box. The ones that did not turn to dust in my hands went on the table next to the knife.

A small flame. I lit the candle at the center of the table.

A large piece of glass.

Yellow eyes reflected a mix of hatred and resolve back at me from the mirror that hung on the wall. I ran my fist into the glass. Cracks sliced my reflection. I liked it better that way. I grabbed a large shard off the floor and wiped the back of my hand against my skirt.

The last ingredient for the spell leapt off the page of Izella's book.

Blood, with intent, from the heart. My glass-torn knuckles would not suffice.

The handle of the knife was smooth and familiar in my palm. There was no doubt about it. It was always meant to be mine.

"Nora?"

I wheeled around. Jack stood in the doorway, staring at the broken glass on the floor.

"What happened?"

My lips twisted into a smile. I tightened my grip on the knife.

"I'm going to the ball."

The candle flickered. I turned the knife to my chest.

Then Jack was behind me, knocking the blade out of my hand. It fell to the table. Rose petals fluttered to the floor.

"Stop it!" He grabbed my wrists, holding me in place as I lunged for the knife.

"Let go. You're hurting me," I said, even though he wasn't.

I wrenched away from him. Jack caught me around the waist and wrestled me to the ground, pinning me with his knees. I wheeled my fists at him, and he cried out in surprise as I landed a punch to his cheek.

Jack's hands found mine again, and he pinned my arms above my head. I twisted against him as tears sprang to my eyes. He was ruining everything.

I felt his breath heavy on my cheeks and stopped struggling.

"Get off me," I choked out.

He let go of my arms and crawled away to sit against the table. Even when he seemed to have given up, he still positioned himself between me and the spell.

"What is wrong with you?" he said. "You were going to hurt yourself."

I sat up. My hands clutched at the floor as I looked for something to hold on to. I didn't want to explain myself, not to him, not to anyone. I didn't want to say that the hurt was what would make everything right for the first time in my life. Jack rubbed his face where his cheek was already beginning to swell.

I pushed up off the ground. Jack matched me move for move.

"I found Izella's necklace," I said. "It's hanging around Siobhan's neck. Portia gave it to her. It didn't go missing—she had it this whole time. She couldn't have Alcander, so she must have taken the next most precious thing my mother had. She took away Izella's protection. It's her fault she died. Not mine." I shook my head as my eyes darted back and forth across the floorboards and I fought to stay in the room. "Not mine."

"Nora." Jack shook his head. "I don't think—"

"No, you don't think," I said. "You don't know. You're supposed to be here. I'm not. I should be the one getting ready for the ball. Portia took that away from me too. She and Alcander both. Just because I look like my mother. Just because I lived and she died."

My skin was not enough to contain the sparks coursing through me. I felt like I would burn up from the inside if I didn't let them out.

"Alcander thinks he can marry me off to some servant in the Fall just because I disobeyed him? I'll show him I'm better than that."

Jack looked like he'd taken another blow. "Alcander is sending you away?"

I began to pace, looking for a way past Jack to the table. "I'll show both of them. Him and Portia. They don't want Izella's face haunting their house anymore? Fine. I'll look like someone else at the ball. They won't even know it's me. They won't know I'm the one who will get the life they want for their daughters. I'll marry the Prince myself. Then they'll see." I darted around Jack, but he caught me and pulled me back, turning me to face him.

"Nora, stop it." His fingers clenched around my arms, and he locked his elbows so I couldn't move. "You weren't even invited to the ball."

"Oh, yes, I was! The invitation was addressed to all of Alcander's daughters, not just the ones preening in front of the mirror. I'm a daughter of this house too. And I'm just as good as they are."

"What are you going to do, steal the carriage so Portia and Alcander will know just what kind of a lady you are?"

"No, I'll—" I stopped straining against him. He was right. My plan extended no further than Izella's knife and my blood.

"They would know it was you," he said. "You can't think that putting a dress on would make you look like a different person."

"A glamour would," I protested. For reasons I didn't understand, I desperately needed his approval. "No one would know it was me."

Jack eased his grip on my arms. I looked past him at the ingredients on the table, waiting for my blood and my will to turn into something new. But Jack's hand was tracing the arc of my cheek, and a small, warm part of me wanted to spend the night here, safe in the kitchen house, perhaps even having conversations I'd been avoiding about those hands and how well I thought they fit into my own.

A horse trotted past the kitchen house. Carriage wheels crunched against the ground behind it. Alcander's family was leaving for the ball.

I almost wanted to stay in the kitchen house. Almost, but not enough.

"Your heart is racing," Jack said.

I could feel it in my chest, a bird throwing itself against the bars of its cage. But I didn't understand how Jack knew until I looked down at his other hand, lightly pressed around my wrist. My whole body was vibrating, and his fingers were right there, on my pulse.

My mouth fell open as the thought came to me. The spell called for blood from the heart, but perhaps another source would suffice. I made to pull away, but Jack held me fast.

"Izella's glamour only covered her scars," he said. "It didn't make her look like a different person."

"Mine will." At least I hoped it would. I looked down at the puckered skin on my arms. I imagined Izella's scars being neat and orderly. Businesslike. Mine were twisted and haphazard, the marks of skin unevenly pressed against hot stone or brought too close to the fire. They were not marks of intention, of control.

"I won't look like a servant," I said. "Not like me at all. I'll be beautiful."

Jack said, "I think you're beautiful now."

"But you don't count."

I realized I'd made a mistake the moment the words escaped my lips. I hadn't meant them. I absolutely meant them. Jack's eyes widened, and his mouth opened as though I'd punched him. Again. He took a step back.

We stood there, staring at each other, neither one of us wanting to be the one to break the silence. I had run my fist through the space between us as surely as I had the mirror. My knuckles were still bleeding.

"It doesn't matter what I think, does it?" he said, finally, rubbing his cheek. "You're going to do it anyway. And I'm going to stay. At least I can make sure you don't hurt yourself any more than you've already decided you want to." He stood aside, leaving a clear path between me and the table.

As much as I wanted him to understand, there were things I couldn't explain to him. I could hardly explain them to myself. I walked past him and picked up the knife from the table. The handle had cooled, but it still felt like mine. My hands trembled as I smoothed back the pages of the spellbook. The glamour spell was written in a thin, willowy hand. I wondered if Izella was the one to put her quill to this page, or if I was just another in a long line of women who had used the spell. But where Izella had used her glamour as a shield to hide behind, I would be using mine as an instrument of creation, to make someone new and different. I had to believe that was the case. Otherwise, I would be just as much of a liar as she was.

I read the instructions three times before I touched any of the ingredients.

I poured the honey onto the shard of glass, making sure it didn't spill over the edge and onto the table, then burned the rose petals and the lavender with the candle flame. The kitchen filled with a flowery, smoky scent. My eyes began to water. I was surprised I still had tears left. As I sprinkled the ashes into the honey, my cinder-covered face stared back at me. My eyes burned gold. I turned away and wiped them before the tears fell onto the glass and ruined the spell.

There was only one more ingredient. Jack tensed behind me as I lifted the knife. He leaned over the table, starting to say something.

"Please," I whispered, and he stepped back.

I hadn't sharpened the blade in months. Greta's reminder about using the whetstone echoed in my ears. But even now, the knife seemed so quick that it could pierce all the way down to the bone without my even touching it. The table swam in front of me.

I could feel everything then: the air brushing my face where Jack's hand had been, the grain of the handle in my palm, Jack next to me, wanting to leap forward and knock the blade out of my hand again, the darkness that impinged on the corners of the room. The darkness that was just as tangible as the knife and the mirror and me. The darkness that was a part of me. If I could just get the smallest bit of it out, I could breathe again.

I heard a voice in my head, taunting me for not being strong enough and recognized it as my own. I didn't know what to do, how deep to cut, how much blood was too much, how much wasn't enough.

The image of Izella's necklace passing from Portia's hand to Siobhan's floated in front of my eyes.

I touched the tip of the blade to my wrist. I felt only a pinch as I stared at the silver laying shallowly in my skin. It didn't seem real—it had to be just a trick of the spell. Then, a burst of pain radiated up my arm, pain so intense that I gasped and pulled the blade across my wrist and out.

A pale pink line appeared along my skin. I uncurled my fist, and the line gaped open, exposing purple and white, raw flesh inside. The pain left me breathless.

My stomach lurched. Yellow-green flowers burst in front of my eyes. I could hear Jack, loud and urgent, behind me. Blood slid out of the gash, slicking my palm and dripping from my fingers to splash onto the table. My hand quaked as I held it over the shard of glass and gave my offering to the spell.

Then Jack was wrapping a cloth around my wrist to stop the bleeding. His words had a panicky, frightened tone to them. The cut had not even been the length of my little finger, I thought. How could there be so much blood? I stumbled as I pulled away from him to turn back to the spellbook. The incantation for the glamour was brief. My voice cracked as I stared into the glass.

"Hide that which others should not see; make secret that which is just for me."

Sir Milton said that magic depends on willpower. At that moment, looking at my reflection, crimson, gold, and ashen in the glass, there was nothing I wanted more.

The tickling began at my wrist. Ignoring Jack's protestations, I lifted the cloth he wound around my arm as the tickle turned into an intense itch. My chest hitched as I watched the torn flesh smooth over, the blood lifting and vanishing as though it had never escaped my skin. The itch intensified, spreading from my arm up to my chest and down to my feet. It covered me like a second skin, a solid one, heavy as lead. I couldn't breathe through the bands that wrapped around my chest and throat. A scream, my scream, echoed off the ceiling. It felt like the last sound I would ever make. Jack threw his arms around me, muffling my scream against his shirt. I fought against him—I was already being crushed by the weight of the magic. His arms were just another binding.

As quickly as it had started, the sensation lifted. There was still a tightness like a corset around my torso, but I could breathe past the feeling of weak hands that remained around my throat. I felt Jack's shirt against my face and the tracks my tears left on the fabric. I could hear his heart thudding in his chest. He ran his hand through my hair.

My hair, which didn't trap his fingers in its snarls.

Without opening my eyes, I felt the top of my head. The hair that brushed against my skin was smooth, with a gentle wave. I pulled back and saw the change first in the shock on Jack's face. I looked past him, into the shard of glass on the table. The honey and ash were gone, replaced by a stranger's face. The girl's pretty lips curled up into a smile.

It was me, but not. Me, but different. Not me at all. My cheekbones were higher, and my cheeks had that rosy glow that Siobhan had to pinch herself to get. My nose was thinner, and my hair had turned from bloodred to a shiny, rich auburn. The eyes that marveled back at me were brown, shot through with strands of gold. I held my arms out in front of me. The scars that marred their surface were gone, replaced by pristine, cream-colored skin. They were no longer the arms of someone who spent her time next to the oven. They were the arms of a girl who had her meals brought to her. I turned to Jack with a smile on my newly reddened lips. He refused to meet my eyes.

I didn't want to mar my new face by showing hurt. "What's wrong?" I said.

"Nothing," he said. "It worked. You look fine."

"Fine?" I turned around, incredulous. My servant's clothes—the green skirt, white shirt, and deerskin vest—were now a rich indigo gown with a skirt that nipped in at the waist to show off the figure I hadn't possessed just a few minutes before. Blue cords laced up the front of the dress, weaving back and forth in a pattern that mirrored the flowery lace that covered the corset. Even the cloth Jack had wrapped around my wrist had changed into a bracelet glittering with sapphires.

"This is so much better than fine."

"You look like someone else," Jack said.

"That was the idea." I glanced at the door. "I'd better go if I want to beat Portia and Alcander to the Castle. If I take Honeycomb, I can ride there faster than their carriage will take them. I think I remember the way."

Jack bristled like he was ready for another fight. "And what if Honeycomb bucks you off because she doesn't recognize you? You'll land in the dirt. It will be all over for you then."

"She wouldn't do that," I said, matching his ire. "She likes me, unlike you right now."

"I don't know," Jack said. "She might not recognize you either. Because you're definitely not yourself. I don't like it."

I looked back at the glass on the table.

"I do."

I started for the door.

"Wait, Nora—"

"What?" I wheeled back around.

Jack pointed at my feet.

I lifted the hem of my dress and looked. I was barefoot. My shoes were under the table. I must have lost them in the scuffle when Jack knocked me down.

The weak hands of the glamour tightened their grip around my throat. I couldn't go to the ball barefoot, but my plain leather slippers would let everyone know that I was an imposter. I thought of sneaking into the main house and stealing a pair of Siobhan or Annabelle's shoes, but there wasn't time. Plus, their shoes would all be Runes green, not placeless and purple-blue like the dress I conjured for myself. I paced frantically, trying to think of other options as Jack climbed the ladder into the loft, leaving me alone in the kitchen. I heard a trunk opening and him rummaging around. Just when I thought he'd become so fed up that he was leaving me to my own devices, he came back down holding a pair of light blue shoes and thrust them into my hands.

"Here."

"Where did you get these?" I stammered. Silver threadwork edged the blue satin.

"They're Ma's from when we worked in the Vale."

"But, Jack—" This felt wrong. He had so little of Liana's left.

"Just take them." He climbed back up to the loft before I could say anything else.

I slipped the shoes onto my feet, and immediately my hopes were dashed. The shoes were too big. Back on the table, my knife whispered in the candlelight. The silver blade was edged in red. I couldn't go through that again.

Please change, I thought. I had to hide the fact that it was not just the shoes that were ill-fitting on me.

The shoes tightened around my feet. I could swear that my corset tightened as well.

"Jack!" I called. There was no response from the loft. I turned to the door.

"Nora," he called back, so quietly that I almost didn't hear him. He peeked over the edge of the loft. All I could see was the candle that reflected in eyes that were solid, dull brown. "Don't fall too hard."

I straightened up and smiled.

"I'm not going to fall at all," I said and walked out the door.

CHAPTER 15

*H*oneycomb gazed warily as I approached. I held out my hand for her to sniff, and she pulled her head back and whinnied.

"Come on, Honeycomb," I said as I put the saddle on her back. "It's me."

She shook her head back and forth as though she were trying to dislodge the reins from my hands and took a few nervous steps forward. I hitched up my skirt, stepped into the stirrup, and swung up onto her back, whispering in her ear until she calmed. My voice, at least, was familiar.

I looked back at the kitchen house only once before leaving the Runes behind. The sick feeling in the pit of my stomach reminded me that Jack was still back in the loft, probably buried under a blanket, letting in neither the light nor the fact that I'd just left him alone.

No, I corrected myself, he wouldn't be. He didn't like being closed in small places. I hoped he could understand—the kitchen house was too small a place for me. If I could just get Honeycomb going fast enough, I could leave everything behind, not just the Runes. I could leave myself behind too. I shored up my grip on the reins as I sat taller on Honeycomb's back and forced my eyes away from the kitchen house. I would deal with Jack later.

I spurred Honeycomb to a gallop down the forest path. I wasn't familiar enough with the route to the Castle to look for shortcuts. As the sun set, the sound of other carriages became my guide through the woods. I rode ahead of the snippets of conversation and bursts of laughter that came from carriages covered by dark blue cloth from the Summit or silver-blue Vale roses. Up ahead was the gold-and-green carriage I had seen so many times before, ready to take my sisters places I would never go. Victor, the footman, sat in front with his eyes fastened to the road. I rode right past them, ignoring the urge to look back and see if anyone noticed me.

As I left them behind, I was overcome with a feeling of power. I felt different. Beautiful, even. I never had to go back to the Runes. I could take Honeycomb all the way to the Fall and tell Sir Reginald's valet thanks but no thanks, I had better prospects. I could ride to the Ken and see the ocean. I could go to the Farlands and join the sorcerers who lived in caves and were said to come out only when the moon was new. My wrist pulsed under the sapphire bracelet. I didn't want to fix the thing that was broken inside me. My strength came from that hurt. I had to show Alcander and Portia just how strong I was.

~

I slowed Honeycomb to a trot. I had outpaced almost every wagon on the road, and the forest around me was silent. In the daytime, the path to the Castle was clear, but now I was less sure. I couldn't wait for Alcander's carriage to catch me. I had to get to the Castle first.

As soon as I convinced myself that I had turned onto a side path and was going in the wrong direction, I heard cobblestone under Honeycomb's hooves. A soft glow emanated from between the trees. I didn't want to deal with the groomsmen who would bring the carriages and horses to the royal stables. The more inconspicuous I could make my entry, the better. I stopped Honeycomb just before we reached the Castle grounds and tethered her to a tree a short distance from the road.

"Stay here," I said. "I'll be back soon."

I kissed her nose for luck and continued down the path on foot, following the wave of carriages that drove up to the oak-lined road. This time, the guards sitting in the towers were unarmed, and the doors that led onto the ground of the Castle proper were wide open. The sword that spanned the doors was broken in two, granting peaceful entrance. Small candles floated in glasses strung from the branches of the oak trees. Fireflies circled the path that led up to the Castle, giving the impression that the guests were surrounded by tiny floating flames.

I followed behind a family with three daughters and a young son as they passed through the gate, also on foot. The glow from the trees and the fireflies made their clothing gold one moment and blue or green the next. They could have been from anywhere. Until we got under the lights inside the Castle, we were all placeless.

The walls of the grand foyer were lined with mirrors that multiplied each guest a hundred times over. I was reminded of my face in the kitchen house mirror in the moment just before its pieces fell to the ground. There, I had one reflection made smaller and broken by cracks. Here, I was one of a hundred versions of myself, all beautiful and all of my own creation. My reflection's eyes flashed gold, and I saw my hidden face through the glamour. When I blinked, it was gone. Deep blue stones that I had not noticed in the light of the kitchen house twinkled in my hair. I was as lovely as the girls around me once more. I wondered if they also found it so hard to breathe.

Music swelled through the hall as I followed the crowd to a landing on top of the stairs that descended into the ballroom. Strings and horns sounded off the domed ceiling. White columns circled the room, branching out as they stretched upwards to form a latticework pattern at the top of the walls. I ran my hand over the column behind me. The white stone was highlighted with grey-brown crackle. It was supposed to be a birch tree, I realized. The ballroom, like the Castle, was in a clearing in the middle of a forest. The ceiling glowed with blue-and-gold light. Could it be magic that made white clouds float over the ceiling? My head rushed as the size of the room hit me, and I took a step back.

"Excuse me." A familiar green dress pushed by. Portia was followed by Alcander, Siobhan, and Annabelle. I stopped breathing as they passed. Siobhan's hand shook as she gripped the railing at the top of the steps. Portia poked her in the back, forcing her to stand up straight again. Annabelle glanced over to make sure Portia and Alcander weren't looking before giving the tiniest of waves to someone already on the dance floor.

"Lord Alcander and Lady Portia of the Runes and their daughters," announced a herald standing at the top of the steps. They descended, Annabelle rushing down ahead of her parents, Siobhan hunched over with nerves again. It would be so easy to walk down behind them as one of Alcander's daughters. I slipped past the herald as he took the name of the next family to enter. I was not used to walking in shoes with a heel. It felt a bit like treading on a surface that was constantly in motion. I was thankful that my skirt hid my awkward gait.

Ahead of me, Annabelle had already vanished into the crowd of dancers. Portia and Alcander went to talk to some of the older lords and ladies as Siobhan was pulled into a circle of girls who looked just as nervous as she did. Everyone had their place. I found mine at the fringes of Siobhan's group as I tried to pick up information about Prince Edward's whereabouts. All I could gather was that the royal family had not yet made their entrance.

I wandered away as the girls' conversation turned to who made their dresses and which gentlemen they would dance with while they waited for the Prince. Nearby, skirts twirled, and tunics flashed in reds, blues, and golds as faces whirled by too fast for me to tell who anyone was. I thought I saw the green swish of Annabelle's dress and was sure I heard her laughter. It was the sound of someone who was here for the joy of it. None of those sounds came from Siobhan's group. Sweat sprang onto my forehead, warm and clammy at the same time. I brushed a hand across my brow, but it came off dry. My damp nerves were hidden under the glamour with my scars.

I hugged my arms around my waist. I hadn't eaten since breakfast. Servants with trays of food wove through the crowd. I made up my mind to follow one of them when I heard my name being called.

I looked down, panicked, sure that this time, the glamour was gone. But my dress was still satin and lace, and the ringlet of hair that I found in my hand was still smooth and auburn. I struggled to breathe through the boning of my corset and the feeling of hands at my throat. Did Izella really live like this, feeling like she might suffocate every day?

Lady Bess came out from the crowd wearing a sparkling white grown and a string of diamonds across her forehead. Her blue-white hair fell in waves down her back. She was stunning.

"How did you know—?" I glanced away from Bess at Portia and

Alcander, who had just taken to the dance floor. They whisked by without looking at us.

"Mist magic, remember?" Bess said. "I can see past the glamour." She must have sensed my nerves as I picked at my lips because she added, "No one else can tell. Maybe Papa, but that's it." She gestured over to where Sir Milton stood in a circle of men and women all dressed in white and pale blue. Gideon stood next to him, holding a glass of gold wine and laughing. Milton had his hand on the younger man's back.

"It's good," Bess said, and it took me a moment to realize she was talking about my glamour. She wasn't smiling. "How did you do it?"

The sapphire bracelet twinkled on my wrist, and the image of the bloodstained cloth that was underneath flashed before my eyes. If Bess could see through the spell, then she must know how it was put on.

"It was in my mother's spellbook," I said.

"Mm-hmm." Bess looked down at my wrist. "I didn't know you practiced."

"I don't," I said. "I mean, I didn't until tonight. I had to see the ball for myself, you know?" It was a weak excuse.

Bess looked around. "It's something, isn't it? Just…you'll be careful, won't you?" She sounded concerned, but I prickled at her words. I was fine. I hadn't done anything wrong. I did a good job with the spell—I must have if only she and Sir Milton could see through it. Her concern was misplaced.

"Of course," I said. "Are you here to dance with Prince Edward?"

Bess laughed. "Goddess, no. I'm betrothed." She waved to Gideon. He smiled back and pressed his hand to the gold key he wore around his neck. "I gave him my key last night. I knew he was the one the moment I met him, but it took a year of his apprenticing before I could get Papa to agree."

"Congratulations." I was relieved I would not have to vie with the Lady of the Vale for the Prince's attention. If that were the case, I might as well go home now. For just a moment, my thoughts went back to the Runes, to the kitchen house, and to Jack, lying on my mattress so he could stare up through the window at the escape of night sky. For just a moment, the suffocation of the glamour loosened, and I could breathe again.

"Even if I wasn't betrothed, I wouldn't be here for Edward." Bess looked over at the stairs, where a large group had gathered as the herald announced the royal family's entrance. "To have to compete with that? No, thank you." She looked back at me, and alarm sprang onto her face. "Nora, your glamour."

As I looked down, the hands of the spell tightened around my throat once more. I only saw the green of my serving skirt for a moment before it turned blue again. My heart pounded. The glamour had gotten me into the Castle. Now that I was here, I couldn't have it flickering on and off.

Bess put her hand on my shoulder. "Think about your intention."

I closed my eyes for a moment, picturing not the kitchen house but the map that was on Alcander's desk when he called me into his study just a few hours before. The Fall stood out on the parchment in vibrant, bloody red.

When I opened my eyes, the musicians went silent, and everyone had stopped dancing. The royal family appeared at the top of the stairs. King Philip and Queen Catalina were flanked by Prince Edward and Princess Callista. The King and Queen whispered a few words in their children's ears before descending to meet their guests. Edward and Callista were swiftly surrounded by admirers. Across the ballroom, I saw Portia nodding at Alcander as Siobhan elbowed her way to the front of the pack of girls.

"I have to go," I said to Bess.

"Good luck," she said. "You'll need it to get to Edward through that group." She chuckled. In another life, we would have been friends. In this life, maybe we still could be.

"You know, I can see why Jack likes you so much," I said.

"And I know why he likes you so much," she replied, glancing back at where Gideon stood with Sir Milton. "Don't break any hearts tonight, okay?"

"I'll try not to," I said.

I turned my attention to the crowd that had gathered around the Prince and Princess as Bess made her way back to the group from the Vale. The Princess flipped her long, blonde hair over her shoulder and laughed at the attention of her suitors. Her lavender-and-pearl dress flared out with the motion of her hips as she turned from side to side to survey her options. She took one gentleman by the hand and led him into the throng of dancers. Prince Edward was clearly less comfortable with the girls that surrounded him. I hovered at the back of the group, unsure what to do. It was like I had arrived at a banquet just as the servants were clearing away the dishes. I was just another anonymous face in the crowd, one that was too far away to even be in Edward's line of sight.

Edward reached out to find his first dance partner, and his hand alit on the arm of the closest girl: Siobhan. My hopes sank as I stepped aside, and they walked to the dance floor. I might have gotten to the Castle first, but Siobhan had always been closer to the Prince. Edward placed his hand on her back, and Siobhan straightened up as though Portia had poked her. I could see her counting her steps as they began their waltz. Annabelle danced nearby, one arm on the shoulder of a young man in green, the other holding up her skirt as they performed a much more elaborate version of Siobhan's and Edward's dance. She grinned and wiggled her eyebrows at Siobhan as they passed by.

Siobhan danced competently but with none of Annabelle's or Edward's grace. When the song ended, Edward bowed, and she curtseyed, and a girl dressed in gold rushed over to cut in. Siobhan returned to the group and was swiftly surrounded by girls asking if the Prince had sweaty palms and whether they talked while they danced. I wondered if anyone else noticed the tears swimming in her eyes.

Rather than waiting their turn with Edward, a few girls left to find lords to dance with, and soon the dance floor was full of young couples. I clung to the safety of the wall, reluctant to leave even when a gentleman in a crimson tunic approached and asked me to dance. Could he be Sir Reginald's son, here from the Fall? Or perhaps Sir Reginald's valet had snuck out just as I had and was trying his hand at winning the Princess. I shook my head and looked down at the floor, and the man asked the girl standing next to me to dance instead.

I could have spent the whole night paralyzed, unable to get near Edward, watching as my chance to prove my worth twirled away. As another song ended, Edward bowed to his partner. When she was pulled away by friends, the girl on my right straightened up, ready to start towards him. I moved first.

"Prince Edward," I said as soon as I was close enough for him to hear me. "May I dance with you?"

He turned towards me, and for a moment, I feared I had acted out of turn. But he smiled and offered me his hand. I couldn't decide whether the glint of interest that flickered in his eyes was real or part of my imagination.

The scene played out in front of me: Edward would declare that he had found his dance partner and did not desire to dance with anyone else for the duration of the ball. His arm would be strong at my back, and I would be smooth and graceful, all satin and silk as the musicians played.

Then it happened. His hand was on the small of my back. I placed my arm gently on top of his, resting my hand at his shoulder. We looked into each other's eyes, the band struck up a fast reel, and I realized: "I don't know how to dance."

The music drowned out my words as Edward moved us along with the other dancers. His feet rose and fell in time with the music, kicking and turning when the rhythm crested. I glued my eyes to the floor and tried to mirror his steps. From the safety of the wall, the dance looked simple. Here in the middle of it, everything was different. Just when I thought I'd figured out how my feet should move, everyone stopped to jump, clap, and start the dance in a different direction.

"What is your name?" Edward asked. I wrenched my eyes off the ground to meet his. I remembered those eyes, brown and full of mirth, from when I had served him at Portia and Alcander's banquet years before. How those eyes had laughed when I offered him one of Liana's cabbage rolls.

Edward winced as I stepped on his foot.

"I'm sorry," I said and looked back down at my feet. The music was speeding up. Edward twirled me under his arm, and my hand slipped out of his. Forgetting the need for my feet to move in time to the music, I rushed back to him, tripped on my skirt, and stepped on his foot again.

"I'm sorry." My regal exterior couldn't hide my lack of a proper upbringing. I wished I could shrink away, but I was surrounded. "I'm so sorry." A few couples stopped dancing and watched us. Siobhan stood at the edge of the dance floor with a mix of amusement and horror on her face. I could read her thoughts: *At least I wasn't the worst.*

"I have to go." I took a few steps back. A girl in a blue dress pushed me out of the way and took my place next to Edward.

~

A small crowd had gathered around Annabelle and her partner, who danced with all the beauty and elegance that I lacked. I watched them for a moment before turning out of the ballroom. As I left, I caught my reflection in the polished white wall. I was still beautiful, at least. Humiliated, but beautiful. I sat on a stone bench just outside the ballroom, leaned my head back against the wall, and closed my eyes. Four or five more songs had ended when I heard feet stop next to me.

"Are you all right?" Annabelle and her dance partner stood above me.

"Too much mead?" he asked.

I tried to stand, but my feet tangled in my skirt. "I'm fine. Thanks."

Annabelle offered a hand to help me up. I took it, and she hauled me to my feet. We stood for a moment, looking at each other, before I remembered she didn't know who I was.

"You're a wonderful dancer," I said.

She brightened. "Thank you! You hear that, Daniel?" She took his hand. "It's all about having the right partner." Daniel flushed and put his arm around her. "Have a good night," she said, and they returned to the dance floor hand in hand. When they passed Portia and Alcander, Annabelle let go of Daniel's hand, and he moved away from her just enough so that it would not look like they were walking together. As soon as they passed from Portia's view, she took his hand again.

Did Annabelle know that her act of kindness had caused me to be sent from the Runes? If she hadn't let me free to go to the Vale, I would be back in the kitchen house, and the only scars on my arms would be from the oven. But if Alcander didn't send me away now, he would find a reason to do it eventually. Now, at least, I had a chance to escape.

I looked back into the ballroom where the King and Queen took to the dance floor. Queen Catalina moved like a swan, her arms rising in graceful arcs as her long sleeves flew out behind her. King Philip mirrored her, dancing like I imagined he might swordfight. Nearby, Princess Callista twirled under the arm of a gentleman in a red tunic. I couldn't see Edward in the crowd, but he had to be there, dancing with yet another girl who was doing a better job than I did. If I had any hope of getting another dance with him, I needed to remember that I was supposed to be a lady, someone of breeding who knew how to hold herself together in front of royalty. Not someone who would sit slumped against the wall, looking like she had too many glasses of mead.

I watched the unspoken push and pull between the dancers as they wove back and forth. This was something that took time to learn. I could understand why Siobhan spent so long trying to master the dance when she could have easily impressed Edward with her skills at the pianoforte or her singing. Dancing required two people moving as one. Annabelle was right: you needed the right partner to make the dance work. As long as Edward hadn't found that partner yet, I still had a chance.

∾

I turned away from the ballroom. I would regroup, go find Edward, and try again. I walked down a hall with enormous tapestries hanging from the walls. Each of the first five tapestries represented a province of Colandaria. I stood in front of the one that showed the Runes. A great tree stood in the center with its branches covered in ivy. The tapestry showing the Vale was threaded with misty blues; the silvery threads that made up the stream looked like they were moving. I turned away from the red hanging that thundered with a giant mountain waterfall and continued down the hall.

The weaving of the thread reminded me of the dancers in the ballroom: just as I couldn't figure out each tiny movement of the dance once I had to do it, the hangings were a mess of colored lines, too separate to make out a coherent image up close. Once I took a few steps back, the picture became clear. In the large tapestry in front of me, a silver thread that seemed like a mistake among the greys, browns, and pewters became the highlight on a knight's helmet where it was hit by the sun. The sky that seemed like a tangle of white, yellow, and blue thread turned into a group of ghostly female figures looking down over a group of knights burrowed behind a stone rampart. I ran my hand over the ghost-women's skirts.

"It's called 'The Protectoress.'"

I spun around and found myself face-to-face with Prince Edward. With my eyes fastened to the floor, I didn't have a chance to really look at him while we danced. Now I had no choice. The torches in the hall glittered off the gold edging on his tunic. He was handsome, but not regally so, like King Philip. I could imagine seeing him traveling from province to province as part of a troupe of musicians or a band of performers. He had softer, less chiseled features than the King. And on his face, the most unexpected thing: a smile.

"Those are the men's families watching over them during the Border Wars," he said. "That one there"—he pointed to the knight in the center, who carried a violet shield with a white rose on it—"that's my father. And that"—he pointed to the knight in the palest armor whose silver shield bore the insignia of a rose wrapped around a sword —"that's the White Knight, the protector of Colandaria. No one knows who he is, but he comes when he's needed. It's all very mysterious."

"Are the others mysterious too?" I didn't recognize the voice that came out of my mouth. It didn't match the nerves that fluttered like wings up and down my back, urging me to fly away.

Edward pointed to each of the knights. "That's Sir Stephen of the Ken, Sir Reginald of the Fall, Sir Alcander of the Runes, Sir Rupert of the Summit, and Sir Milton of the Vale. Sir Milton's grandmother made the tapestry. It was a gift to my father when he went off to war."

The figure that Edward had named as Sir Alcander wore pewter armor and carried a green-and-gold shield. He bore little resemblance to the man in the ballroom. The man in the tapestry looked brave.

"It's a lovely piece," I said.

"You ran out," Edward observed. There was a crinkle of amusement on his face.

It was as though the glamour slipped down my throat to control my words. "So did you."

"I snuck out. There's a difference." Edward gestured back towards the ballroom. "There is only so much dancing and so many girls I can take at one time. Unfortunately, no one in there would let me have a break."

I remembered his trepidation about picking a bride from the conversation I'd heard over the Castle wall. "It must be hard having so many girls try to make an impression at once."

Edward nodded. "So far, you're the only one who's left any impression at all."

"And I left it on your shoe," I said, looking away to hide my embarrassment.

Edward laughed. "It's all right. Most of these girls are trying too hard. It's impossible to know who anyone is when all you see is the face they're putting on for you."

I glanced down at my bracelet. The blue stones twinkled back at me.

"So what were you doing instead of going to your dance lessons?" Edward asked.

Baking bread. Serving dinner. Gathering herbs before they all dried up for lack of rain.

"Studying," I said, "with my mother."

"What subjects?"

I couldn't believe we were still talking. He looked at me like the lady I needed to be.

"History, about the Border Wars. Geography."

"Oh," Edward said, glancing at the wall hanging behind us. "I guess you didn't need me to tell you about the tapestry, then."

I smiled instead of answering.

"Are you and your mother close?" Edward beckoned for me to walk with him.

I nodded. "We were, but she died a few months ago." It was easier to think now that we were moving and I didn't have to look at Edward's face when I spoke. I looked at Liana's shoes appearing and disappearing under my skirt. "It was a fever and a terrible cough." The lies tasted like truth.

"I'm sorry to hear that," Edward said.

"My father remarried already," I heard myself saying. "I'm trying to avoid my stepmother and stepsisters tonight. We don't exactly get along."

Edward laughed. "You'd fit in well here. I spend a good deal of time trying to avoid my familial duties. Like now, for example."

On our right, two guards stood in front of a wide entryway. They nodded at Edward, who gestured for them to leave as he led us into the room. The walls were lined with stained glass windows, some of which were open to let in the nighttime air. Torches blazed in sconces between them. A wide carpet stretched across much of the room and up to the marble steps that led to a dais on which two large thrones sat empty.

Edward spread his arms out like he was a barker at the Market. "The throne room. This is the reason most of the guests are here tonight. Half showed up out of obligation, the other half out of some misguided belief that they'll end up the next prince or queen. Callista has no intention of picking a husband tonight, regardless of what Father wants her to do. She just wants to dance with some handsome gentlemen for an evening. And I—" Edward shook his head. "Well, like I said, it's hard to get to know anyone when there are a hundred people around and music drowning out the conversation."

"So you escape to the throne room," I said.

Edward sat on the steps in front of the thrones and put his head in his hands. "Go back to the ballroom and spread the news," he said. "Everyone can go home."

He seemed so much more human now than he did in the ballroom. He was wearing a glamour too, one of obligation to his station. I wondered what else was underneath. I sat down next to him.

"What would you rather be doing right now?" I asked. He looked at me as though he were surprised I was still there.

"Riding," he said after a moment. "There's something about the feeling of galloping down the road with the wind whipping at your face. Burning it, even. It feels free. Like you could go anywhere, be anyone. Do you know what I mean?"

I thought about the exhilaration of leaving the Runes just a few hours before.

"I might. It's like the path is full of chances, and if you can just grab the right one, you can choose your destination, no matter how far away it seems." I worried that I sounded ridiculous, but Edward nodded.

"That's exactly it." He sat for a moment, looking at me without saying anything. The music from the ballroom echoed faintly off the walls. "Do you want to try that dance again?"

I shook my head. "No, I don't think that's a good idea."

"Come on." Edward offered me his hand. "Maybe learning to dance is just a matter of having the right teacher."

With reluctance, I met him where he stood.

"I pity your shoes," I said. He smiled.

"First, a proper hold." He put his arm around my waist again and nodded his approval when I placed a tentative hand on his shoulder. "Start by stepping forwards with your right foot."

I looked down at the shoes that peeked out from under my dress in sky blue satin.

"Don't look down," Edward said, and I raised my gaze to meet his. "Your feet will figure it out on their own."

He counted in threes and moved backwards as I took halting steps forwards. He was a good teacher. The steps slowly became familiar to my untrained feet as we waltzed. In the ballroom, I had the feeling of a hundred eyes all trying to bore through my glamour, looking for a sign that the girl underneath was unworthy of a dance with royalty. I was guilty of that myself as I watched the other girls dance with Edward. Now, I found myself relaxing and listening more closely to the music. Edward reminded me a few more times not to look at my feet, but it wasn't long before I had a hard time keeping my gaze away from his.

"Close your eyes," he said.

"What?" I skipped a step, and my foot landed on his again. He laughed, full of good humor.

"Trust me," he said.

I closed my eyes, and the music seemed to get louder, his hands warmer. He raised the hand that held mine, and I felt a gentle pressure on my back. Without his saying a word, I understood. He wanted me to turn. I stepped out, my hand pivoted in his, and I felt my skirt fan out around me.

I could do this, I thought. This could be me.

Feeling a soft pull on my arm, I stepped back to Edward, opened my eyes, and smiled. For the first time, my movements felt natural, like I'd always had these rouged lips and this noble face.

"You know, you're beautiful when you smile," Edward said. He stopped dancing but kept his arm around my waist. "I mean, you're beautiful when you're not smiling, but when you smile your eyes light up, and did you know there's some gold in them? The gold really comes out when you smile." He shook his head, laughing under his breath. "I am very bad at this. Where are you from? I can't tell from your dress. There's too much violet in the blue for you to be from the Summit, and your shoes look like they're from the Vale."

"I thought we weren't supposed to be looking at my feet," I said. My heart ran on ahead of me.

"Tell me," he said. "I need to know where I can come to call on you, if you'd like me to."

I imagined Edward riding up to the Runes, stately and handsome on his mount.

"I'd like you to."

He touched his hand to his forehead and shook his head. "I don't even know your name. I told you I'm bad at this."

I hesitated. I left Nora back in the kitchen house. Nora wouldn't have a prince knocking on the door, come to court her. But I didn't feel much like Eleanor, either. I never did, not even now. I felt like someone new, someone who had discovered her power and liked it.

"Your Highness." The stern voice came from the entrance to the throne room. Edward's hand dropped away from my back. An older lord stood in the portico with his arms crossed over his chest. His silvery hair and short beard reflected the torches on the wall.

"Ioan," Edward said, just as sternly.

"Your father needs you in the library."

"There's a ball going on," Edward said. "Surely it can wait."

Ioan shook his head. "Your father left the ball. It is a matter of great importance regarding activity in the Farlands." His tone seemed to hold some significance for Edward, whose bearing changed as he turned back to me.

"I'm sorry," he said. "I have to go. Wait here for me. I won't be long." He followed Ioan out of the room.

With Edward gone, the throne room seemed even larger than before. Now I was ready to take up the space myself. I felt like dancing for joy. When I got back to the Runes, I would no longer be under Alcander's thumb. Portia would no longer be able to slam me down like I was the sister she hated. I waltzed around the throne room alone, whirling about using the steps Edward taught me. I imagined the expression on Siobhan's face when Edward came to court me. I was sure I had seen that look in the ballroom in the tears that hovered at the corners of her eyes. She deserved it. Didn't she?

I hopped up the steps that led to the thrones. Someday I might sit there, looking down on my court. I ran my hand over the velvet-covered arms of the thrones. King Philip's was the taller of the two, with a royal backing and a matching cushion. Amethysts were set into the scalloped edges of the wood. Queen Catalina's throne was smaller, covered in matching gold leaf, with lavender velvet. I brushed my skirt behind me, sat down in her seat, and closed my eyes, raising my hand in an imagined wave to my subjects.

I felt freer than I had all day. It was as though the boning that held my ribs in place had vanished and taken the smothering hands that pressed around my neck with them. There was space for all of the sweet air I could take in. I was weightless.

Dread poured down my throat.

I knew what I would see when I opened my eyes. My bracelet of shining blue stones would be gone. On the arm that was raised in a ridiculous wave to imagined courtiers would be only a dirty, bloodstained rag. A dull ache radiated down my arm to pool in my elbow. My hand dropped onto my skirt. My skirt, which was once more the rough green material that I wore every day in the kitchen house. I didn't have to reach up to my hair to know that the glamour was gone. The only thing I could think was that Portia had been right. My blood wasn't good enough. Not for the Castle, not for the ball, and not for the spell.

"What are you doing here?"

The guards Edward dismissed from the throne room had returned. They stood in the doorway, looking at me with angry suspicion. Fear kept me in my stolen seat. I gripped the arms of the throne with stiff fingers.

"Where is Edward?" was all I could get out.

The guards crossed towards me. "That's none of your concern, girl. Get up."

"No," I stammered. "Edward told me to wait here."

The first guard's hand went to his sword. "You're trespassing at a royal ball." He turned to the second guard. "How'd she even get in here?"

"Came in through one of the windows, I imagine," the second guard said, pointing to the wall of stained glass. "Just had to see what the noblefolk are about, didn't you? It's too bad the Prince doesn't have dalliances with servant girls." He grabbed my arm, digging his fingers into my skin. With a hard push, he threw me forwards, down the stairs. My hip cracked against the floor. I cried out as pain lanced up my spine.

"What's this?" The first guard ran his finger over the arm of the throne. It came away red. "Blood? You got blood on the Queen's throne?"

The second guard hovered over me. "Must've cut herself climbing in the window," he said. I felt warm blood trickling down my arm past the rag that didn't do enough to dam its flow. The second guard pulled me up from the ground, pinning my arms roughly behind my back. "You'll be lucky if the Queen doesn't take more of that blood as punishment." His words were coarse and ugly in my ear as he pulled me away from the throne room. My gait was uneven; my right heel slammed down on the floor with each step I took. I strained to look behind me. One of Liana's shoes lay at the bottom of the steps where I fell.

"Wait—" Pain shot through my shoulder as I wrestled in the guard's grip, trying to turn around so I could get to the shoe. He pulled me farther away. I gripped my toes in the remaining shoe to keep it on my foot.

"Think she's a Farland spy?" the first guard said as they marched me out of the throne room.

The second guard shook his head and nodded towards my skirt. "Runes green. She probably belongs to someone in the ballroom. Let them deal with her."

My hair fell in front of my face, making it difficult to see where I was going. The faint music from the throne room got louder until it was almost deafening. I felt the crowd of people moving aside as we passed. My whole body burned with the same hot blood that I now wanted so badly to keep inside. The guards pushed their way onto the band's platform, and the musicians stopped playing. The room fell silent.

"Who does this belong to?" one of the guards shouted.

Tears pinched my face. Where was Edward? Why wasn't he here to help me? I looked out across the crowd as hundreds of eyes stared back at me, registering amusement, embarrassment, and disgust. I couldn't see the royal family anywhere in the room.

"Nora!" I heard Bess say from the back at the same time that Annabelle, who had been standing with Daniel in the middle of the crowd of dancers, began to push her way towards the musicians' platform. Daniel cried out her name as she was intercepted by Portia, who shoved her out of the way, not stopping until she reached me. I couldn't understand what she was saying until she had grabbed me by the hair and her voice was low and icy in my ear.

"—never been so embarrassed in my life! Just like your slag of a mother." She pulled me off the platform. I struggled to pry her hands out of my hair, but she held on with an inhuman grip.

Portia yanked me up the stairs, past the herald, and out of the ballroom. Servants opened the doors for her, and cool night air blasted me in the face. Portia kept moving, pulling my hair so hard that bright stars exploded in front of my eyes, magnified by the candles that dotted the lawn. It felt as if the Castle itself were applauding my humiliation. I tripped on the stairs that led down to the road, and my knees slammed on the marble.

"Fix yourself," Portia ordered as she finally let go of my hair. I struggled to my feet and found that Alcander had joined her, standing behind me as part of a united front. He ordered a servant to fetch their carriage.

I stood between Portia and Alcander, fighting a strong desire to crumble to bits on the ground. As I squeezed my eyes shut against the ache that pounded down from my head, Siobhan ran down the steps.

"Mother! Father! Where are you going?"

"Home," Portia snapped. Victor, whom someone must have fetched from wherever the footmen were spending the evening, drove the carriage around to the front of the Castle. "We have something we need to deal with." Portia opened the half door, pushed me inside, and stepped in after me so I couldn't slip out past her. Alcander followed. I hugged my knees to my chest, making myself as small as possible against the far side of the carriage.

"How will I get back?" Siobhan asked as Portia closed the door without letting her in.

"That boy of your sister's ought to be good for something. Get him to take the two of you." Portia called for Victor to go.

"Daniel?" Siobhan said. "You know about him? But—" The rest of her words were cut off as the carriage moved.

I watched out the door of the carriage as the Castle disappeared, suddenly filled with worry about Honeycomb. I could only hope that in my haste, I hadn't done a good job of hitching her to the tree, and she could get home.

My bones shook each time the carriage bumped on the road. If the ride to the Castle seemed long, the ride back to the Runes was interminable. Portia and Alcander sat stiffly, ignoring my presence even when I ripped the hem out of my skirt and tore off a piece of fabric to wrap around my wrist in the place of the kitchen cloth. The blood had slowed to a trickle, but it still flowed, reminding me that I could never take back my decision to use Izella's magic.

Finally, just as I was sure that I would spend eternity in the carriage with Alcander's and Portia's knees only inches from my face, Victor yelled for the horses to stop. I stayed inside when Alcander and Portia got out, pressing my back into the wall and wishing that I could glamour myself into disappearing.

"Get out," Portia ordered. I stumbled to the ground. The shoe that I still had fell off my foot. Portia swooped down to pick it up.

"What is this?" she demanded, waving it in my face. "This isn't yours. You stole it."

"No!" I protested. Alcander followed as Portia dragged me into the main house. A fire blazed in the hearth in the parlor. Portia pulled me close as the flames danced in her eyes. Her beauty was terrifying.

"None of this belongs to you," she said. "You can't steal your way in here. Your mother tried, and look where she ended up."

Any hope I had of being whisked away from the Runes by Prince Edward was gone. Portia would make sure of it. I was going to be sent to the Fall in two weeks' time. What else did I have to lose?

"It would have been mine," I said, "if you hadn't killed my mother. You're the thief."

Alcander grabbed my arm and jerked me around to face him. The blood from the cloth around my wrist smeared on his hand. As he stared at it, the realization of what I'd done dawned on his face. With one swift movement, he grabbed Liana's shoe out of Portia's hand and threw it into the fire.

"No!" I gasped, diving after it. Flames scalded my hands. Alcander pulled me back, shackling his arms around my waist as blisters erupted on my skin. He turned to Portia, speaking in a low voice.

"Put her with the ashes."

Terror tore me in half. I struggled in Alcander's grip, wheeling my arms to try to hit him. He walked me down the hallway after Portia, who flipped through her keys until she found the one she wanted.

"Please, don't," I cried.

She fit the key into the lock. This time, there was no glamour of torches and books to provide an eerie comfort. There was only ash and death.

I kicked Alcander as hard as I could. My foot connected with his knee. His legs buckled, but he stayed upright and threw me into the room. I landed hard on the ground.

"Maybe this time you'll learn," Portia said as she slammed the door in my face, plunging the room into darkness.

"No, no, please," I cried, pounding the door and sending bright flashes of pain across my burned hands. I threw my shoulder into the wood as hard as I could. The shock of the impact shook the door, but the lock would not give way.

I could picture Alcander's face on the other side of the door, and I knew.

He would burn me too if he could.

CHAPTER 16

I flew to the wall, searching for the missing stone. I had a desperate hope that Yllianne had hidden something else there, something that would create a barrier against the darkness. Wet pain burst through my hands as I clawed over rough stone and mortar. When I reached the corner, my foot landed on the stone I had pulled out during the brief moment when the room was filled with hope instead of ashy regret.

A hollow gaped open in the wall above the stone. I reached in as far as I could, scraped around the edges, and found nothing. The darkness sucked up my voice as I screamed into the walls. There was no echo. I threw myself against the door until my shoulders could not bear another blow.

I slid down the door, wincing as my shirt caught and tore on the splintered wood. Someone would come. They had to.

Hunger gnawed at my belly, a dull growl that rose to a fiery need. I pictured the food I'd seen whisked around on trays at the Castle—small, round pastries and meat that practically dripped off the bone—but whenever I got close to tasting it, it turned to ash in my mouth. I needed something to wash it down. If I only had something to drink, I could put out the fire burning in my stomach.

I counted to ten, sure that someone would come for me when I reached the end. Soon, I had reached a hundred, then a thousand, stopping only when my thoughts became hazy and I couldn't remember what numbers came next. That was when the spiders came. I could hear the *ping-ping* of their legs as they crawled out from the hole in the wall, making their way down the stone to the ashy floor to swarm over me. I clenched my eyes shut against the tiny pricks of their feet as they left a pin-dotted trail of soot on my skin. When I could not bear it any more, I flipped my skirt aside and slapped at my legs again and again.

I stayed a sunken puddle on the ground. If I slept, I dreamt of nothing and woke with a pounding heart, my throat crying for water. I felt tears, sticky on my cheeks, drying up along with the rest of me. Voices sounded outside the room—Portia, Alcander, Siobhan, Annabelle, other servants. Someone was struck down in front of the door, but the sounds faded, just figments of the room.

Then, while moving my hands uselessly across the floor, I felt it. The texture of the dirt was different, clammier. I had a sudden, clear memory of myself at twelve, shut up in this room for asking Robert if he was my father. The floor was damp then too, making the ash cakey to the touch. I felt like I was pulling a full wagon through mud as I hauled myself over to the damp earth and dug.

I jammed my hands into the ash, digging with all the energy I could muster, working past pain. What little hope I had fluttered away as I felt the tiny pile of earth next to me. I must have been digging for hours, but I had barely scraped the surface. I jolted out of an empty sleep to dig again. Those two imperatives became my whole world: dig, sleep, dig, sleep. I was sure that when I came out of the room, I would be old, older than the old woman in the woods whose name I could not remember.

My hands had gone numb by the time I found it, and I had to press my face to the floor to make sure it was really there. Water. I lowered my lips to the ground once more and drank. What sloshed around in my mouth was mostly mud, but I forced myself to swallow it anyway. My stomach lurched, and it took all my willpower to keep from throwing it back up on the floor.

Someone screeched with delight. The sound, high-pitched and steely, sliced through my head. I didn't know if it had been moments or days since I found the water. There was a bustle of activity in the hall.

"The Prince!"

He was here. He had come to rescue me.

The noise died down as the activity moved elsewhere in the house. I forced my eyes to stay open, waiting for a sign that the voices were not just in my head. Some time later, I recognized the click of Portia's heels against the stone floor, her gait practiced and urgent. They were right outside my door now. My head swam as I leaned against the rough wood.

"Thank you for your time. I'm sorry to have bothered you this evening."

Edward.

"Your Highness, can't Siobhan try on the shoe? Her memory of the ball is hazy from the wine. She doesn't remember half the conversations she had."

"Mother!"

Edward's laugh.

"Lady Portia, I don't think that is the case. Are there any other girls in the house?"

Silence.

"Well, then, I must be leaving."

No! I'm here! I knocked against the wood. The sound pounded in my head, but nothing could get through that door, not sound, not light, not me.

"Do come back, Your Majesty, if you don't find the girl you're looking for. I'm sure Siobhan would love to see you again."

"Mother!" More insistent, embarrassed this time.

Then, new feet running down the hall. Familiar, but with panic that made them alien.

"Wait, Your Highness—"

"Ignore him. He probably wants you to try the shoe on the cook." A laugh, cruel and dismissive. I couldn't hear Edward's response.

There was a scuffle, the thump of a body hitting the floor. Portia's yell: "Give me those!"

The click of a key in the lock.

The door fell open, and I fell with it. No light came into the room. Had someone extinguished the torches in the hall? No, my eyes were wide open. It hurt to close them; the insides of my lids scraped my eyes each time they shut. The whole world had gone as dark as the room with no windows.

Strong arms locked around my waist and pulled me into the hall. I tried to say something, tried to move.

"Nora." A hand stroked my cheek. "I've got you."

My face pressed into a soft shirt. A hand pressed urgently against mine. *I'm here.*

I wanted to tell Jack I could hear his heart beating, but no sound would pass my lips.

"What in the name of the Goddess is going on?" Edward, from above.

Portia. "Your Highness, you don't understand."

"What possible explanation could you have for—"

"Has she been eating mud?" Siobhan, closer to my ears.

Jack's arms tightened around me.

Shouts whirled through the air, cycloning above my head until silence broke through, empty and clear.

CHAPTER 17

I heard singing. I was sure of that much. I was back in the great house at the Vale, standing next to a small, round table with Sir Milton, Lady Bess, and Gideon. The space in front of me opened up to night, and stars twinkled in the dark. I felt the urge to reach in, to lose my fingers, then my hand, then my arm as I tried to touch the stars. The voices kept me in Sir Milton's study. I tried to match their harmonies, but as soon as I opened my mouth to sing, the night winked out. That magical overtone, the music of the stars, would not appear when I added my voice to the spell. A low ticking sounded close to my ear. I looked up at the shelves, where the orbs of mist hovered over their bowls and found myself drawn to the one that screamed, drawn to the spectral hands that reached out from the mist and mouths that opened in cries that I was sure I could hear if I could just get close enough—

When I wrenched my gaze away, I was back in the kitchen house, twelve years old and feverish. I lay in front of the fire as Greta held a ladle to my mouth. There were things I wanted to tell her, but I couldn't speak past the soup that poured down my throat. I needed to apologize. I was wrong about going to the main house. I was wrong about so many things. Sweat beaded on my forehead, lifting from my skin to join the mist from the Vale that passed through the kitchen house and took me with it, out the window and into the forest. The mist whispered regrets that I could not hear over the ticking, which became more urgent as I moved closer to my destination. I followed it over trees bare with drought. As I looked back, the mist snagged on branches and tore off to clothe the trees with cloudstuff.

I followed the sounds until I reached the Castle lawn, still lit up with candles for the ball. The harvest moon hung large and yellow in the darkening sky. The mist floated across the grass, extinguishing the flames until the Castle stood grey and sterile.

The mist and I went through open doors and down to the ballroom, where I danced with Jack as musicians played behind us. He wore his serving clothes, stained with dirt from the garden, but he danced like nobility. The ticking was louder here, louder even than the music. As Jack spun me under his arm, my indigo dress swirled around me, and I recognized the noise for what is was: Annabelle's metronome clocking time. I kicked up the mist on the floor, and it made its way up the walls, taking the place of the petrified trees that stretched to the ceiling, leaving us back in the misty forest. Fog rained down from the sky, and as my vision became hazy, my hand slipped out of Jack's, and he disappeared, his fingerprints still lingering on my skin.

I was in the dark, alone.

~

I sat up with a start. A corona of light burned in front of me, fading as my surroundings came into view. I could still hear singing. My head swam, and I sank back into soft pillows, shielding my eyes with my hand. My wrist was wrapped with a clean white bandage that tingled faintly where it touched my skin. The singing stopped, and a girl's face appeared above me.

"You're awake!" She pushed a lock of mousy brown hair back behind her ear and looked over at the window. "Oh, sorry!"

She ran to the other side of the room and shut the curtains that hung on either side of a large window. I struggled to sit up again as more of the room came into focus. The furniture was sparse: only a chair, a small table, a cabinet, and the bed I lay in, which had soft sheets that smelled of lavender. For a moment, I wondered if I were still in the room with no windows. Perhaps this space and my caretaker were tricks of its glamour. I ran my hands over the smooth wood of the bedpost. I couldn't still be in the room. The sunlight filtering though the gauzy curtains felt warm and real.

"Here." She handed me a cup of water. "Drink this."

The water was cool, tasting faintly of dandelion. It was one of Greta's remedies for after a fever. I asked for her.

"Who is Greta?"

I shook my head. "Never mind."

The room didn't have any of the familiar features of the main house at the Runes, no carvings of ivy or oak furniture. I felt a momentary panic at the idea that this could be the Fall, that Alcander had gotten rid of me, and there was a stranger in a neighboring room waiting for marriage. As the girl bustled about over by the table, I finally noticed the deep violet of her skirt. As improbable as it seemed, there was only one place I could be.

"Am I in the Castle?"

"Of course you are," said the girl, who told me her name was Regan. "You don't remember coming here?"

"No. The last thing I remember—" I recalled shouting and a hand stroking my hair. "—I was in the Runes. How long have I been here?"

"Two weeks, just about. They brought in healers to see you, but you were asleep most of the time. You were pretty groggy whenever you were awake. I fed you some soup when I could. You thought I was this Greta person. Who is she?"

I thought of Greta's kind eyes and the oven burns on her skin. When I looked down at my arms, for just a moment I was afraid that the Castle healers had done away with the scars that tied me to Greta and Peter. It was almost a relief to see them still there, twisted and white. My hands were the same now, covered with dark pink that had begun the slow process of healing.

"She raised me," I said. She's my mother, I thought afterwards.

"You asked for her a lot. And for others too. Peter and Jack and Edward. Did you mean the Prince?"

Heat rose to my face. "Is he here?"

"No." Regan waved her hand towards the window. "He's probably in the Ken by now. They said in the kitchen that that's his last stop before he comes back here."

I tried to hide my disappointment as she finished her work at the table and brought over a tray with a small bowl of broth balanced on top. I took the bowl and a spoon from her and dove in. I was hungrier than I realized.

"Oh!" Regan exclaimed. "Someone wanted to know when you woke up." She darted out of the room as the salty broth pulled me back to the kitchen house. I wondered why I was alone in the Castle. Had anyone from the Runes come to check on me? Did they even know where I was?

A familiar face appeared at the door, waving a hand with three working fingers.

"She wakes," Sir Milton proclaimed as he came in the room. "I'm glad to see it. I'll send word that you're up and about."

"I'm not about quite yet," I said, smiling. "What are you doing here?"

"I was asked to come," he said. He looked as though he were about to say something else, then changed his mind. "They wanted to keep you at the Runes, but after three days in that room, you needed more healing than Greta could do on her own."

I blinked my surprise. Surely I had been in the room longer than that. I felt like I had aged decades in the dark.

"Edward saw to it that you were brought here so the royal healers could try their hand. Lucky for you, I've also picked up some restorative tricks in my time. Actually, Bess was the one who figured out the mist bandage, but I'll gladly take the credit." With a wave of his hand, the bandage around my wrist disappeared. Underneath, the line I had etched into my skin was mending. Milton eyed it with approval and waved his hand again. The bandage reformed. When I looked closely, I could see all the way through the mist that tingled around my wrist.

"From what I understand, you got out of that room just in time," Milton said. "Any longer and we might not have been able to bring you back."

I closed my eyes. I didn't ask how Milton knew what happened at the Runes. I didn't want to think about the room with no windows at all. Questions pricked at my mind until I asked, "What was the Prince doing at the Runes?"

Milton raised an eyebrow. "You've created a rather big mess. Edward is traveling the country looking for you."

"He is?"

"He and Ioan, the court sorcerer, are going door to door looking for the girl who lost a shoe at the ball. It was Philip's idea."

Something about it being the King's idea, not Edward's, to search for the girl from the ball didn't sit quite right with me.

Milton continued. "Ioan detected traces of a glamour, meaning the shoe had been changed to look different or to—"

"—fit better," I finished for him.

"Imagine my surprise when they showed up at the Vale with a shoe I gave to Liana," Milton said.

"Jack gave them to me," I said. I recalled what had happened to the shoe's mate and was filled with regret. I hadn't done my job of looking after them.

"Ioan believes that only the girl who originally cast the spell can make it work again."

"But if they know the shoe was glamoured," I said, "then they must suspect that the person wearing it also had a glamour on."

Milton nodded. "Edward doesn't know who he is looking for. She could be anyone."

Edward knew that the girl he taught to dance might not be who she appeared, and he was looking for her anyway. I didn't know what to make of this. He was in another room when the guards paraded me in front of the assembly like a discarded piece of trash. He hadn't seen the shame I'd felt, the shame I'd brought on the Runes. To him, I was still the girl in the indigo dress, whoever she might be.

"They'll be sending a message to the Runes that you've woken up," Milton said. "Someone will come to get you. I'm sure King Philip will want an audience with Alcander before you're sent home."

The thought of seeing Alcander and Portia again nauseated me. Surely the King wouldn't let them take me back to the Runes. I would be back in the room with no windows as soon as I arrived.

Milton put his hand on mine. "I've said this before—the Vale is here for you if you want it."

I thanked him, and he turned towards the door. "By the way," he said as he walked out, "I mentioned to Philip that you were at the ball, and you never had a fair chance at trying on the shoe."

If I could have gotten out of the bed, I would have hugged him. "Thank you," I said again, and I meant it.

⁓

Two women came in to check on me later in the afternoon. They had me sit up and poked me with strange instruments. One of them conjured a tiny, glowing ball that moved back and forth in front of my eyes as the other held a horn to my chest and listened to my heartbeat. I didn't know if they were sorcerers or healers. They talked only to each other, but between all the unfamiliar terms they used, I gathered that they thought I was well enough to go home. They looked over me with pride, like I was a problem they had solved. It was so different from the care that Greta gave when anyone in the kitchen house needed help. Milton said that she couldn't have healed me on her own, but I still wished she were in the Castle. I needed a familiar hand.

In the evening, Regan returned with dinner.

"I made it myself," she said, full of pride as I made my way over to the table. There were two spoons, three different forks, and a knife on the tray she placed in front of me. I stared at the utensils, not sure where to begin. I didn't want word of my lowly habits getting back to the royal family. The smell coming up from the roasted pheasant on the plate made my mouth water.

"Just use the big fork," Regan said after I just sat there for a few minutes with my hands hovering over the tray. "The big one is for the meat. The smaller one is for the vegetables. The rest of them seem like a waste to me."

"Decoration, maybe?" I smiled at her and picked up the biggest fork. "Do you want to sit?" I took a bite of the pheasant. It was delicious. I could taste hints of thyme and sage and something else I couldn't identify. When I finished, I sopped up the juices with a chunk of bread. I was sure the King and Queen wouldn't use their bread as a utensil, not when they had six different pieces of silver to choose from, but comfortable habit took over. As I imagined the royal dining room, much larger than the one at the Runes, I remembered something Jack had said long ago about his dislike for banquet tables. I sighed as I popped the last piece of bread into my mouth.

Regan sat across from me and talked as I ate, going on about the gossip circulating among Castle servants—who was filching biscuits from the pantry, who was seen gallivanting with whom, and which footman had been the last to catch a peep of the new stable girl they all thought was so attractive. I couldn't keep up with all the names and relations she threw out, but I was glad for her company. When she mentioned the preparations for the ball, I joined in the conversation.

"You'd have been amazed," she said. "There was so much food left over. What a waste. But we made short work of in the kitchen, believe me!"

"It must have been delicious," I said, picturing the powdered pastries I hadn't been able to taste.

"You didn't have any?" Regan said. I was surprised that she assumed I had been at the ball. I wondered if she'd seen my serving skirt when I arrived at the Castle.

"No," I said. "I didn't have time. But I saw it, and it looked wonderful."

She smiled, and color came to her cheeks. It didn't seem like she was used to compliments. "I wanted to be one of the ones who got to go around with the plates at the ball, but they made me stay in the kitchen. What was it like?"

"Overwhelming," I said. "Extravagant. Like nothing I've seen before." I told her what I could remember about the guests and the music. She laughed when I described the King and Queen dancing.

"Did you dance with Prince Edward?"

I nodded. "Twice. It didn't go so well the first time. I stepped on his shoes a lot. I'm surprised he could walk afterwards." I joined in Regan's laughter. "I even lost my shoe," I said in a fit of giggles.

Regan stopped laughing. Her eyes widened, and she stood up from the table.

"It's an honor to serve you, my lady." She curtseyed before running out of the room.

"No, wait—" I called after her. I was so glad to have a friend here. I didn't want to suddenly be treated like royalty. When she came back in to get my plate and turn down the bed, she worked without talking and avoided meeting my eyes. After she left, the small room felt too big for me.

Regan drew an extra set of curtains to block out the moonlight before she left. When I blew out the candles on the wall, shadows danced within shadows, reminding me too much of the darkness of which I'd been a part. I opened the curtains back up. The first clouds I'd seen in ages covered the full moon. Only a fuzzy ball of light shined through, but it was enough.

I couldn't sleep no matter how hard I tried. As I thought about the next day, emotions jumbled in my head—the fear of seeing Alcander and Portia, excitement at the possibility of Edward's return, worry that I wouldn't be able to make the spell work again if he tried the shoe on my foot. My blood wasn't good enough to keep the spell intact the first time. Why should it work now?

The sheets tangled around my legs as I turned over. The downy bed was much more forgiving than the straw mattress on which I slept in the kitchen house. I felt like I might sink into the feathers and never be able to crawl out. I grabbed the blanket and lay down on the floor below the window. There, under the moon, the night and I drifted away.

~

*H*orror was evident on Regan's face when she came in with breakfast.

"What are you doing on the floor?" she cried, ignoring my protests that I could stand on my own as she helped me up.

I rubbed my eyes. "It was more comfortable than the bed."

Regan groaned and walked me over to the tea and scones she'd put on the table. She waited until I began to eat before going over to the cabinet, opening the doors, and paging through the clothes inside. The dresses that hung there were worthy of the ball.

"Are those the Princess's?" I asked.

"No, they're extras. There has to be something in here that will fit you. You can't just wear your underwear when you meet the Prince." Regan gestured to my sleeveless white shift. I looked down at the scalloped lace around the neckline. What she called underwear was nicer than anything I had at the Runes.

"What happened to my old clothes?" I asked as Regan sorted the dresses into piles on the bed.

"I don't think they made it out of the laundry. They weren't in any state for you to wear again, anyway."

I was surprised at the dismay I felt at the idea of my serving clothes being tossed out with the trash. They might not have been much, but they were mine.

"But think," Regan said, swooping over to me with a dress in hand. "It's been three weeks since the ball. Prince Edward needs to fall in love with you all over again." She clasped the dress to her chest. "It's so romantic!"

I sipped my tea and tried to quiet the shaking of my hands.

"This one will be perfect." She held the dress out to me. It was made of heavy, hunter green satin. An underlay peeked out in contrasting gold fabric; the same color covered the chest and the insides of the sleeves. An ivy vine was embroidered along all the edges in shiny gold thread.

"It's beautiful," I said. It reminded me of the dresses Siobhan and Annabelle had worn to the ball. It was a dress I could have worn, if only I were able to go without having to hide my identity. Regan helped me into it, tying the gold cords at the front in a much more complicated pattern than I could muster. She sat me down and brushed my hair, apologizing every time I winced as the brush caught on the snarls. After dusting my cheeks with powder, she pulled a mirror out of the cabinet and held it in front of me.

"What do you think?"

It was hard to believe that I was the girl in the mirror. I was beautiful, almost. I couldn't get past the lump in my throat to answer her, so I just nodded. Regan produced a pair of gold slippers and deemed me fit for a royal audience.

I stood up. The dress was heavier than I expected, and Regan had laced the corset so tightly that it felt like I was wearing the glamour again. I could only hope it would be enough to hide me from Portia and Alcander. Word came around that they were due at the Castle anytime now.

I felt apart from myself as I followed Regan out of the room and through the Castle halls. I was too nervous to look around, so I kept my eyes fastened to the spot where Regan's apron was tied in a neat bow at the back of her neck. She stopped at the end of the hall and opened a door. Over her shoulder, I could see the stained glass of the throne room. This was not the entrance I went through with Edward; it was closer to the head of the room, where King Philip and Queen Catalina were already seated in their thrones. Princess Callista stood next to her mother and turned her head to see us standing in the doorway. She nodded in my direction.

"Come on." Regan jabbed me in the back until I entered the room and stood at the base of the steps that led up to the thrones. She curtseyed to the King and Queen and rushed out of the room. I looked towards the door, feeling the urge to make a quick exit myself, but Regan peeked her head back in and gave me a vigorous nod of encouragement.

I bowed to the thrones.

"Good morning, dear." Queen Catalina's voice was gentle. "It is good to see you well again. Please, have a seat." She gestured to an ornate chair to the left of the thrones, close to King Philip's seat. I hesitated before sitting, remembering what happened the last time I had ascended the dais. I was sure that if I did it again I would be back in my serving garb, once more choking on ash from the room with no windows. But when I swept my skirt behind me and sat, King Philip nodded his approval.

"Let them come in," he said. Servants opened the large double doors at the other end of the room, and Alcander and Portia filed in with Siobhan and Annabelle trailing behind them. Instead of shrinking back, I sat up straighter and raised my chin. Siobhan's eyes met mine, and her face turned almost as green as her dress. Portia looked like she wanted to rush to the front of the room and rip me limb from limb. It was only Annabelle's hand clutching hers that kept her in place. Annabelle smiled at me and offered a small wave before grimacing as Portia's grip on her hand tightened. Alcander stared out the window. I sat up even taller, daring him to look at me. He couldn't, not when I was being presented to him as Lady Eleanor of the Runes, just as noble as he was.

King Philip turned back to me. "Is this your family?"

My heart leapt as two more people entered, trying their best not to be noticed. Greta wrung her hands together. Peter put his arm around her as he looked up at me. Portia glanced back at them, rolling her eyes in annoyance.

"Yes, Your Highness," I said. Siobhan looked over at Alcander, confused. He did not meet her eyes.

Where is Jack? I mouthed to Greta. She shook her head.

"Alcander," Philip said. His tone was that of a man who expected obedience. Alcander's head snapped away from the window. "I find myself in an unprecedented situation. Only a few men have been judged worthy of being named knights of Colandaria. I expect those who are given this highest honor to be our best, our most righteous and noble. It is abhorrent enough that you would treat a servant in your household the way you have treated this young lady. But to think that she is your blood? This I cannot fathom."

"You're her father?" Siobhan turned on Alcander.

He didn't look at her as he spoke. "Not now, Siobhan."

"Yes, now! She's my sister? Owl Eyes? But how? Why is she—?"

"Shut it," Portia hissed. Annabelle wrestled her hand from Portia's grasp and went to Siobhan, whispering in her ear until the King tapped the arm of his throne for attention. I wondered if Sir Milton had been the one to tell King Philip who I was. I looked back and forth from the King to Alcander, whose eyes were fastened to the throne.

"Your ancestral family home is not mine to take from you." Philip stood up. "But your title is. From today onwards, you will no longer be known as Sir Alcander of Colandaria. I can only hope that your children will do better."

Alcander bowed his head. Color drained from his face until it was as grey as the stones on the floor.

"Your Highness," was all he said.

King Philip went on. "As for the young lady, it is her decision where to go and what to do after this morning's session ends. If she wishes to return to the Runes and be properly instated as a member of the household, she may do so." He looked towards the back of the room, where Edward entered with Ioan, whom I recognized as the man with silver hair who escorted Edward away from the throne room during the ball. "However, if my son has anything to say about it, she may choose to remain here at the Castle."

He sounded so certain, but unless Edward had already tried the shoe on every other girl who attended the ball, there was no way for King Philip to know that I was the one his son was looking for. As Edward walked towards me, his hopeful smile faltered. A cold feeling crept up my spine. The almost-beauty I was now didn't hold a candle to how I'd looked before.

"Were you at the ball?" Edward asked.

I could hardly hear him over the blood pounding in my ears. I nodded.

"Did we dance?"

My nerves lifted, and I laughed. "We tried. I left my first impressions all over your shoes. I did better after you gave me a lesson."

"What did we talk about?"

He was testing me. He must have asked these questions to the girls at every estate he visited. Some of them might have even guessed the answers and tried on the shoe, but they wouldn't have been able to reactivate the glamour.

"You told me about the tapestry in the hallway—the Protectoresses. We talked about how we were both trying to avoid our families." I looked past Edward to where Siobhan watched me with wide eyes. "You talked about how riding is the only thing that makes you feel free. I said I knew what you meant, but I'm not sure I do." The truth jarred me. "I'm not sure I've ever known."

Edward studied my face. "You look like someone else," he said. I couldn't tell if this was a good thing. He turned to Ioan and gestured for the older man to get something from his satchel.

"Prince Edward will try the shoe on the girl," Ioan said to the assembly, holding up Liana's shoe. The light from the open windows bounced off the silver threading. "If she can activate the spell, the Prince will have found his bride."

Edward looked over at his father with alarm. A transaction passed between them too quickly for me to understand. Whatever unspoken argument had just taken place, King Philip had won. Suddenly I went from being the girl the Prince was searching for to being a few minutes away from becoming his betrothed.

I looked over at Alcander as Edward knelt down and slipped the shoe onto my foot. He couldn't keep his eyes off me now. Edward was no valet from the Fall. I'd won the game we'd been playing for the last seventeen years. I wouldn't have to go back to the kitchen house ever again. My skin tingled as the shoe tightened around my foot.

"It's you—" Edward gasped.

"No!" Portia shouted. Alcander's head hung in defeat. Siobhan stormed out of the room with Annabelle on her tail, trying to comfort her.

But Edward was still talking. "My…" he trailed off, glancing at Ioan.

In a flash of purple and white, Regan dashed from where she was watching in the doorway and whispered in Ioan's ear. Ioan passed the word to Edward.

"My Eleanor," Edward finished.

Hearing him say my name out loud, I felt like I'd been struck. Why hadn't anyone told him my name before? Why hadn't I?

You look like someone else. The words echoed in my head in Jack's voice instead of Edward's. When I lifted my foot, Liana's shoe stayed on the ground.

"No."

No one heard me. Behind me, Queen Catalina stood up to congratulate Edward. Greta and Peter looked at each other with the same confusion that played on Edward's face.

I grasped for what was true about this moment. Liana's shoe never fit me, not really. The glamour I wore at the ball was just as suffocating as the air in the room with no windows. The spell made an illusion of me. I didn't know how to float with the folds of my skirt or how to eat with dangling sleeves. But somehow, with the shoes and the dress and my new face, I became the person Edward was looking for. I said the right things, smiled and laughed in a particularly intriguing way, and was the perfect image of what he wanted. But I couldn't keep the spell up at the ball any more than I could now. When the magic wore off, what would Edward be left with? He didn't know Nora, the kitchen servant who was more comfortable sleeping on the floor than in a royal bed. I was not a lady, and a dress didn't make me one.

I remembered King Philip's ultimatum: pick a bride at the ball, or he would pick for Edward. Edward might have wanted to court me, but I was Philip's choice for his son's marriage. By betrothing us, how was he doing anything different than Alcander tried to? Edward didn't know me any more than I knew Sir Reginald's valet. Neither of us even knew the other person's name.

My lies—the lie I'd made of myself—had spurred this whole disaster into motion.

Everyone fell silent, eyes on me once again.

"My name—" I said, "My name is Nora. I'm sorry. I can't—"

I didn't know what else to do. I pushed my way out of the throne room. Greta called to me as I went by, but I couldn't stop. I had to get out of the Castle, away from the mess I'd made. I ran through the halls until I found the exit and stumbled down the steps under the clouded sky. I clutched at the dead grass on the lawn. Tears stung my eyes. I didn't want to imagine the scene going on inside.

The sky cracked open, and rain began to fall in large, slow drops that mixed with the tears running down my face. I sobbed into the ground, pressing my face into my hands and breathing in the rich, damp earth in hitching gasps. I wished for someone to tell me what to do, to tell me what I wanted. There was no answer.

Then it came to me so clearly, and I knew that I had always known.

The green dress in which I'd felt almost beautiful just moments before weighed down on me. I had to get it off. My hands twisted in the cords that Regan had so carefully laced. I pulled at them until they loosened. In just my shift, I felt more myself.

"Nora!"

Greta and Peter ran down the steps. Greta stopped, looking at the dress on the ground. She picked it up and crouched next to me as Peter came to my other side.

"I'm so sorry," I said through my tears.

"It's okay," Peter said. I held tight to the arms they put around me. We might not look the same, but our scars made us family. Squeezing my shoulder, Peter got up and headed towards the stables. I leaned on Greta as we sat in the rain.

"Why did you come?" I asked.

"Alcander made Peter come. He was supposed to follow the carriage on horseback, and you were supposed to ride back with him. I couldn't let him go alone."

I nodded. Even if I had gone home to the Runes, it wouldn't have been with Alcander.

"But, Nora," Greta said, "How could we not come? You're our daughter."

They were still here. The parents I'd always needed; the parents I'd always had. They were the ones who knew me. I threw my arms around Greta and hugged her like I did when I was a child.

"Nora, you need to know—things have changed at the Runes. It's —" Her voice hitched. "—different now. Peter and I won't be there much longer." I looked up at her, trying to figure out what she meant as Peter came back, leading Honeycomb behind him. He nodded at me.

"We'll see you soon," he said. "We'll tell you all about it then."

They were giving me lease to go, to take Honeycomb wherever I wanted. I looked towards the forest path. There was only one place I wanted to be.

CHAPTER 18

$\mathcal{M}$uddy water sprayed onto my skirt as Honeycomb's hooves pounded against the ground. Wind whipped past my face, sending my hair flying out of its bindings. My path was clear. I didn't have to go back to the Runes. The King himself said as much. I could ride all the way to the Farlands if I wanted to. For the first time, I felt the freedom Edward spoke of, the freedom of possibility.

I didn't have to go back to the Runes, but I did.

Izella's tree stood in the middle of the field, leafless and proud. I rode past it, not stopping until I was in front of the kitchen house. I leapt off Honeycomb's back and threw the door open.

"Jack!" My voice echoed from the walls. I ran to the ladder and climbed into the loft. "Jack?"

The kitchen house was empty. Jack's mattress was propped against the wall.

My chest caved in with something greater than disappointment. I sat heavily on my mattress and looked up at the window as rain slid down the glass. I closed my eyes. The scent of the breakfast Greta and Peter made that morning floated up to the loft, even now, hours after they had gone. Those smells—eggs and butter and a hint of thyme—they were the smells of home.

After a few minutes, I got up and rummaged through the chest in the corner until I found one of my extra skirts. The material was coarse and familiar. The waistband soaked up the wetness from my shift when I pulled it on, but I didn't care. The weight of the skirt was just enough to ground me. Next to the chest, someone had placed Izella's spellbook and box and, on top of them, the knife I carried since childhood. I picked them up and reached under my mattress. My hand closed around the opening charm, which had resumed its crystal form, waiting for my blood to turn it into a key once more. A bit farther under the mattress, I found the tree Liana gave me, the one she had carved from a branch of the hazel tree in the field. I touched my finger to the beak of the owl that nestled in the knothole before placing the carving in my pocket.

Down in the kitchen, I lit the fire in the hearth and pulled a chair up to the flames to warm myself. When I was ready, I reached for the knife. I turned the handle over in my palm, running my fingers over the carvings for the last time before tossing it into the fire. I held the spellbook in my lap. In it was an ancestry that could be mine, if I wanted it.

I didn't.

I placed the book on top of the fire and watched the flames lick at the pages. The edges of the parchment blackened and lit up, and the deep red base of the flames looked almost like blood. The box went in next, followed by the opening charm. I doubted that the crystal would burn; just like the blade of the knife, it would be left when the fire had burned out. But there were always bits of memory left over, even when everything else had turned to ash.

As smoke curled up to the chimney, I whispered the Final Rites. "Izella. Goddess grant safe journey to the World Apart. May the tether that ties you to this world be unbound. Though your footsteps no longer fall upon the ground, we carry their echoes in us." I would carry her echoes, but the face that I wore would be mine alone.

The door opened. I looked up at Jack standing there, soaked from the rain. Emotions jumbled in my head—relief, joy, warmth—but it was anger that propelled me to where he stood in the doorway.

"Where were you?" I said. It was almost a shout.

"Nora? What are you—?" He blinked water out of his eyes.

"I needed you at the Castle, and you weren't there."

His face darkened. "It wasn't my place."

"Peter and Greta were there," I insisted. My anger dissipated. I wasn't actually mad at him. I was frustrated at myself for starting things this way. Yet another mistake to add to my list.

"Don't you dare say I wasn't there for you." Jack pushed past me into the kitchen. "I took a beating from Alcander trying to get you out of that room." He wheeled around, pointing at his face, where bruises had faded to yellow on his chin and cheek. "And another one after the Prince hauled you off to the Castle. Turns out pushing the lady of the house to the ground and taking her keys is a fireable offense."

"They fired you?" I reeled.

Jack's anger was just beginning to crest. "I went to the Castle every day for a week to try to see you, but no one would let me in. This might come as a shock to you, but no one there really cares what a servant wants. I had to get Sir Milton to go for me. So don't ever say I wasn't there for you."

"I'm sorry," I said. This wasn't going the way I wanted it to. The feeling I'd been overwhelmed with on the ride back to the Runes, the feeling I'd always known in the back of my mind as truth, was stuck on my lips.

"Why would I want to watch you get betrothed to the Prince?" The rain that pounded the doorway and smacked against the windows almost drowned out his words. "Try thinking of someone else for once. Your feelings aren't the only ones that matter. You don't think about how the things you do affect the people who love you, like I love you."

As soon as the words came out of his mouth, Jack went for the ladder to the loft, leaving me with their echo. I couldn't lose him, not now.

"Where are you going?"

"Ma's last carving," he said. "The one she made for you. I didn't take it when Alcander kicked me out. I had to wait until no one was here before I could come back to get it. That's what happens when you're not welcome in your own home anymore."

I took the tree from my pocket. "This one?"

Jack stopped with one hand on the ladder.

"It didn't fit," I said. "The shoe, I mean. Your ma's shoe, when Edward put it on my foot. It did for a moment, but then it didn't. I didn't want it to." I put the carving down on the table and took a step towards him. "When my glamour went away at the ball, I thought it was because I'd done something wrong with the spell or because my blood wasn't good enough. But that wasn't it. Sir Milton said that magic depends on willpower, and I didn't want that—the throne, the Castle, the Prince. I don't want this either." I gestured out the window to the main house. "I want the people who know me better than anyone and love me anyway. You. I want you." I took another step towards him and said what I knew had been true for years. "I love you."

The words hung in the air between us as my hand found its way into his.

Jack's edges softened. "Take us out of the kitchen house, and we don't have a bed to sleep on."

Sir Milton's offer sounded in my head. "So we go to the Vale."

Jack smiled, looking down at the ground. "We're already there. I'm staying in the great house for now. Sir Milton is taking me on as a gardener. He offered Greta a job as a healer for the whole province. I think she's taking him up on it. Peter asked for a position working on the great house's grounds. You could come with us. Be Greta's apprentice."

Excitement stirred inside me. It was exactly what I wanted. Home. Family. And Jack, I hoped.

When he looked back up at me, his brown eyes had bloomed green. "You're wrong, by the way," he said. "I don't know you and love you anyway. I love you because I know you."

Neither of us moved. Water dripped off his hair and down his nose. Then, the whole world shifted, and my lips were searching for his. We breathed each other in.

I smoothed back the hair that had fallen in his face. His smile could have stopped the rain from falling.

"Milton might give us some land to build on," he said. "But we can't expect any more than that."

"That's more than enough."

"It will be hard," Jack said, pressing his palm to mine.

I twined our fingers together. "But it will be home."

I looked around the kitchen house for the last time, and I knew. *I'm here.*

THANK YOU FOR READING

Did you enjoy this book?

We invite you to leave a review at the website of your choice, such as Goodreads, Amazon, Barnes & Noble, etc.

DID YOU KNOW THAT LEAVING A REVIEW...

- Helps other readers find books they may enjoy.
- Gives you a chance to let your voice be heard.
- Gives authors recognition for their hard work.
- Doesn't have to be long. A sentence or two about why you liked the book will do.

~

Don't miss out on your next favorite teen or new adult read!

~

**Join the Fire & Ice mailing list at
www.fireandiceya.com**

Perks include:

- First peeks at upcoming releases.
- Exclusive giveaways.
- News of book sales and freebies right in your inbox.
- And more!

ACKNOWLEDGMENTS

It has been a fifteen-year journey to bring *Owl Eyes* to the printed page, and there are so many people without whom this book might not exist. Thank you to the teachers of the University of Pennsylvania Theatre Arts Department who unknowingly let me steal the bottle of stage blood that inspired so much of this book. To Rebecca Romeo, who was there at the beginning, and Alyc Helms and Shari Arnold, who gave guidance at the end. To the amazing people of the Rosemont College MFA program, especially Tawni Waters and everyone in the Fall 2012 Novel Workshop. To my parents, Joan and Ed Lazer, who read and gave comments and edits on fifteen years' worth of drafts, and to my husband Eric Hawthorn, whose critiques and support have meant everything. Thank you to Caroline Andrus and Nancy Schumacher for taking a chance on this book, and to Heather Maloney for the edits. Finally, I owe an enormous debt of gratitude to all of the teachers who were there along the way. They are all phenomenal women and writers, and it has been an honor to work with each one of them: Deb Margolin, who allowed us the freedom to figure out who we truly were and in whose class *Owl Eyes* was conceived; Karen Rile, who guided me through the very first draft; Rachel Sherman, who was there in the middle; Carla Spataro, whose tireless efforts have made not only me but every other Rosemont student a better thinker and writer; and Carmen Maria Machado, a writer I only wish I could be like, whose brilliant notes helped this novel find its final form. Finally, thank you to Jacqueline Fitzgerald Hennessey, my very first creative writing teacher, for encouraging me to bring all my weird little stories to life. Colandaria has been an idea in my head for about twenty-five years, and I'm so grateful to all of you—and you, the reader of this book—for joining me there. I hope you'll come back again.

ABOUT THE AUTHOR

Molly Lazer is a former associate editor at Marvel Comics, where she worked on books such as *Fantastic Four, Captain America, New Avengers,* and cult favorite comic book *Spider-Girl.* After returning to graduate school to receive a degree in education, she began a career as a high school reading, writing, and drama teacher. She also serves as a professional critiquer for Comics Experience, helping aspiring comic book writers finesse scripts for publication.

Author Photo by Saúl Gomez

In 2016, Molly received a MFA in Creative Writing from Rosemont College. Her short stories have been featured in numerous literary magazines including *Gone Lawn, LIT,* and *Silver Blade.* She lives outside Philadelphia with her husband and twin sons. *Owl Eyes* is her first novel.

www.mollylazer.com

 facebook.com/mollylazerwrites